HOMEFRONT

JESSICA SCOTT

Printed in the United States of America

First Printing 2015

ISBN: 97-8-1511457-39-2

Author photo courtesy of Buzz Covington Photography
Cover design by Jessica Scott
For more information please see www.jessicascott.net

DEDICATION

To Sandee
You are deeply missed.

ALSO BY JESSICA SCOTT

Falling Series

Before I Fall

Break My Fall

If I Fall

The Homefront Series

Homefront

After the War

Face the Fire

The Coming Home Series

Because of You (ebook)

I'll Be Home for Christmas: A Coming Home Novella (ebook)

Anything for You: A Coming Home Short Story

Back to You (ebook)

Until There Was You (ebook)

All For You

It's Always Been You

All I Want for Christmas is You: A Coming Home Novella

Nonficton

To Iraq & Back: On War and Writing

The Long Way Home: One Mom's Journey Home from War

Homefront

PROLOGUE

Tal Afar
Late 2006

Shit days were nothing new. In fact, Sergeant First Class Gale Sorren was on a thirty-six day streak, and there was no sign that they were coming to an end any time soon. But he had to keep going.

No matter how much he might want to take a knee.

The funeral detail was somber and professional, the flight line dead silent now that the aircraft had killed its engines. His throat closed off. His eyes burned. He held his salute as the caskets moved slowly past, one after another in slow procession. His arm trembled from holding it for what felt like a lifetime, but there was no way in hell he was going to drop it.

Three of his boys were heading home tonight.

There was no sadness. No raging grief. Only a sober, silent tribute to the fallen.

The rage would come later. Much later. For now, there was too much work to be done.

He dropped his salute and listened to his boys remember their brothers. Recounting their heroism. Their bravery.

Gale said nothing. There were no words that could get past the block in his throat. So he let his men remember their friends while he stood watch.

He stood there, long after the rest of the battalion had left the airfield. The Air Force security guard came and went and came again. The kid finally gave up trying to get him to move hours later.

It was probably for the best.

A stone skittered across the blazing asphalt. He watched it tumble to the edge of the tarmac and land in a pothole.

He glanced over at the source of the stone's movement. Tellhouse, one of his fellow platoon sergeants, walked up. Tellhouse was a sergeant first class like Gale. Promotable, too, which meant they were both going to be looking for other jobs soon. Gale didn't really want to leave his boys mid deployment because he got promoted out of his position.

Gale liked Tellhouse for the most part. Except for his temper. They needed to work on that. After all, there couldn't be two of them enrolled in anger management training. Sarn't Major would crush the both of them. The problem was they both tended to get pissed off about the same things at the same time.

Tellhouse pushed his eye-protection up higher on the bridge of his nose. "First Sarn't needs you at the company."

Gale made a noise and tried to summon an ounce of give-a-shit over what the First Sergeant wanted. Maybe if the fucker left the office once in a while, Gale wouldn't be strung out trying to take care of three platoons instead of just his own. Thank God Tellhouse was competent or Gale might have lost his shit a long time ago.

Finally, he shifted his weight and moved.

Maybe someday he'd find the grief for his soldiers.

But that day was not today. Not when they had a mission gearing up in about six hours.

He breathed out deeply and fell into step with his fellow NCO. The walk was solemn and silent and filled with things neither of them could say. The war was nothing new. Both of them had spent more than their fair share of time in Hell.

But sometimes, days like this just got the best of you.

He stepped into the dark interior of the company ops.

Funny how a few pieces of plywood and a couple of extension cords suddenly made an office. He stopped short, though, when he saw the battalion command sergeant major standing with the first sergeant. Not extremely out of the ordinary, except that Gale had the distinct impression Sarn't Major was waiting for him.

Gale swallowed the tight knot in his throat that wouldn't seem to budge. "What's the occasion?" he asked, looking between the two senior NCOs.

First Sarn't handed him a sheet of paper. "You got a Red Cross message."

The knot in his throat swelled, blocking his airway as he looked down at the handwritten note.

The room spun out at the edges when he saw Jamie's name.

The words blurred together. *Hospitalized. Stitches. Psychiatric ward.*

He breathed deeply and looked at his NCO leadership. "When can I leave?"

It was the sergeant major who spoke. "I can't let you go. Your daughter's life isn't in immediate danger. She's safe. Your ex-wife didn't request your presence."

A loud buzzing filled Gale's head, blocking out the sound of the sergeant major's words. "My daughter's in the hospital," he finally managed. "I need to be there."

Sarn't Major shook his head, his expression flat and emotionless. "That's not going to happen, Sarn't."

Gale couldn't say what happened next. An urge to do violence slammed through him. He imagined driving his fist into the sarn't major's face and beating the lines off that sun-worn leather skin. All the rage, all the fury, boiled up in a single violent flash.

The next thing he knew, he was back outside. Tellhouse's hands were driving into his chest, holding him against the wall. "Stop. Sorren, fucking stop."

Tellhouse's words finally penetrated the fog. Gale blinked rapidly and looked at the other platoon sergeant. He stopped struggling to get free.

Tellhouse took a step back but still kept his body between Gale and the door. Gale stood there for a moment, reality crashing through the haze of violence, grief, and rage. Helpless, potent rage. "I need a few minutes," was all he could manage before he executed an about face and walked away.

Then there was no rage. No more red-tainted visions of violence. This was something more. Something he couldn't name and couldn't process.

Jamie was in the hospital. His *daughter* was in the fucking *hospital* and Melanie hadn't requested his presence.

He barely felt the gravel beneath his boots as he walked back to his CHU. He was stuck half a world away in a fucking war that he no longer even hated, and there was nothing he could do.

He closed the door to his CHU. Locked it behind him with a solitary, metallic click.

He stood for a moment in the Spartan emptiness. There was a light coat of dust on the old leather chair he'd gotten from a major on his way out of country.

A box of unopened Pop Tarts had fallen over.

All around him was dust and dirt. There was an explosion somewhere in the distance. A pop of gunfire at the test fire pit. The war was fucking everywhere.

He stood there in the center of his CHU. There was something broken inside him when he couldn't even cry over his fallen soldiers anymore.

Something broken that he was unable to name, that he couldn't be there when his little girl needed him.

The air conditioner in his CHU kicked on. His cheeks were suddenly cool.

He lifted one hand at the unexpected sensation.

His fingertip came away wet.

He unclenched his other hand. The Red Cross message was still there, crumpled at his fingertips.

The Red Cross message that told him his daughter was in the hospital.

The wetness on his cheeks grew colder, spread down his neck as the words on the paper blurred.

He dropped to his knees, doubled over as the violent, unrestrained grief ripped him apart.

CHAPTER ONE

Fort Hood, Texas
2009

If there was a hell, First Sergeant Gale Sorren was certain this was it. In fifteen years, he'd never been assigned to Fort Hood, and while he'd been begging to be assigned here for years, he remembered with punishing clarity why people had recommended he avoid the home of America's First Team for so long.

It was fucking hot and it wasn't even summertime yet.

He'd thought he knew hot. Hell, he'd spent enough time at Fort Benning and in Iraq to be intimately familiar with just how hot the planet could get.

But somehow, Fort Hood took hot to a whole new level. It was a dry heat, his last sarn't major had said when he'd given Gale the news that he was getting his assignment wish and being sent to Hood.

It was just past the ass crack of dawn and the sun slowly slipping over the horizon, and it was already a hundred degrees. And it wasn't even summer yet. Next to him, his commander, Captain Ben Teague, was busy being a smart ass. It was his totem animal, or so he said.

"I wonder if the sarn't major would let us run in just our PT belts."

Gale shot him his best *are you high* expression. Teague grinned and raised his hands. Teague was Gale's commander and technically that made him Gale's boss but the commander/first sergeant relationship was… How had Sarn't Major Cox put it once when Gale had threatened to kill one of his platoon leaders for getting drunk with the soldiers back at Benning? It was an arranged marriage. A unique description, Gale supposed.

"I'm thinking that might get us both fired," Gale said mildly.

"Really?"

"No, not really. It'll get the sarn't major's boot surgically implanted in my ass." Gale stopped a soldier and told him to tighten his PT belt around his waist. The new Corps sergeant major had a thing about uniform violations and a loose PT belt was a cardinal sin these days. "Besides, it could be worse."

"How?"

"We could be patrolling Sadr City in this weather in full kit."

"You know—" Teague snapped his fingers— "that is an excellent point." He shoved his hands in his pockets as they walked toward the PT formation area. "I really wish we didn't have mandatory fun today."

They were both in ACUs. Gale resented the hell out of any morning that didn't start off with PT, but he damn sure resented it when he was forced to skip PT to go to *breakfast.* What kind of animals started their days with food? Give him coffee and a good six-mile run any day of the week. "Don't get me started."

"At least there'll be coffee." Teague frowned and glanced at him. "There *will* be coffee at this kind of thing, right?"

"Do I look like I have the slightest idea what we're doing today?" Gale needed to be spending time with his formation, not doing whatever the hell they were going to do this morning. He was still getting to know his troops and their issues—and there were a lot of them. Issues, that is. "It's not like I spend my free time checking the battalion's social roster."

"Hell, I don't know what you do on the weekends other

than bailing kids out of jail." Teague glanced over at him and Gale braced for more sarcasm. "Do you even have free time—oh hey."

Instantly his commander's expression softened. Gale followed his line of vision to see Teague's other half, Major Olivia Hale, talking to the battalion commander.

"I know what you do with yours," Gale mumbled and tried not to be jealous of the new and shiny love between his commander and the battalion's lawyer. Major Hale nodded at Teague in acknowledgment and turned back to her conversation with the battalion commander.

It was the subtlety of her gesture that convinced Gale that she and Teague had a good chance at making things work. They were a good fit. She kept Teague honest in more ways than one, and they were both very good at keeping things professional at work.

It was a nice change from all the drama Gale dealt with on a daily basis. Angry spouses, cheating soldiers, and everything in between. Life in the Army sometimes felt more like a reality TV show than a professional organization.

He peeled away from his commander and headed to the front of the formation where his platoon sergeants were talking with each other. Sergeant First Class Iaconelli was the headquarters platoon sergeant, and while Gale had his misgivings about a recovering alcoholic on the team, Iaconelli had proven to be a rock since he'd come to work for him.

"Are we set for the range tomorrow?" Gale asked Iaconelli.

Iaconelli nodded. "Roger, Top. Final checks today before lunchtime."

"Make sure we pull some camo out for shade." When one of the other platoon sergeants started to protest, Gale talked over him. "We don't need to practice being hardcore in the heat. We need to be able to shoot, and we can't do that if soldiers are dropping from dehydration."

Iaconelli nodded. "Got it, Top."

Gale jerked his chin, and Iaconelli stepped away from the formation. "You talked to Foster today?"

Foster was on convalescent leave for surgery to repair a torn meniscus. He was also struggling with an addiction to methamphetamines. "Roger. He called in like he's supposed to."

"How is he doing?" If Gale had serious misgivings about Iaconelli, he had even more about keeping Foster in the ranks, but these men meant a lot to Teague. He was keeping a very close eye on both situations, however. If the time came that he needed to recommend the commander take action, Gale would do what needed to be done.

"He sounded steady. I'm going to swing by and check on him after PT."

"Good. If you get even a hint that something is wrong, I want every pain pill counted."

"Roger, Top." There was resentment in Iaconelli's answer, too obvious for Gale to ignore.

"Something you want to say?"

Iaconelli looked out over the formation, grinding his teeth until the muscle in his jaw looked about to snap. "It's hard enough staying sober without everyone looking at you like you're using all the time."

Gale studied the other man silently. "Are we still talking about Foster?"

Iaconelli didn't look away. "It doesn't matter. But maybe give him the benefit of the doubt?"

Gale folded his arms over his chest. He wasn't looking for a fight with one of his platoon sergeants. If Iaconelli needed to get this off his chest, then so be it. Finally, when Iaconelli let the silence stand, Gale spoke. "The fact that he's still in the Army and recovering from surgery while he's trying to get clean *is* benefit of the doubt."

"You don't know him," Iaconelli said.

"And you do. And that closeness blinds you to the reality

that he's got a long hard slog ahead of him to stay sober." No point in pulling his punches, regardless of whether they were talking about Iaconelli's personal issues or Foster's.

"Oh I'm very much aware of the road he's on." After another moment, Iaconelli turned and stalked back to the formation. Whatever was eating at him wasn't going to come out today. But soon. The situation needed watching. Closely.

Gale let the other man go. He didn't need to get into a dick-measuring contest with his platoon sergeant. Foster wasn't one of Gale's boys. He was just another soldier, another face in the crowd. If he soldiered, Gale would let him continue to soldier. If not, he was going home. Gale had a war to train his men for and he needed every single body able and fit to fight.

Another soldier who was distracting from the mission of prepping to head back to Iraq wasn't going to garner much sympathy from Gale.

The cannon sounded, and Gale called the formation to attention and present arms as reveille trumpeted over the installation. They saluted the flag, and there was a moment of somber pride as the colors were hoisted up at the division headquarters. When it finished, Gale turned the troops over to Iaconelli, who took charge of the formation for PT.

Teague fell into step with him as they headed toward the parking lot.

"So. You call your ex yet?"

Gale sighed but said nothing. He never should have told Teague that Melanie lived in Harker Heights and that he was still summoning the courage to call her.

"I'll take that as a no?"

Several weeks had gone by since Gale had reported to Hood. He'd told himself that he needed to get situated first. That there would be time.

But he was lying to himself. Because the truth of the matter was he was afraid. Afraid of seeing the daughter who'd nearly died almost two years ago. Afraid to look at her and see the hate and the blame and the guilt looking back at him. Oh, he knew he wasn't going to win any parenting awards for stalling. He should have been on the first plane smoking and to hell with what the sarn't major had said.

But he hadn't been. He'd damn near been court-martialed back in Iraq and it had taken Sarn't Major Cox almost eighteen months to save his ass. The fact that Gale was on his second tour as a first sergeant despite the assault said a lot about how well connected Cox was. Only Cox and Tellhouse knew his history from downrange in this unit and Gale intended to keep it that way if he could.

But even the charges and the job didn't excuse Gale's action or lack thereof. He told himself that Skype calls and text messages were enough, that she was okay. That Mel had a handle on things.

But even those were convenient lies. Fear was a powerful thing and yeah, he was afraid. He'd finally gotten his wish of being stationed near his ex-wife and their daughter and he was paralyzed by fear. Fear of what it meant to live in the same town as Mel and Jamie. Fear that if he tried to be a dad after all these years that he would fail miserably. Or worse, that Jamie no longer needed him because he'd been gone too long.

He was afraid to face the bitter truth: that Melanie didn't need him after all these years.

Maybe she never had.

***

Melanie Francesco stirred her coffee while the captain next to her made idle conversation about one of the local pawnshops burning to the ground.

Melanie was reasonably certain that the fire had not been an accident, but she wasn't in a position to comment. She was a liaison between the business owners and the real estate council and random speculation like that could cause problems for her office.

She fought the urge to check her cell phone for the tenth time that morning. She told herself that Jamie was fine. She'd dropped her off at school that morning after the requisite fighting about whether or not the sky was blue or if the sun was actually going to come up tomorrow. Because all they did was fight.

The fights were exhausting, but it was the fear that kept Mel up at night. Fear that Jamie was slipping away again and Mel wouldn't be there to save her next time.

The captain moved away, leaving Mel alone. She stole a quick glance at her phone. No text but no missed calls from the school either. Relief crawled over Mel's skin. Jamie was still in school then.

She tucked her phone back into her purse as she spotted a friendly face—someone she wouldn't mind actually talking with—and made a straight line for Major Olivia Hale. "I didn't know you'd be here."

"Mandatory fun and all that," Olivia said with a smile. Melanie envied the woman—even in ACUs, which were not exactly made for women's bodies, Olivia looked stylish and effortlessly well put together.

Melanie smiled back. "Life isn't the same without you on the Council harassing the slum lords trying to screw over soldiers."

"It was one of life's true pleasures," Olivia said dryly.

"There is no one to play the Faux Outrage Drinking Game with me anymore. The monthly meetings are epically more boring." She sipped her tea, watching the room. "How's life down in the new unit?"

"It's good. I have a sense of purpose again." Olivia smiled warmly.

Melanie set her tea on a nearby table. "So what are we doing here? And I'm not interested in the official bullshit line, either, so don't waste your breath."

Olivia grinned wickedly and it was the smile that Mel remembered all too well. The smile the other woman used when she was about to rip someone a new one. "Well, since you put it that way." She took a sip of coffee. "We're trying to build relationships that will strengthen the community. We've got a massive problem with soldiers being involved in misconduct off post and we want to get civilian agencies involved before the police get involved."

And just like that, all the pieces clicked into place. "So you're bribing the landlords with shitty coffee and donuts in the hope that we'll call you guys instead of the cops?"

"More or less." Olivia set her coffee down and retrieved a folder from the table. "We've got this handy little quick reference guide with all the unit phone numbers. Kind of a cheat sheet of names and numbers to call. We even laminated it to make it durable. Isn't it nice and shiny?"

Mel shot her friend a wry look. "Is this even legal?"

"I'm not going to offer an official opinion on what I think of this program."

"Why don't you approve?" Mel asked, keeping her voice low.

Olivia sighed. "Because it enables some people's misconduct to be hidden away and covered up. I prefer we work things through official channels. Transparency and all that." Olivia's smile could have cracked glass. "Community outreach with the realtors keeps problems handled through informal networks instead of the Bell County legal system."

Melanie opened her mouth to speak but the words locked in her throat.

The tea in her stomach turned bitter and cold as her guts twisted with recognition and surprise at the last person she'd expected to see here today.

Gale.

Her heart slammed against her ribs as anxiety and something else knotted in her belly. For a moment, she thought about turning away. About hiding from the man who'd just walked into the room like he owned it.

But it was too late.

Because across the conference room, near a tray of donuts and a box of coffee, her ex-husband's eyes met hers.

The world tilted beneath her feet. He was supposed to be stationed at Fort Lewis, halfway across the country. And instead he was here. In this room. At this moment. *As a first sergeant?*

Closer than he'd been in over two years. His jaw was iron, his shoulders broad and strong. It was criminal how good that uniform looked on him. And damn it, she was not going to notice these things about him.

But despite herself, she noticed everything about him. His dark brown eyes were hard and filled with shadows now. Colder than she remembered. A smarter woman might have been intimidated by him. A younger woman might have already been wringing out her panties. But she remembered him for the boy he'd been. The boy she'd loved.

The boy she'd left.

He was not that boy anymore. And she was no longer the scared uncertain girl trying to find her way in the world.

"Are you okay?" Olivia's voice came from very far away.

"Yeah. Excuse me a sec?" She hated bailing on her friend but this was not a conversation she wanted to have with an audience.

She offered a tense, flat line in place of a smile as he approached. Defenses up, that's what she needed. She could not do this with him right now. "I'm not exactly sure what the correct greeting is," she said, doing her damnedest to keep her voice level.

As though they were perfect strangers, talking about unimportant things.

The hush between them swelled into a living thing, pulsing with raw and ragged emotions.

"I can explain." His voice was rough and deep.

"How long have you been here?" Her words were too sharp on her own ears. She sucked in a deep breath, trying to stave off the riot swirling in her belly. No matter how much time they spent apart, every single time they were around each other things went to shit in a rapid, predictable manner. She really wanted to avoid that at the present moment.

"Long enough." Gale cleared his throat and had the decency to look embarrassed. "I should have called you."

"And yet you didn't, so there we are." She turned, looking for her cup, needing space, needing distance between them before she broke apart into a million ugly pieces in front of her peers and coworkers and a half dozen random strangers.

Gale's hand was rough and strong on her shoulder. "Mel..."

"Don't." She moved away from his touch, barely keeping her voice low. "You don't have permission to touch me." Mel bit her lips together, inhaling a deep, hard breath. Gale lowered his hand and they stood there at an impasse.

A few months. No call. No note. Nothing. Hadn't tried to see Jamie. *Just move to town and don't say a word.*

That told her all she needed to know about where she and Jamie stood in his priorities. Just like always, the Army won. She bit down harder, trying to divert the pain in her heart to the pain in her lip. "Jamie will be happy to see you," she said finally.

She didn't mean to throw Jamie in the middle but that's the way things were with them. It was the way it had been since...since always.

He stiffened. His hands flexed by his sides. Like he needed to do something with them that hopefully didn't involve her.

"I meant to call." There was a rough edge to his voice. A blade, like cut steel, ragged and raw.

"I'm sure you did." Her words were brittle. She headed for the door in what she hoped was a relatively inconspicuous manner.

She needed a few minutes to put everything back in the

box she marked "Gale" and did her best to ignore.

Because she'd be damned if she was going to cry over this man one more time.

CHAPTER TWO

Melanie kicked the front door closed and sorted the mail: junk, bills, Jamie's latest catalogue from that store in the mall that Melanie hated. She was, of course, the worst mother in the world because she wouldn't let Jamie shop there. Mel was all for women owning their own sexuality and all that but she drew the line at hyper-sexualizing her daughter. If they both survived Jamie's adolescence, maybe Jamie would thank her later.

She had her doubts, though. She put the envelopes in stacks, almost on autopilot until she came to a tan, card-sized envelope with a Fort Lewis return address. No name but then again, she didn't need to read the name to know who it was from.

Her heart fluttered a tiny bit as she opened the belated birthday card. It was a squirrel holding a sign and wearing pink heart sunglasses. *Happy Birthday Mel. - Gale.*

In the fifteen years since their divorce, he'd sent a card every year and every year he'd screwed up the date. Still, it was a nice, if empty, gesture. He'd missed far more than just birthdays since their marriage had fallen apart all those years ago.

If she hadn't seen him today, maybe she would have smiled at the stupid squirrel. But she had seen him today. Had been sorting through her reaction all damn day. She wasn't angry. She wasn't sad.

She was… she didn't know how to handle the news that he'd moved to Killeen. She'd never expected that. How had he even gotten here? The last time Jamie had asked her dad to move closer to them, he'd said something about burning in hell before the Army sent him to Hood.

And yet, here he was. He'd caught her off guard. Completely off guard. And she hated that more than anything.

There was a thump on the ceiling. Then the sound of feet moving from her daughter's bathroom down the hall to Jamie's bedroom. It was a normal sound. Nothing about it should have set her heart to pounding rapidly in her chest. But there was something off. Something that set the hair on the back of Melanie's neck on edge. She'd ignored her gut once before.

And she would never make that same mistake again. She rushed upstairs to find the bedroom door locked.

"Open the door, Jamie." Her voice was deadly calm. She was proud of herself, actually. She managed to smother the kick of panic that sucked the air from her lungs.

"Just a sec, Mom."

"I'm going to count to three, then I'm kicking this door in." She'd done it before. Jamie knew better. She *knew* not to lock the door. Fear gripped her throat, her voice tightening. "One." More scrambling. "Two."

The door swung wide, and her daughter rushed to fill the space. "What's up?"

Melanie inhaled deeply. No drugs. No smell of antiseptic or rubbing alcohol. Jamie stood there, one arm behind her back. "What were you doing?"

"Homework." Jamie blinked innocently.

Melanie didn't buy it for a second. "What's in your hand?"

"Nothing, Mom."

Fear licked at her spine. Jamie was lying. Again. She grabbed the arm Jamie held behind her and shoved the sleeve up.

Pale scars crisscrossed Jamie's forearm, but no fresh marks. Relief slithered over her skin.

Jamie yanked away, her mock innocent expression shuttering closed into the belligerent look Mel knew all too well. "I'm fine, thanks," she said.

"You're not allowed to block the door." Melanie folded her arms as they prepared for the all-too-familiar battle.

"I can't have any privacy?" Defiance looked back at her from Jamie's eyes, eyes that looked so much like her father's, except they were lined with a heavy black liner that no matter how many times Mel kept throwing it away, her daughter kept coming replacing.

Melanie sighed heavily, praying for patience. "You know the answer to that question."

"You know, you treat me like a criminal. I might as well act like one."

Melanie held out her hand. "Phone."

"You have no right—"

Her temper snapped beneath the weight of the fear. "I have every right. You live in my house, you live under my rules. When you go to college, you can make your own rules."

Jamie slapped her cell phone into her mother's outstretched hand. "I can't wait."

The texts were blank. All that meant was that Jamie had gotten better at deleting them before Melanie caught her. She was hiding something. Mel just couldn't figure out what.

"Come do your homework at the table."

"I'm fine in here."

Melanie lifted her eyes toward heaven, grinding her teeth. "It wasn't a request, Jamie."

Jamie made a disgusted sound and slammed the door shut with a bang. Melanie briefly considered for the hundredth time taking it off the hinges entirely.

But that wouldn't really do any wonders for trying to rebuild trust like their therapist kept trying to get them to do, now would it?

She walked straight into the kitchen. She started to pull salad out of the fridge, then stopped. She leaned against the counter and focused on breathing slow and steady. Tears burned behind her eyes. Every single day was a new version of the same old fight.

Makeup. Phone. Homework. And those were the easy fights. They took up most of her energy, keeping the real fear buried. Waiting. Lurking in the dark for the right moment to strike back and remind her that she'd almost lost Jamie once.

That it could be happening again and Jamie would be able to hide it this time.

No, their therapist didn't really understand the fear that Mel lived with. The fear of the tiny nicks in her daughter's flesh. The blood that had circled down the drain, that left a faint stain that taunted Melanie with the epic levels of her failure as a parent.

The fear that her daughter was only pretending to be okay but was slowly spiraling out of control again, and there was nothing Melanie could do to stop it.

Not for the first time, she wished she'd found someone to share the load with. But the few times she'd dated hadn't really gone anywhere serious. She had her hands full with Jamie. Most men, even the good ones, wouldn't stand for being second place. She didn't blame them, honestly.

But damn, she was tired of being alone.

"Mom?"

Mel lowered her hands. Jamie stood near the wide arch that led into their living room, her books clutched to her chest. For once, she didn't look like she was ready to fight at the drop of a hat. For a brief moment, she saw her little girl, looking at her with worry in her eyes when she'd caught Mel crying once. For a moment, it was just Jamie standing there.

Mel would do anything to hold onto that moment. To make it last longer than a few heartbeats.

Melanie lifted her chin and straightened. Took a deep breath and tried to change the tone of their evening. "Sorry. Rough day at work. Any preferences for dinner?"

"Macaroni and cheese?" Jamie said hopefully.

"Sure." She wasn't going to win any Parent of the Year

awards for feeding her kid mac and cheese out of a box, but then again, your kid ending up in the hospital for cutting herself pretty much already ended any chances of that.

Oh, she knew on an intellectual level that what Jamie had done wasn't her fault. That it was a mental health issue and blah blah blah.

But that didn't stop the guilt that rode on Melanie's chest. That burned beneath her heart every single day. Why had she missed the signs? What could she have done better? Why did she and Jamie have to fight so much?

It felt like they'd been fighting since the day she'd been born.

Jamie paused where she'd been setting her books on the kitchen table. She looked sideways at Mel and said cautiously, "It must have been a really bad day at work."

"It was." She couldn't come up with the words she needed to tell her daughter about Gale. How would Jamie react? Mel honestly didn't know. Jamie hadn't seen her father since before his last deployment.

Melanie offered a faint smile that she wished she felt and tried to hold onto the oh-so-fragile peace between them. "So how's school?" She knew she was supposed to ask questions that didn't involve responses like "fine" or "good." But she didn't know what to ask anymore.

"Fine. Sold any houses this week?" Jamie asked. Such a neutral question.

As though Mel hadn't just been treating her like a suspect a few minutes before. Like Jamie hadn't just caught her mom standing in the kitchen fighting tears. "I've got a closing on Thursday."

"That's good, right?"

"It is." Mel pulled a box out of the pantry. Food was another thing they fought about. Mac and cheese was one of the few fail-safe dinners. The doorbell rang. Mel paused and looked toward it. The UPS man was the only person who ever came this late in the afternoon. "Start the water?" she asked.

For once, Jamie didn't argue. Mel wasn't going to second-guess the moment's peace. She was sure there would be another fight before they went to bed. It sucked. There was no other way to put it.

She opened the door looking down, expecting her latest book.

Instead her gaze fell on a pair of dusty combat boots. Boots that damn sure weren't supposed to be on her doorstep.

And they damn sure weren't supposed to belong to Gale.

CHAPTER THREE

Gale had done dumber things in his life. But at that moment, he was having a hard time remembering any. Oh he'd had a plan. It had involved apologizing and trying to explain. As half-assed plans went, it wasn't the worst idea ever. But after seeing Mel earlier, he realized he was letting fear rule his life. He'd wasted far too much time already.

He wasn't really sure what his reception would be.

Okay, that was a lie. He was pretty sure Mel was going to take one look at him and rip his spine out because he hadn't called first. He'd be lucky if she let him explain before having his ass carted off to jail. And wouldn't that be a joy to tell Captain Teague or Sarn't Major Cox?

He'd been sitting in the cul de sac near her house for the past hour, unable to get that morning out of his head. Replaying it over and over again. He'd almost driven away. Twice.

Then he got sick of himself for being such a damned coward.

Now that he was here, he had no idea what to do.

They both stood there on either side of the door and neither of them said a damn thing.

Melanie hadn't moved. There was no expression in her eyes. No anger. No hate. None of the potent, violent emotions that had slammed into him across the miles and the years when he'd told her he wasn't going to be able to come home and help with Jamie.

What do you mean, you're not coming?

You didn't request my presence, Mel. They're not letting me.

Your daughter is in the hospital and because I didn't write the words "I request your presence," they won't let you come home?

Why didn't *you write the fucking words?*

He shoved the memory away violently. He couldn't face that day again. Not now. Maybe not ever.

Now, there was nothing but cool detachment looking back at him.

A cool detachment that flooded the dead space inside him and tried to make him feel. Tried and failed. Frozen. He was frozen. His heart pounded in his ears. All he could do was stare at the woman his ex-wife had become.

Time hadn't changed the shape of her face or the curves of her body. She'd cut her hair. He wasn't sure how he felt about the soft sleek dark hair brushing her shoulders. He remembered it being longer.

It was so much easier to distract himself with how she'd changed than to face the reality of the time that had passed between them and everything he'd missed along the way. He'd seen Jamie before he left on that last deployment but that had been almost three years ago now. Three years was a long time to not see your daughter.

It wasn't nearly long enough for him to get over just how badly he'd fucked up. As a husband. As a father.

There was nothing he could do to make things right. There was no success as a soldier that could make up for those other failures.

He knew that now. After years of hoping to unfuck things, he'd finally accepted there was nothing he could do to undo the damage he'd done. He'd given the Army everything he'd had.

And he could never get that back.

The war, work—all of it was a convenient excuse for being a shitty father and a terrible ex-husband.

He swallowed the dryness in his mouth and shoved his hands in his pockets because he didn't know what else to do with them. "Hi, Melanie."

And wasn't that fucking eloquent? Christ.

"Daddy?" A squeal from the kitchen. "Daddy!"

Jamie bolted toward him from across the house. She rushed past Mel and into his arms, and Gale found himself hugging someone who was no longer a little girl.

"Hey, Peanut." He breathed in the scent of her hair. His daughter. His eyes burned. He'd almost lost her.

His arms tightened a little more as the memory of helpless agony and regret crashed over him. He bit back the emotion, refusing to let his daughter see him cry.

He set her back to look at her. She was taller now, her hair long and straight and dark. But most importantly, she was healthy. And whole.

She looked so much like Melanie when they'd been younger.

"You're all grown up." His voice was thick. She was no longer the little kid with too much leg that he'd taken to the Dallas Zoo when she'd been nine. To the San Antonio Zoo when she'd been eleven. He could still feel Jamie's little fingers curled around his hand when she'd been little enough to look up to her dad with adoration in her eyes that he'd done nothing to deserve. That little girl was long gone, now.

He hadn't spent nearly enough time with that little kid and now she was all grown up into the beautiful young woman standing in front of him.

Jamie practically vibrated with excitement. "I can't believe you're here! Why didn't you tell me you were coming?" She rounded on her mother. "You didn't tell him he couldn't come, did you?"

Melanie flinched beneath her daughter's verbal assault. In that brief moment, he saw the tired lines around her mouth, the fatigue in her eyes, and he wanted to ask what was wrong.

Instead, he focused on Jamie.

"*I* didn't tell *her* I was coming." He took a deep breath, taking the edge out of his voice. "And don't talk to your mother that way."

Jamie rolled her eyes but kept smiling at him. "Sure, Dad. Whatever. Are you staying for dinner? Please say yes."

Gale looked at Melanie and held his breath. Melanie didn't look irritated. She looked…tired, more than anything.

Gale swallowed. He'd made things worse by coming here tonight. Granted, he'd had a shitty plan in the first place but things were rapidly going to hell. He took a step backward. "I'm sorry, Mel. I'll… Give me a call and let me know when a better time is?"

She met his gaze silently. Across the gulf that spanned the distance between them, for one brief moment, he saw the girl she'd been: carefree and daring and full of life. The lines around her mouth had been from smiles once, her eyes bright and shining and laughing.

But that girl was gone now. Vanished beneath the smooth mask of polished professional Mel. She shifted subtly and the illusion vanished, leaving the harsh reality of their lives standing between them.

"There's never a good time around here," she said mildly before she headed back toward the kitchen. "You can stay if you'd like."

Gale stepped into her home. She'd painted since the last time he'd been here. There was a new rug in the living room and a big picture of a faded, black and white barn with a bright red door. Dark cherry hardwood gleamed beneath his dusty boots. The furniture was something heavy and solid. He guessed their old raggedy secondhand rocking chair was nowhere to be found.

He felt out of place, but what did he expect? This was Melanie's space, Melanie's life.

He wasn't a part of it.

He walked into the kitchen, not wanting to get caught mentally inventorying her place. Mel stood by the stove and Jamie leaned on the counter, moving a wine glass out of the way. Gale had half a thought that Jamie couldn't be drinking. Mel wouldn't allow that. Right?

"So when did you get in?" Jamie asked.

"A few months ago. I was getting settled before I called."

"Glad to see we're a priority in your life," Jamie said dryly.

He ignored the arched eyebrow Mel shot in his direction before she turned away. He supposed he deserved that. He looked around for anything to talk about. Damn it, when had he become so inept?

"You are." The words were flat and lifeless. Hollow. His gaze landed on a biology textbook on the table and he seized on it as an excuse to talk about anything other than why he hadn't come by sooner. "You're taking biology?"

"She's *failing* biology." In went the macaroni to the water and Gale didn't miss the emphasis on "failing." Steam rose over the pan but Mel didn't turn around.

"Biology is so boring," Jamie said, not trying to keep her mother from hearing her complaint.

Gale glanced at Mel and didn't miss the tense set of her shoulders. Her back was stick straight.

"You need to do well in school, kiddo. You want to go to college, right?"

Jamie rolled her eyes. "Yeah, sure."

"No idea what you want to be when you grow up?" Gale said, leaning over to look at the papers scattered near her book. He wasn't sure if it was supposed to be homework or what, but he could tell that it was an unorganized disaster. His need for organization started pinging and he fought the urge to sort through the pages.

"Not really. I mean, I think I want to go into journalism, maybe. I like writing. And honestly, when am I ever going to use this stuff in real life?"

"Writing is an important life skill." Gale stuffed his hands into his pockets. "But I used biology all the time in Iraq."

Jamie's eyes went wide with curiosity. "Really? How?"

"Biology was actually important over there. We had to watch out for different viruses and bacteria in the food. The feral animals are all vectors—"

Jamie's face lit up. "Oh, I know what that is. It's something that transmits a disease, isn't it?"

Gale saw Melanie glance over at their daughter. Her expression was slightly more relaxed now but guarded. Why could he do nothing right with her? Then again, maybe showing up on her doorstep at dinnertime unannounced was a bad place to start if you wanted not to piss off your ex.

Yeah, he had the shitty ex-husband role down to a T. He should probably count himself lucky that she'd let him in the house to begin with.

"Yeah. See? Real world biology." Mel pulled the milk out of the fridge. Gale badly needed something to do other than stand there. It felt strange and out of place to have her cooking with him just standing there. He took a step closer. "Is there anything I can do?"

She paused, her deep blue eyes hesitant. Not angry, though, so he supposed that was a start. "It's boxed macaroni and cheese." Mild words belied the edge beneath them.

Gale opened his mouth to speak then snapped it closed. He couldn't blame her. He should have called first.

Damn it.

Mel stepped away and started mixing the macaroni again as it boiled. He couldn't say why he was here or what he'd hoped for. It was stupid, really. The truth was he was a better soldier than a husband or father, and he always had been.

Hell, there was a reason why he worked so hard. He was good at the Army. It wasn't a job to him. It was who he was. It was what he was good at. He knew how to lead soldiers, how to get their confidence up to be the first man in the stack. How to whip their asses when they got arrested for stupid shit, then get them back into shape so they could still go downrange and kick some ass.

Here in Mel's kitchen, surrounded by the only two women in his life, he felt…awkward.

He didn't like the feeling. But after the last deployment, he'd made a promise to himself that he was going to get his ass to Hood come hell or high water. He was going to figure out how to be a damn father.

And now that he was here, he had no fucking clue what to do.

CHAPTER FOUR

"Did you really move here?" Jamie asked after a moment.

The hope in Jamie's voice chipped away at the stone that encased Melanie's heart. Even if Gale had moved here, Gale wouldn't really be here. The Army would always take him away again. Or give him an excuse to leave.

He had never been there when they'd been younger. Oh, he'd been around just long enough to marry her and then it had been off to Kuwait for a year or some other place that had needed him more than his family had.

He'd deployed to Bosnia right after the divorce. She remembered sitting at her mother's tiny two-bedroom apartment, holding a colicky Jamie while they both cried their hearts out. She'd been so afraid for him, even after their marriage had ended.

She stole a long look at him while he was paying attention to Jamie and her homework at the kitchen table. The years had been good to him. He'd always been tall but he'd filled out. His shoulders were wider than when they'd been younger, his arms bigger. He'd finally grown into those hands she'd loved when she'd first met him.

There were flecks of grey now in the closely shorn black hair at his temples.

His eyes, though—his eyes were so different. They were still the same deep dark brown with impossible lashes that she'd first noticed when he'd been a gawky kid at eighteen and she'd been so impressed that he was going to be a soldier. Now, though, they were lined with fatigue and worry and too much time in the Iraqi sun.

"Yeah, Jamie. I'm going to be stationed here for the next few years." He cleared his throat and Mel didn't miss how he was pointedly avoiding looking in her direction. "And then I think I'm going to retire."

She dropped the spoon. It clattered to the counter, splattering yellow goop across the counter. "Damn it," she muttered.

She never expected that he would be anything other than a soldier. He'd been born for the uniform. It was part of what made her fall for him way back when. And it was what had made her leave him when she realized that she would never be the priority in his life that she selfishly needed to be. The idea that he would ever be anything other than a soldier had seemed impossible when she'd been up for weeks with a crying baby and she hadn't seen her husband because he'd been in the field.

She felt his gaze on her back as she cleaned up the mess.

"So where will you settle down?" she asked, not looking at him. Her voice was edgy. Off.

"I was thinking I'd try to find a job around here. Maybe as a contractor or something."

"Really?" She didn't need to see Jamie's face to hear the unfiltered joy in her daughter's voice. It was instant forgiveness to a father who hadn't been there. She should be happy that Jamie didn't hold his past actions against her dad. But that joy burned in Melanie's heart as something she would never have from her daughter.

Melanie was the one who'd made it to every school play, who'd patted Jamie's back when she'd been sick, who had taken her to the doctor. Melanie was the one who lay awake worried about her now, terrified that the scars on her arm were hiding a sign of something worse to come.

And Gale was able to just walk in, announce that he was going to settle down in the area, and her daughter was bursting with instant forgiveness. She took a deep breath. This was not a bad thing. She would not be pissy about this.

She turned slowly, schooling her features. "I think that's really great," she said cautiously and hoped there was no edge to her words.

It was hard. So damn hard.

Gale watched her silently for a moment then turned his attention back to their daughter, his expression unreadable. "Yeah. I've been gone too much. I haven't been there for you. Or your mom." He rubbed his big hand over his jaw, darkened with five o'clock shadow. "I can't get that time back. But maybe I can be here now."

Melanie focused on scooping mac and cheese into the waiting bowls. "Order up," she said, forcing a lightness into her words that she didn't feel. "I'm going to go change. Jamie, please empty the dishwasher when you're done eating."

"Ugh."

The sound was like nails on a chalkboard. Melanie almost snapped at her but bit it back fiercely. She could do without sniping at her daughter for the duration of however long Gale would be here. Gale could have dinner with his daughter without her pissing in it. Just because all Melanie ever did was fight with Jamie didn't mean she had to do it tonight. Maybe they could have a meal without one of them leaving the table in tears.

"You're not going to eat with us?" Gale asked.

"I need to…I need a minute to change," Mel said. It was a retreat and they both knew it. "You should get caught up with Jamie. She's missed you."

She padded out of the kitchen and gently closed the bedroom door behind her, surprised by the regret and sadness dancing in her thoughts.

It wasn't the first time she'd wondered how things would be different if she'd had the courage to stay. To be the devoted Army wife while Gale was off being the soldier he needed to be. About what would have happened if she'd stayed married to a man who loved the Army more than her. They'd been poor when they'd first gotten married but they'd been happy because she'd thought she loved him enough for both of them. Then she'd gotten pregnant before either of them realized what had happened and everything changed.

Gale had started working harder, hoping to get promoted early. He'd been worried about money and the cost of the baby. And Mel had been worried about raising the baby right on little money.

And so they'd struggled. And as they'd struggled, things had gotten worse and worse between them until Melanie finally broke and their marriage had shattered in the wreckage.

What if she'd been stronger? She'd tossed the thoughts over in her head and reached the same conclusion she always did—the divorce had been inevitable. She hadn't wanted to spend her life waiting for a man who would spend more time at war than he did at home.

Leaving had seemed like the way to protect her heart from the life of disappointment she'd been facing. Looking back now, though, she wasn't so sure. Things had been hard with Jamie. Harder, too, when she thought about all the nights she'd lain awake watching the news and worrying about Gale when he'd been deployed.

Of course, she'd never admit that she'd worried about him when he'd deployed. He'd always kept her informed of when he was leaving, when he would expect to be home.

When he would pop in for a week or so and spoil their daughter, then escape again into the ether of his latest assignment.

And when he left again, she would try not to miss him. Because she did. She always did. That hadn't changed with the divorce.

Many things had, but not that.

***

"So how's school?" Gale asked, chasing a half-moon noodle around his plate. He hated macaroni and cheese. He'd always hated it, primarily because he'd grown up eating it so much when he was a kid.

It had been a cheap way to feed four kids. He didn't blame his parents. They'd done the best they could by him and his brothers while Mom had worked third shift at the mill and Dad had worked the woods until the mud and the rain and the snow pushed them out of the forest. Still, he hated mac and cheese all the same. It was so funny when people found out about it. It was as if he'd said he hated kittens and kicked puppies.

"Fine," Jamie said.

"Just fine?"

Jamie rolled her eyes and Gale's jaw tightened instinctively. The simple gesture struck straight to Gale's last nerve. He paused. The whole roll-your-eyes thing was the one thing that his soldiers could do to make him completely lose his shit. But Jamie was not one of his soldiers.

"Yeah, Daddy, fine." She looked up at him from the massive plate of carbs and fake cheese. "You're not going to start nagging me about school like Mom, are you?"

"Probably," he said mildly, still toying with that noodle. "School's important."

She tipped her head at him and Gale saw a flash of Melanie when she'd been just a little older than Jamie was now. Defiance and spark. God, but she'd been a pistol when they'd been kids.

"Really? That's why you're in the Army, right? Because school's so important."

Gale set the spoon down with forced gentleness. He couldn't say what was grating down his spine but something about Jamie's tone was striking all the wrong nerves.

And that said a hell of a lot about his parenting potential. He'd been around her for all of fifteen minutes and he was having a damn anxiety attack. "Twenty years ago school wasn't like it is now. The jobs weren't the same. You need to do well in school so you can get a good job and support me and your mom when we're old and broke." He grinned and wished he actually felt the smile on his lips. But he was good at faking things these days. Smile and wave and no one asked any questions. "If you don't have a good enough job to pay for an old folks home, we'll have to live with you."

Jamie made a disgusted sound, completely unimpressed with his sarcasm. Obviously, he needed to learn to speak teenage girl as opposed to teenage boy. He could speak that language. Hell, half his company was seventeen to twenty years old. But talking to a young knuckle dragger was a hell of a lot easier than trying to find common ground with this mysterious member of the female species sitting across the table from him.

He was suddenly acutely aware that he had no idea how to act around this particular female. It was like his little girl had been replaced with an alien life form of rolling eyes and bad attitude.

"Yeah, 'cause work is the most important thing, right?" She pushed her plate away and slid her chair back. The conversation was going from bad to worse and Gale couldn't figure out what the hell he'd done to derail things so badly.

"Your mother asked you to do the dishes," he said.

"I have *homework*." She made that sound again and stalked from the room while Gale sat there, stunned and speechless.

What the hell had just happened? He hadn't seen her in years and she was rushing off to do homework? How the hell was that for a welcome home? He was not used to people walking away from him. He was a first sergeant in the U.S. Army. People did not just walk away.

His blood pressure spiked, and he took a deep breath. In through the nose and out through the mouth like the anger management coach had taught him the first time he'd been sent there by his commander. That had been five years ago, when he'd thrown his helmet at some young, smart-mouthed lieutenant who'd refused to listen and had gotten three of their boys shot up as a result. Then came the incident downrange last time. Clearly his training wasn't worth a damn if it failed when he needed it most.

He'd never been a believer in the deep breathing techniques, but hey, it was better than his instinctive reaction might have been. What he wanted to do was yank her little ass back into the kitchen and make her do the dishes and then some. If he had his way, he'd have her cleaning the kitchen grout with a toothbrush and scouring powder.

What he actually did was sit at the table and take deep breaths like the deadbeat father he was.

"That was fast," Mel said from the doorway to her bedroom. "She knows how to push all the right buttons, doesn't she?"

It was amazing the transformation a simple change of clothes could do. Mel was wearing a plain white t-shirt and well-worn jeans. The clothes hugged the curve of her hips. Hips that used to fit perfectly in his palms, once upon a time—and where the hell had that thought come from?

Still, he couldn't look away. Melanie was a beautiful woman, sophisticated and so far out of reach it wasn't even funny.

He cleared his throat, pulling his thoughts away from the dangerous detour they'd just attempted. "Is she always like that?" He picked up Jamie's plate and slid the rest of the mac and cheese into the trash.

"Pretty much since puberty," Melanie said as she started emptying the dishwasher. "I've seriously considered boarding school. Possibly the Citadel."

Gale didn't know if he wanted to laugh or be horrified. "It can't be that bad, can it?"

Mel deliberately looked away, avoiding his eyes. Finally, she looked up and her eyes were filled with a kind of regret. "She's always been difficult but—" Melanie pressed her lips together into a flat line and looked toward the living room where Jamie had vanished. "This is going to make me sound like the worst mother in the world but she's been a monster since she started getting her period. Days go by where she doesn't speak to me at all. And after..."

Gale stood rooted to the spot. He didn't know what to do, what to say. He paused, looking over at her. There was a deep sadness around her eyes, in the tension around her mouth.

Because he could think of nothing else to do, he reached for her, covering her hand with his own. Her skin was smooth and soft, the bones fragile beneath his touch. "I'm sorry I haven't been here, Mel." A hesitant admission.

She looked up at him, her eyes filled with unsaid things. Her gaze flicked to their hands and he was suddenly conscious of the roughness of his palms, the grate of calluses on her skin.

She slipped her hand from his. "We can't change anything now, can we?" Soft words that slid between his ribs and sliced at his heart. She started taking the dishes from the dishwasher while Gale stood there helpless and mute.

He wanted to help. He needed to do something. But there was nothing for him to do but stand there and feel useless while she emptied the dishwasher. He glanced down at the trashcan. Maybe...nope. The bag was fresh and empty.

"Why are you here, Gale?" She didn't turn back to look at him when she asked the question that tore out his heart.

He swallowed the lump in his throat. "Because I haven't been."

She flicked the dishwasher closed and leaned against the counter, folding her arms over her chest. "Why now?" No anger in those words.

Gale rubbed his thumb against the cool granite countertop, swiping at an imaginary spot. A far cry from the cheap Formica they'd had in that trailer once upon a time. "I had the opportunity to come to Hood and I took it." His answer felt lame and amateurish but he could find nothing better. He didn't need to tell her about the assault or Sarn't Major Cox saving his ass by getting him down here. Funny, he could walk around in the middle of a shit storm with the world blowing up around him, but right then, standing in his ex-wife's kitchen, anxiety clutched at his insides and squeezed his lungs. "I figured maybe I could be closer to Jamie and—" *You.* But he didn't say that out loud. Fear choked the word off. "I wanted to try to be a father while I still had the chance. You know, before she moved out and went to college and started doing body shots on the weekends."

"That is a terrifying visual." Melanie braced her hands on the counter. Gale tried not to notice how the movement stretched the fabric across her breasts. Because nothing said trying to make amends by staring at your ex-wife's tits like a lovesick puppy.

He kept waiting for the argument to start. The same argument they had year after year.

She would slap at him for being gone. He would slap at her for leaving. She would blame him for never being there. He'd apologize for the U.S. starting the wars that took him away.

They'd end up at the same bitter impasse.

Instead, Melanie sighed heavily, her eyes closed, her expression weary. "I'm glad you're here."

It was not a response he'd expected.

***

"Come again?"

She almost smiled at the surprise in his words but she didn't. Because her heart was bruised and tired tonight and it was nights like this that she often found herself dreaming of stupid, foolish things.

"I'm glad you're here," she repeated. She could have lied and changed her words but she doubted that he really hadn't heard her. Besides, part of her *was* glad he was here. "Maybe you can be the bad guy once in a while."

She finally dared to look up at the man standing in her kitchen. He was so different from the man she'd married once upon a time and a lifetime ago. The changes were more than the thickness in his body or the weariness etched into his skin. There was something darker about him now. Not tainted, but no longer innocent. Something that made her wonder at the things he'd seen and done in the name of God and country.

The house was silent around them. She'd worked hard to provide the trappings of a nice life for her daughter. Polished and gleaming and hollow. Empty of the toys Melanie used to trip over when Jamie was younger. Empty of signs that a family lived here. Instead, it felt like two ships passing in the night and Jamie was pulling further and further away from her every day.

Maybe with Gale here, things could be different. Maybe they could draw her back from the precipice she balanced on. Make their daughter hate her a little bit less and try to recapture the hints of a family that she'd always tried to provide.

Melanie offered a watery shrug. She was just tired today. That's all. "It's just that everything is a fight with her. Getting her to school in the morning, doing her homework." *I'm afraid, Gale.* But she didn't say it. She couldn't give voice to the fear that choked her. "I'm just tired of fighting with her." She smiled weakly. "You should move in and I'll move out for a little while. Have at her."

Gale folded his arms across his broad chest. He was a massive man, still in his prime, and he was standing in her kitchen. "Is she still going to counseling?"

Mel closed her eyes, hating the elephant in the room. "Twice a week."

"Meds?"

"Anti-depressants." Her voice broke. Rationally she knew that Jamie's mental health issues were not her fault, but the guilt wasn't buried deep enough that she could avoid the hurt.

"Mel." She opened her eyes and he was there, in her space. Close enough that she could see the small scar on the edge of his lip, the five o'clock shadow against his jaw. "It's not your fault." Quiet words overlaid on steel.

Her throat constricted and it was suddenly difficult to swallow. She waved one hand, trying to fake flippancy and failing miserably. "Oh, you know, mommy guilt and all that."

Her cheeks heated beneath his gaze but he didn't step away. Neither did he move. "What about you?" he asked softly.

"What about me, what?" He was standing too close. She should move or make him. It was her house. And yet she didn't.

She had no claim to this man. No, she'd given that up years ago when she'd walked away, taking a colicky baby and sentencing herself to hard years alone. There were plenty of men interested in the ex-wife but once they discovered the little girl, no one had wanted to take on the baggage of someone else's kid. So Mel had embraced the solo life and done her best by her daughter.

"How are you dealing with everything?" His voice rumbled deep in his chest.

"Fine," she said, because there was nothing more she could say without spilling everything. And she was so damn tired of carrying the load alone.

If there was one thing she knew with absolute certainty it was that Gale was good at making promises, not so much on delivering. She was sure that the moment she leaned on him, she'd find herself alone, leaning into the wind.

He was still watching her, still too close. Finally, he shifted and leaned against the island, creating at least the idea of breathing room between them.

"I'm holding a first sergeant job in the First Cav so I'll be busy but it's not my first time doing it." He adjusted his feet, crossing them at the ankle. "I'd like to come around more," he said.

Melanie's heart sank with his words. "You won't have time,

Gale."

"I'll make time."

She folded her arms over her chest, mirroring his position. Needing the barrier between them. "Why now? What's this big impetus for showing up and wanting to be a father to a kid who'd rather spit at you than talk to you?" She held up a hand. "Oh wait, that's me."

His dark eyes were filled with sympathy and something she couldn't identify. "Maybe I've been doing it all wrong."

She tipped her head. "Doing what wrong?"

"Life. The Army. All of it. Maybe I've been doing all of it wrong."

There was more there. Things he wasn't saying. Regret stood between them, empty and hollow and filled with aching things.

Melanie looked away from the intensity looking back at her. She scuffed her toe against the tile. "I guess I don't know what to say to that," she mumbled finally.

"How has she been?"

Melanie looked away from the raw ache in Gale's eyes—from the fear that mirrored her own. The unspoken question in those words that he couldn't voice. The question that haunted her dreams and twisted them into nightmares. "I haven't caught her again."

"That's good, right?"

"I hope?" She rubbed her hands against her upper arms. "She scares me. What kind of parent am I that I'm terrified of what my daughter can do to herself?" She took a deep, shuddering breath. "All I keep thinking about is when she was in the hospital. I came home today and she'd locked herself in her room. Gives me a heart attack every time she doesn't answer right away."

Gale stilled. "What do you mean, locked herself in her room?"

Mel sighed heavily. "Every time I find her door locked, I

get this bolt of fear that I'm going to find her—" Her voice dropped to a whisper. "Cutting again," she said after a moment.

Her heart jammed in her throat as familiar anger rose from a place she'd been unable to cleanse. He hadn't come home. Oh, on an intellectual level, she'd understood that his commander hadn't allowed it. But as she'd sat in that hospital room and done battle with a daughter who'd sliced her own skin, she'd been angry that he'd left her alone. Again.

The upstairs door slammed again and Melanie's mouth pressed into a hard line. Gale looked up at the ceiling with her.

"Is it wrong that I want to go upstairs and check the bathroom?" Her voice cracked on the words.

"I don't think so." Gale took a single step closer. Close enough that when he lifted his hand to her shoulder, she could see the stubble on his jaw. This time when he reached for her, she didn't pull away. She simply stood there, drawing strength from the man in her kitchen. It was weak and it was foolish but at that moment, she didn't care. "She certainly knows how to go for blood, doesn't she?" Gale mumbled after a moment.

"It's the same fight, Gale. Every. Single. Time. She's so stubborn." A strand of hair fell from behind her ear and she tucked it back, not missing how his eyes followed her movement.

Mel cleared her throat. It was tempting, so tempting to stand there with him and pretend like everything was normal. That the last fifteen years and some change hadn't happened. Bigger things were at stake here than any latent feelings that being around Gale might stir up. Still, the validation that her fear and concern weren't unreasonable felt nice for a change. Far better than the cruel abuse she levied on herself for not doing better with Jamie.

"I want to help," he said. He swallowed and rubbed the back of his neck. "I know it's late and I should have been here years ago and I don't deserve it but I'd like a chance. You know, to be around."

She looked up at him. "I've never stopped you from seeing Jamie."

"I know. I just…I want." He glanced toward the stairs where their daughter had flounced off. "It looks like I'm going to need some pointers on how to handle her."

Melanie smiled softly and for the first time, a hint of the shadows in his eyes faded a little. "I'm probably not the person you need to ask. I'm not doing very good at this whole parenting thing."

He slid his hand up to cup her cheek. "You're doing the best you can."

The tenderness of the gesture overwhelmed her. His hand was big and strong and gentle, so gentle. Like he was afraid she was going to shatter beneath his touch.

In truth, she might. Because in that single touch, her heart swelled, breaking free of the stone she'd deliberately built to protect herself from her feelings for this man that had never gone away, no matter how much time and distance she'd put between them.

***

He stood there looking down at her, at the beautiful, tired woman his ex-wife had become. Her lips were parted, just a hint. He could lean down and close the distance between them. And it was tempting, so tempting to taste her again. To see if she was all that he remembered, all that he'd dreamed about for so many years.

This wasn't why he'd come here tonight. He'd long ago given up hope that there could be anything between him and Melanie again. There was too much pain, too much bitterness.

But in that moment, he felt something he'd thought long dead.

He felt hope.

Almost, he leaned in closer. Almost, he could taste her lips on his.

A muffled vibration broke the tension. He closed his eyes and breathed deeply as his cell phone broke the mood and shattered it on the polished granite countertop.

“Do you have to get that?” she said after he made no move to answer it.

He met her gaze, not bothering to hide the stark regret that burned in him at that moment. “Yeah.” He looked down at the phone. Sarn't Major Cox.

He turned to step outside to answer it because it was work. It was always work that took him away from her.

"I need you and the other first sergeants in my office, time now," was Cox's greeting.

"Roger, Sarn't Major." Because there was no other response he could give. He hated himself when he stepped back into her kitchen. "I have to go," he said.

"Of course you do." Resignation laced her words.

"I'm sorry, Mel."

She hesitated, long enough that he turned to go. "I know," he heard faintly as he let himself out.

She didn't stop him. He didn't blame her. There was too much hurt and bitterness.

And he was unable to find a way across the chasm of fifteen years and the many disappointments that stood between them.

CHAPTER FIVE

Gale looked up at the knock on his office door. Tellhouse, the Assassin Company first sergeant, stood in the doorway. "You get the message?"

It was strange being assigned with Tellhouse again. Gale had honestly hoped he'd left his past at his last duty station when Sarn't Major Cox had him pulled down to Hood.

Something had changed since the last time he'd served with Tellhouse but Gale couldn't put his finger on it. Either way, Tellhouse helped him get caught up on everything and hadn't once mentioned the problems downrange.

"What message?"

"Sarn't Major wants to see us."

And there went Gale's plan to get caught up on evaluations between PT and first formation. "Lovely." Gale sighed. "Any reason why?"

"Two arrests this weekend for domestic assault."

Gale scrubbed his hand over his jaw. "Shit. Who got arrested?"

"A guy in Chaos Company and a private in Headquarters Company."

"And so *we're* all going to get our asses handed to us?" Gale said.

"Yep, that about covers it. You still gonna argue with me about collective punishment?" Tellhouse leaned against the doorframe.

"Seeing how Assassin Company hasn't had any arrests in going on two months, you're clearly doing something right,"

Gale said, grabbing his headgear. It pained him to admit that to Tellhouse. The idea of collective punishment went against everything Gale thought about leadership but to each his own. Tellhouse was convinced that his methods were effective and, well, clearly something was going right in Assassin Company. "Doesn't mean I want to be supervising kids on the weekend when that's what I've got sergeants for." They stepped out into the sweltering heat. "No clue what the Sarn't Major wants?"

"I figure it's part of the same old song and dance." Tellhouse fell into step next to him. "He's apparently off his medication so he might be a little crazy today."

Sometimes it felt like crazy was part of the job description. And Cox might be partially—or mostly—crazy but he was still damn good at what he did. If Gale had to lose a little skin off his ass to make the sergeant major feel better, then so be it. He'd known Cox for a long time and had seen some of the shit that loosened a few bolts. The soldiers might joke that Sarn't Major Cox was on medication for several ailments but getting blown up a couple times would be enough to give anyone nightmares. Cox had at least three combat action badges and two Purple Heart awards. Even his drivers were afraid of him because of his mercurial moods.

He paused on the back dock of his operations. A skinny kid with purple and black hair slouched past them, glancing warily at Tellhouse and Gale. "New recruit?"

Beside him, Tellhouse spat onto the dirty concrete. "My kid."

"He on drugs?" Pants that were at least five sizes too big jangled as he stomped up the steps into Tellhouse's company. There was something skittish about the kid.

"Not that I know of. He knows his hair pisses me off. But his mother insists he's just going through a phase." There was a hard edge to Tellhouse's words and Gale glanced over at him to find him glaring at his son with something more than disapproval.

"He's just a kid, man. We all did stupid shit that pissed off our parents when we were kids."

Gale's dumbest stunt had been getting Melanie pregnant right after they'd gotten married. As long as he lived he'd never forget the watery feeling in his guts when he'd shown up at her place with her hand locked in his to tell her parents what they'd done. He'd never expected a baby would change their world so dramatically.

Married or not, he distinctly remembered thinking that her old man was going to kill him. It was disconcerting to be reminded of how badly he'd screwed up at life before he'd even gotten a chance to get started. Not that he regretted Jamie. Not by a long shot. But Mel's dad had looked at Gale with disappointment. It was strikingly different from the pure animosity that ripped across Tellhouse's face when he looked at his own son.

Tellhouse stuffed a wad of dip in his bottom lip as they walked toward battalion headquarters. "He's a fucking waste of good sperm."

"That's a fucked up thing to say about your own kid."

"You have no fucking idea what this kid has put me through. I never wanted him in the first place."

"Jesus Christ, man. Cut the kid some slack. Shit, do you have a cousin or something he can go live with?"

Tellhouse grinned. "I'm just fucking with you. You know me better than that."

Gale studied his friend for a long moment, not entirely convinced that Tellhouse was just screwing around. "Sure. Whatever."

Tellhouse shot him a funny look but said nothing. They walked the rest of the way in silence.

He thought he'd rather deal with purple hair and chains on clothing, thank you very much, instead of a kid who'd carved bloody lines into her own skin. She'd terrified her mother and given Gale an anxiety attack in the middle of Iraq.

But he said none of that to Tellhouse. And somehow, Gale doubted that Tellhouse would appreciate the comment.

***

Melanie stared at her cell phone for the seventh time in the last five minutes. Her blood pressure was still pounding on the inside of her ears.

Jamie wasn't in school.

She fought the panic that gripped her lungs as she opened up her calendar. No, today wasn't an early release day and the school hadn't messed up Jamie's schedule like it had done before.

She tried to call Jamie again. No answer. Fear was a live thing in her belly as she closed out her e-mail. Maybe she was at the house.

She grabbed her keys and purse and headed for the door. Her ten o'clock meeting was going to have to wait. As she pulled into traffic, her phone vibrated furiously in the cup holder. Ignoring her no-driving-and-talking rule, she snatched at it.

"Jamie?"

"Hey." Gale's voice was deep and smooth over the phone. Disappointment raced over her skin. "What's wrong?"

She clicked on the speakerphone and waited impatiently to turn left toward her house. "I'm heading to the house. I think Jamie skipped school."

"Does this happen often?" A loaded question asked after a long pause.

"It happened a few times before I found out she was…you know." She hated that word. She squeezed her eyes closed, forcing down the memories.

"I'll meet you at the house."

That simple statement made her pause. "I—you don't have to."

"I'd like to help, Mel." A world of unspoken things in that simple sentence.

She could tell him no. She could tell him she didn't need his help. She could push him away and handle things the way she always did, by herself.

But the words didn't come.

Because she was tired. Tired of fighting. Tired of arguing. Tired of facing alone the fear that her daughter would move beyond the impulsive urge to cut into something with far deadlier consequences.

"Okay," she said. That single word lifted the weight from her shoulders. "I'm heading there now."

"I'm already on my way."

There were a hundred questions she could ask him about why he was doing this. Why now? "Thanks, Gale."

He made a noise and the line went dead. It was strange thinking that he would be there. They'd never gotten a chance to be a team because they'd both given up on their too young marriage. They'd been too young for a child. They'd been too young for life.

Despite her walking away from him when they were younger, the man who'd shown up on her doorstep the other night was a far cry from the boy she'd fallen in love with. She wondered what the war had done to him. How it had changed him and molded him. But she didn't have time for that now.

Gale pulled into the driveway right behind her. He drove an F150—an older model but it looked like he took care of it. Rough around the edges and built for a life of hard work.

Kind of like the man who stepped out of the truck.

His uniform didn't hide the size of his body or minimize the strength of the man. And why did she keep noticing how much he'd changed? He stopped just short of stepping into her space.

Mel adjusted her purse, palming her keys, and headed for the front door. She met his gaze and instantly realized her mistake. He was edgy, coiled energy, poised to spring. She looked away and stepped into the foyer.

She could deal with him later. For now, right now, she needed to find her daughter.

He followed her into the house silently. But his presence did nothing to alleviate the terrible feeling of being alone.

Just like always.

***

Gale followed Melanie into the house. He'd done this a time or two before. Not with this house, but he'd gone into troubled homes before. Had to break up more arguments between soldiers and their wives or their husbands. It was always tricky when it involved the kids. He glanced up the stairs, listening carefully for anything out of the ordinary.

He'd never thought he'd be entering into a situation with his own family, though.

"Jamie!"

"There's music on upstairs," he said when the ringing in his ears finally stopped and he could hear clearly once more.

Mel tipped her head and listened. Gale tried to hear if there was anything else beneath the dull echo of sound but all he could hear was the beating of his own heart.

Mel climbed the stairs quickly. Gale followed closely, feeling out of place behind her. He was used to leading the way up the stairs, not following. And even though they weren't conducting a clearing operation, it felt funny not being first.

Except that on the way up the stairs, he could savor the gentle sway of her hips as she climbed. And he was neither a saint nor a monk.

He enjoyed the view.

Maybe he'd tell her so sometime.

But not today.

Not when they were supposed to be a united front with

their daughter, who was determined to push as many boundaries as she could.

"Jamie!"

Beneath the music, there was the sound of human movement. Relief contrasted starkly with the sound of the dark, pounding, violent music that Gale recognized easily: the same stuff his boys listened to when they were getting psyched up before patrols. Gale glanced at his ex-wife. "Does she always listen to Five Finger Death Punch?"

Mel shrugged helplessly. "I never thought I'd miss the Disney days," she admitted. "I try to keep her from listening to truly horrible stuff. But yes, she listens to heavy metal." Mel frowned. "How do you know this band?"

"It's really popular with the boys."

"You listen to it?"

He shrugged and wished he didn't notice the slight curl at the edge of her lips or the curiosity in her eyes. "It's good to run to."

A smile teased the corner of her lips. "Huh. How about that."

"What?"

"You used to listen to country."

He jerked his chin toward the door. "I still do. Maybe we can get our daughter to lay off the angry metal music and back to Kenny Chesney or something less likely to give her old man a heart attack."

Smiling, Mel reached for the door handle. It didn't budge.

She slapped her palm against the doorframe. "You have two seconds, young lady!"

The door yanked open in one. "What!"

Jamie's eyes were red and mascara streaked down her cheeks. Gale's heart twinged at the sight of his little girl in tears.

Mel, however, didn't miss a beat.

"What happened?" Mel asked. "And more importantly, why aren't you in school?"

"I failed my last biology test." Angry, frustrated words. Gale stayed silent, simply observing interaction between mother and daughter. They'd done this dance too many times, he realized.

Except for his daughter's quick glance toward the floor. If Mel noticed the movement, she said nothing.

"Don't lie to your mother," he said quietly.

She looked up at him angrily. "I'm not lying, *Dad*."

"This is the last time I'm going to warn you about blocking the door," Mel said. "And you belong in school, failed test or not."

Jamie made an *ugh* sound. "Will you both please leave?"

Neither of them moved.

"I feel like there's more to this than just a bad biology grade." Gale didn't move, didn't take his eyes from the bedroom door. Something wasn't right but he couldn't put his finger on it. He was tempted to push the door open and see what else was going on. He was reasonably certain that anything he did right now was going to go over like a condom on a collection plate.

Which meant exactly zero as far as constraining his options.

Especially since he wasn't sure exactly what was triggering his bullshit meter but his Spidey senses said that there was more to what was going on in that bedroom than their daughter was letting on.

He didn't want to raise a red flag, though. This was Mel's territory and while he was happy to be her moral support, he didn't want to push any boundaries that may or may not exist. Knowing that Jamie was okay was enough for now.

"Ten minutes," Mel said. "Then you're going back to school."

"*Fine.*"

Gale followed Mel out into the hallway and the door clicked shut behind them. Not quite a slam but really, really close to one. About as close as Jamie felt like she could get without really crossing the line.

He looked down at Mel. Her eyes were less strained than a moment before; some of the tension around her mouth had faded. "Hey." His hand on her shoulder stopped her. Her shoulder was tense beneath his touch. "You okay?"

***

The simple question broke her. It shattered the chains that held the lid on her emotions. Her eyes burned. She turned her face away, unwilling to let him see her cry. "I have to be, don't I?"

His hand on her upper arm was more gentle than she remembered. He seemed patient and calm, two things she'd never associated with him. For the briefest moment, she stood there and let herself pretend that the intervening decade and its wars hadn't dragged them apart. That they'd managed to stick together when there had been more month than money.

That she hadn't screamed his name alone in the darkness when she'd sat in the hospital while the doctors stitched their daughter back together, wishing he was there instead of off to that god forsaken war.

For the briefest of moments, she stood there, stealing a moment of comfort from a man who'd always let her down.

Because she could do nothing less and she was afraid that if she moved, she would shatter into a thousand tiny pieces.

CHAPTER SIX

"She is going to go back to school, right?" Gale asked when they were downstairs and away from the pounding heavy metal upstairs.

"Yes. Ten minutes or thirty, it doesn't really matter. But I want to give her time to calm down." Mel glanced over at him from the fridge. "What kind of sandwich do you want?"

"I get food out of the deal?"

She fought the urge to smile at his question. It was strange having him here. Strange having him in her home. Strange having him stand by her side as she battled with their daughter.

She'd been fighting with her daughter for so long she'd forgotten what it felt like to not argue. To remember that there had been a time when they'd laughed and she'd painted Jamie's toenails and hadn't felt the anger pulsing off her little girl in violent purple waves.

"Where'd you go just then?" he asked gently.

Mel gave herself a mental shake and looked up to see Gale watching her. "Nowhere," she said after a moment.

He didn't look away, didn't acknowledge her dodge in any way.

She opened the fridge, pulling out lunchmeat and cheese and setting it on the island. "I forget what you like on your sandwiches," she said.

She stepped back to close the door and he was there. Right behind her. Everything fell away. In the hushed solitude of the house, his body pressed to hers. A perfect fit even after all these years. Her hips were flush against him, her back pressed against his strong chest. It was a simple accidental embrace, but suddenly Mel couldn't remember how to breathe.

They simply stood for what felt like an eternity.

She felt his breath catch. A sharp intake of breath that took her mind to a dark and primitive place. His fingers flexed on her waist, a slight touch that sent her mind into a spiral of sex and need and wanting things.

He tightened his grip on her. A momentary insanity, nothing more. Savoring the feel of his big body surrounding her. Making her feel cherished like he had once upon a time.

She closed her eyes savoring the feel of his breath, deep and slow against her back. Almost, she could imagine him cupping her face, angling her mouth to his. Almost, she lost herself in the fantasy of the moment, of the feel of his body against hers.

Then he shifted, reaching across her, leaning close enough that she could smell the soap on his skin, a hint of whatever he'd used to shave with that morning.

"Mayo," he said. He held up the jar as though her entire world hadn't just melted in a rush of heat between her thighs.

She narrowed her eyes as he moved away, setting the mayo on the counter. Mayo her Aunt Fanny, she thought. He'd done that on purpose, and now he was acting like everything was fine while she was still struggling to remember how to breathe.

There was a thump upstairs and Gale looked up at the ceiling, listening intently. "What's she doing up there?"

"Probably throwing something," she said. "She has your temper."

He looked down at her sharply. "I don't have a temper."

Mel lifted one eyebrow. "Since when?"

His lips curled at the edges. "Since I had to go to anger management training after my first tour in Iraq."

She paused, studying him. He'd turned a simple comment into a joke but there was something more. Something deeper. "Why did you have to go to anger management training?" she asked.

"Several reasons," he said after a moment.

There was nothing she could say to that. She wanted to ask. About the deployments. About the war. But she didn't know if it was rude or not, so she left her questions unasked. If he wanted to talk about it, he'd bring it up.

"Did you do stuff like that a lot?"

Gale shrugged and plucked the mustard from the door next to her before turning back to the meat on the counter. "I spent a lot of time learning to control it. I've still got a career. Win-win, right?"

There was a flippancy to his words that made her doubt the lightness in his tone, but she didn't press. She pulled the bread out of the cabinet and pulled out four slices. She looked toward the stairs. "I wonder if Jamie wants to eat."

"Want me to go ask her?"

Mel sighed and thought about her answer. "You'll probably find the door barricaded again, which would mean that Jamie wants to call my bluff about taking the door off the hinges."

Gale stopped her where she was laying out the bread. His hand closed over hers, big and solid and rough. "Mel."

She looked away, not wanting him to see the fatigue that was breaking her. "I don't want to fight with her," she admitted.

"How long has this door battle been going on?" he asked after a moment.

"It feels like forever."

Another thump from upstairs. "What the hell is she doing?"

He didn't move his hand but his grip tightened. She looked up at him, his jaw tense. He hadn't moved. "Gale?"

But he was gone, moving toward the stairs. Fear had her following him. Fear that her daughter and her ex were about to clash and she had no idea if either of them would escape unscathed.

***

Gale took the stairs two at a time and headed down the hallway as quickly and as silently as he could.

He paused outside Jamie's door, his blood pressure spiking as he heard muffled voices from behind the closed door beneath the pounding heavy metal.

He slapped his palm against the thin wood door. "Open the door, Jamie."

The music pulsed louder.

Gale jimmied the door handle, wondering how pissed Melanie would be if he ripped it off its hinges. If he was right, he'd probably get a pass.

He was backing away to get some momentum when the door opened. Just a crack but it was enough. He pushed into the room past Jamie and inhaled deeply.

"Where is he?"

His daughter stiffened and he could actually see her working to come up with a lie. "You don't have any right to come in here like this."

"I have every right," he snapped, then followed his intuition and ripped open the closet doors.

He would have missed the little shit if he'd had normal colored hair but the boy hiding in Jamie's closet had multicolored spikes that clashed with the darkness.

Gale grabbed his upper arm and dragged the kid out of the closet.

"Mom! Do something!"

Gale was vaguely aware that Melanie had followed him up the stairs to their daughter's room.

"A boy, Jamie? Have you lost your ever-loving mind?" Mel was supposed to be the voice of reason and well, she apparently wasn't going to be either of those things right then. One of them had to be calm and rational. Gale lashed his temper back violently, reminding himself that the kid in his grip was just that—a kid.

Not one of his soldiers. A kid. Just like he'd been once upon a time.

Jamie threw her hands up and rolled her eyes. "He was helping me study for biology."

"I bet," Gale muttered. The kid squirmed on the end of Gale's grip. He tightened it. He turned the kid to get a good look at him. "Your father is going to be quite interested in this little tale. Does he know where you are right now?"

"None of your business, gramps," the kid sneered.

Gale briefly wondered how long the prison sentence would be for throwing a sixteen-year-old walking hard-on down the stairs of his ex-wife's house.

"I'll give you one more chance to answer me, then I'm calling the police."

The kid lifted his chin defiantly. Gale's heart pounded in his ears violently. "Melanie, phone." Gale held out his hand.

"Yes! Shit. No, my dad doesn't know where I am."

Gale's smile could have cracked glass. "Excellent. Let's go tell your dad what you've been up to." Gale twisted his fist in the kid's collar and forcibly guided him from the bedroom. It took everything he had to keep his temper reined in.

The need to do violence pounded in his veins. Damn it, his little girl wasn't going to end up repeating the same mistakes he and her mother had made.

"You got this one?" he said to Melanie as he paused near the door, jerking his chin back toward Jamie's room, where a class one tantrum was erupting. Gale took one look and realized his soldiers at their worst had nothing on a highly pissed-off teenage girl.

"Oh yeah," Mel said. There was deep resignation in her voice. "So much for lunch, huh?"

"Don't worry about it. I'll take a rain check." The little bastard squirmed in his grip. "Hold still," he snapped at the punk ass kid. The kid froze. "Jamie, I'll talk to you tomorrow."

"I hate you!"

She slammed the door and Melanie sighed, following Gale down the stairs. "Wow, guess this changes the afternoon agenda," Mel said after a moment.

The kid was struggling for defiance but Gale could have sworn he looked like he was going to piss himself. Two seconds later, Mel returned from the garage with a bright yellow electric drill in one hand. "What are you doing?"

"What's it look like?"

He couldn't remember the last time he'd seen her so pissed off. He didn't envy her. She was going to spend the rest of the afternoon battling their daughter.

He had the strongest urge to touch her but the walking boner in his hand was squirming too much for him to let him go. "I'll come back later to make sure you haven't killed each other," he murmured.

Her tongue flicked across her bottom lip a moment before her throat moved as she swallowed. "I'm sure we'll both be alive," she said bitterly. "But I'd like that very much." A hesitant whisper.

If they'd been alone, he would have kissed her then. But they were not alone, so there was no acting on the suggestions of the good idea fairy on his shoulder, urging him to part her lips and taste her.

But he wanted to.

He had no idea what he'd do if she kissed him back.

***

"This is child abuse!"

Melanie dropped the screws to the hinges in her pocket, then hoisted and carried the door down the hallway, doing her best to ignore her daughter's tantrum.

She offered up a silent apology to her parents for every bad thing she'd ever done as a kid. If she survived long enough to keep Jamie not pregnant, off to college, and not in much more therapy, she'd consider herself a success at parenting.

Right now, she was considering herself an abysmal failure.

She leaned the door against the hallway wall and went back to retrieve the electric drill. She straightened and held out her hand. "Phone."

"No." Jamie folded her arms over her chest, her expression a mixture of belligerent and stubborn defiance that set Mel's teeth on edge.

"Fine. I'll turn it off at the cell phone provider."

"Ugh." Jamie stomped to the bed and pulled the phone out from under her mattress. "Why are you being so mean?"

"Because I'm your mother and I'm not going to let you sneak boys into my house. I've raised you better than that."

"You raised me to be a dried out, frigid old bag!"

Mel winced. Damn but her daughter knew how to fight dirty.

"Watch your mouth," Mel said softly. "Now, let's discuss the consequences for your lying and sneaking and cutting school. No phone for two weeks. No friends' houses for two weeks. No TV, no video games. I will allow you to keep the iPod provided you don't break any of the other consequences. We'll talk about the door when your two weeks are up."

"You are the worst parent ever!" Jamie's words broke over a sob, tears streaming down her face.

"I'll see you at dinner." Melanie offered a flat smile she didn't feel and headed down the stairs, acutely aware of her daughter burning holes into her back as she walked away.

"If looks could kill," Mel muttered. She set the drill on the table behind the couch then went into the kitchen. Today called for wine on more than one count.

She was glad Gale had been here today. If he hadn't figured out that Jamie had a boy in her room—dear Lord, the next thing they might have been discussing was grandbaby names. And what the hell would she have done with the boy had Gale not been there?

What a disaster.

She must have been horrible to puppies and kittens in a past life.

But honestly? She did not remember being this rotten. She was sure that adding Gale to the equation wasn't helping things with Jamie. No matter how much having him around made Melanie feel…supported.

There was a thump on the ceiling and Mel glanced up, wondering what her daughter had done to her room as payback. She hadn't been exaggerating when she'd told Gale that Jamie scared her but the sound of her crying echoed through the house.

When she'd been a toddler, her tantrums had been epic, but Mel had thought she was just needy. When she'd been a preteen, she'd started getting huffy. Then came the day when Mel had discovered her daughter passed out on the bathroom floor in a pool of blood.

She'd completely lost her shit.

She'd put a call through to Gale, who'd been in Iraq at the time. She'd sent the Red Cross message in a blind panic. And she'd waited for the phone call, hoping this time he'd be able to come home and help her deal with their daughter.

I can't come home, Mel.

Instead, she'd dealt with her daughter's latest rebellion. Alone. Like always.

The cutting had terrified Melanie and sliced at her in its own way. Reminded her that she'd failed as a parent. Good parents didn't have kids who cut themselves, right? Those were lies that tormented her when she was alone in the dark. Cutting was a mental health problem. It was not Mel's fault. Except that no matter what she did, there was no shaking the guilt, no ignoring the what ifs. Melanie had always done her best but it hadn't been enough to keep her daughter from scarring herself.

She glanced up at the sudden lack of noise from upstairs. Downing the rest of her wine she walked to the foot of the stairs and listened, then walked down the hall and checked the bathroom, just to be safe. She paused outside Jamie's room. She'd probably cried herself to sleep.

It was exactly what Mel felt like doing.

***

"What were you doing in my daughter's room?"

Gale wasn't in the mood for chitchat with the creepy miscreant in his passenger's seat but he figured Tellhouse wouldn't appreciate him skull-dragging his son all the way home behind his truck.

The kid sighed dramatically and looked out the window with a sulk.

That sigh tried the last bit of Gale's patience. The kid had no idea how close his temper was to snapping the leash that restrained it.

"Son, we can do this the easy way or the hard way. I've been to Iraq. There's no telling when my PTSD is going to act up." Gale had known Tellhouse for years but for the life of him, Gale couldn't remember his kid's name.

"I'm not your son."

"No, you're not, because if you were my kid, you would have one color hair. Now what's your name?"

Another dramatic sigh that was like nails on a chalkboard for Gale's nerves. "Alex."

"What were you doing in my daughter's closet?"

Alex shot him a dirty look. "Filming a porno, gramps."

Gale had a vision of slamming the kid's face into the dashboard like something out of a cheap B movie. But that would be neither right nor legal. He was just a smart-mouthed punk kid, trying to get Gale's temper up. And oh but it was working.

Gale had been young once. Damn, if he didn't feel like that was a million years and a lifetime ago.

Gale worked really hard not to lose his temper. Times like this took a superhuman effort.

There was a time and a place to lose one's temper and wreak havoc. Havoc was good in bar fights. Not so much in company training meetings.

Or when dealing with pissy little shits in the seat next to him.

"You better pray for your immortal soul that you're joking." Gale drummed his fingers on the steering wheel. "What were you doing with my daughter?"

"Biology."

The leather on the steering wheel twisted in his grip. "Son, you say biology and I start needing anti-psychotic medication."

Gale pulled onto Fort Hood and drove the rest of the way to his company ops, choosing to say nothing further. He stopped behind Tellhouse's office. "Let's go."

Alex's eyes widened. "My old man is going to kill me." There was genuine fear in his eyes.

Gale was still pissed off enough to have absolutely zero sympathy, but the fear looking back at him penetrated the anger. For a moment, Gale stood there, looking down at a frightened boy. No longer the defiant little shit he'd dragged cussing out of Jamie's closet. No, this was something different. "You should have thought about that before you cut school and hid out in my daughter's room."

Just like that, the defiance was back. "Ugh."

Gale ground his teeth at the universal sound of disgruntled teen angst. But when Gale followed him out of the truck, he looked back, his eyes wide. Gale kept his expression blank. "Oh, you didn't think I was going to let you just leave, did you?" He patted the kid on his shoulder. "No, your dad and I are going to have a little chat."

He squeezed Alex's shoulder until he saw the boy wince. "Stay away from my daughter."

He released the kid with a shove toward the back door of

Tellhouse's company ops.

Tellhouse looked up from behind his computer. His eyes narrowed instantly when he saw his son. "Sorren? What the…?"

"I think this belongs to you," Gale said as Alex slouched between the two men and tried to disappear.

"Where were you?"

When Alex didn't answer, Gale filled in the empty space. "Hiding in my daughter's closet."

Tellhouse frowned. "Lovely."

Gale shrugged. "Long story. Short version is your son was up to no good in her bedroom. I'd appreciate it if you'd keep him and his overactive hormones tied up until she's in college."

Tellhouse glared at his son. "Wait outside."

"Ugh."

Gale ground his teeth once more. "I hate that sound."

"That makes two of us." Tellhouse folded his arms over his chest. "Did he hurt your kid?"

"Not that I know of. Found him hiding out. Both of them were being sneaky. I'd just as soon not become a grandfather any time soon or go to jail for inflicting grievous bodily harm on a teenager so…"

Tellhouse held up one hand. "I'll talk to him."

"Appreciate it." He started to go.

Tellhouse told his kid to get in the office and shut the door. Gale wished he hadn't heard the other first sergeant start yelling before the lock was clicked.

Gale hesitated at the sound of a hand slapping on wood. On the one hand, Gale was still royally pissed he'd found him in his daughter's bedroom. On the other, Gale had been a horny sixteen-year-old once upon a time.

Tellhouse wouldn't hurt the kid. Right? Gale waited another moment, then left, an unsettled feeling deep in his gut.

CHAPTER SEVEN

Melanie stared at the television, not really seeing the news. The wine in her glass was tepid but she kept swirling it aimlessly.

Except for going to school, Jamie hadn't come downstairs since the epic battle over her door. Which had been two days ago. She stomped out of the house first thing in the morning and stomped back in after school. Melanie had cooked dinner but Jamie hadn't eaten. At least, not with Melanie.

There were dishes in the sink in the morning, though, so she knew her daughter hadn't resorted to an active hunger strike.

Melanie regretted taking the door off Jamie's room. But what was she supposed to do? She'd threatened to take it off so many times and Jamie kept ignoring her. And hadn't the therapist said that there were boundaries and consequences for every action?

It wasn't some vapid paranoia.

It was a fear grounded very much in reality.

She pulled her knees up to her chest and rested her chin in her palm, staring into the swirling white wine. A tiny vortex of sparkling clarity. Too bad she didn't know how to get that clarity with her daughter. She wished she knew how to break the cycle of fighting and bitterness. This epic clusterfuck of a relationship.

Her phone vibrated from the other room. She thought about ignoring it. She wasn't in the mood to deal with any drama from the office. If she was getting called to go in because the intern forgot to turn off the coffee pot again… She tossed back the rest of her wine and padded into the kitchen, the glass dangling limply in her fingers.

A smile toyed at the edge of her lips when she saw Gale's name in the caller ID. It was too easy to smile. Too easy to let herself pretend that all those lonely yesterdays hadn't happened. "Hey."

"Hey." His voice was warm and welcoming on the end of the phone. A bright spot in the shitstorm of her afternoon. "Any improvement on the temperamental daughter front?"

Mel glanced toward the ceiling. "I wish I could report otherwise but no, she's still not talking to me."

"Want me to come over and try to talk to her?"

She frowned, glancing at the wine bottle on the center island, then decided to pour another glass. "I hadn't really thought about that," she admitted after a moment.

Gale said nothing. "I'm not trying to be bitchy," she said quickly. "I just… I'm not used to you being around. That's all."

A resigned, heavy sigh before he spoke. "I know."

Screw it. "Come over. Come try to talk to her. What's the worst that could happen?"

"She could start hating me instead of you?"

Mel smiled even as her eyes burned. He'd been making a joke but it still hurt to hear. "That would be a nice change of pace." Her heart cracked a little in her chest but she wouldn't let him hear her cry.

She hung up the phone and tried to keep her messy emotions from cracking open the vault where she'd locked them. Everything with Gale was messy.

Headlights flooded the living room a few minutes later. She opened the door, surprised to see him in civilian clothes. Casual jeans and a button-down shirt cuffed at the wrists.

She took a step back to let him into the house. Maybe that second glass of wine hadn't been such a good idea. It made her feel loose and warm as he walked toward her. He paused, his eyes warm and dark. "How are you holding up?"

"Been worse, I suppose." She lifted the glass of wine to her lips. It was sparkling and sweet on her tongue.

She felt like every movement was under a microscope. Like she was being watched by a hungry beast. For a moment, Melanie felt something she hadn't felt in the war zone that her home had become. She felt alive. Aware of the heat in her veins, the tightness of her skin.

She reminded herself it was all an illusion. An illusion that started with the man in her foyer and would end with her heart breaking again.

Because Gale Sorren was a soldier. And that meant that anyone in his life always came second to the Army. It was a mistake to let any fantasy take hold. A terrible mistake.

Gale wouldn't stick around long enough to convince her it was real. So why get wrapped up in the fantasy, no matter how nice it was thrumming through her veins at that moment?

The rough hair at the base of his throat drew her gaze. The hard line of his collarbone collided with the edge of his shirt and Mel suddenly had a hard time breathing.

"You're bigger than I remember," she said, needing something to say, to fill the hushed space between them.

"I'm about fifty pounds heavier, if that's what you're getting at." There was a faint curl at the edge of his lips.

"Fifty pounds?" She looked over the broad expanse of man in front of her. Wide shoulders and rough hands. If there was fifty extra pounds on the man, he wore it well.

Really well.

She turned away before he realized she was mentally undressing him. And wouldn't that be fun—and awkward—to explain?

Yeah, that second glass of wine had definitely been a mistake. It was taking her mind on a road trip that started at Gale's throat and traveled down that amazing chest to… She turned away, flicking on the outside light as the sun sank into the central Texas hills.

Oh Lord, she needed to go on a date. Or take a hot shower. Maybe both.

"Mel?"

His words brushed over her hair. He was standing too close. Her spine tingled from the heat of his body. It took every ounce of control not to lean back against him like she'd done when they were younger.

She didn't know if he'd moved or if she had. But one moment she was standing still. The next he was behind her, his body flush against hers. His big, powerful chest against her back, warmth from his body penetrating hers, wrapping around her and holding her close.

She felt his lips against the top of her head. His hands slipped up her arms. A gentle caress by rough, war-worn hands. He skimmed her exposed flesh. Teased the warmth pulsing through her to a fevered pitch.

It would be a simple thing to lean into him. To close her eyes and lower her head back to his strong shoulders. To let him hold her in a way she hadn't been held since…since the last time his arms had been around her.

It would be such a simple thing.

***

Gale didn't know what had possessed him. But when she'd started undressing him with her eyes, it had done something powerful to the need he'd been restraining since he'd returned to her life.

He'd known when he'd gotten his orders to come back to Fort Hood that he'd wanted to be part of Jamie's life again. He'd hoped beyond hope that maybe it wasn't too late. He'd made that decision when he'd been stuck in Iraq while his little girl was in a psych ward and his wife—his ex-wife—faced that trial alone.

He'd almost quit then and there. But he hadn't. Because as much as he'd needed to be home, he'd been in the middle of a bad fight in Tal Afar.

He knew he'd been a shitty husband and a worse father. He knew that. But still, he'd made choices. Choices that had involved begging Sarn't Major Cox to get him pulled down to Fort Hood.

He didn't know how many favors Cox had called in to get Gale's ass out of a sling and on assignment, but he assumed it had been a lot.

He stood there now, in Melanie's foyer, close enough to reach out and touch her.

And he did. Because he could do nothing less. And the latent hope that maybe, just maybe, he could fix things with Melanie, that he could somehow make up for not being there for her all those years, grew into something he could no longer control.

His breath caught in his throat as he skimmed his hands up her arms. Desire, raw and powerful, sliced through him when she shivered in response to his touch.

It took everything he had not to gather her into his arms and pull her against him. It was enough, for the moment, to simply stand close to her. To inhale the sweet, clean scent of her shampoo. Feel the cool silk of her hair against his cheek.

To know that she had not pulled away.

He traced his hands over her shoulders. Barely touching her. Skimming along the soft skin of her neck.

They stood together for what seemed like an eternity. He couldn't move away, couldn't tear his hands away from the barest touch. He could do nothing more than hold her in his arms and feel her breathing against him. Her back shifted with each breath, bringing her closer with each tiny inhalation.

He ached to kiss her. Ached to turn her in his arms and press his lips to hers. To see how different she would taste now with a lifetime apart between them.

But he was afraid that this was all nothing more than an episode of insanity.

One he didn't want to end.

He wasn't sure if she moved or if he did, but the moment faded. Slowly, reality intruded and he lowered his hands as she stepped away.

She turned to face him. Her hair had fallen in her eyes and she lifted one hand to slide it behind one ear.

"Jamie's upstairs." Her voice sounded off. Heavy and sultry. Her eyes were dark and clouded with shadows, and something else.

Something he thought he knew but was afraid to name.

He cleared his throat before he spoke. It was a long time before he found the words he needed to say.

The words he wanted to say started with *please* and ended with them naked. He wasn't sure that would go over well.

And besides, he wanted to keep the moment untarnished in his memory. It had been so fucking long since he'd held her.

"So what's our negotiating position?" he asked.

"On what?" She frowned and looked down at her wine glass.

"I'm going upstairs. Are there any things that are expressly forbidden? I don't want to undermine you."

She smiled and it was warm and sunny. "You sound like you know how kids play mom against dad."

He grinned down at her, fighting the urge to stroke his fingers over her cheek. She was so fucking adorable. "It's part of the duty description of being a first sergeant," he said mildly.

She frowned. "I'm quite sure I have no idea what you're talking about."

"Soldiers will try to get between you and your commander. It's up to the commander and the first sergeant to present a united front."

She opened her mouth to say something then closed it.

He stepped close. "What?"

"I—" She paused, refusing to lift her gaze to meet his. "I guess I hadn't thought about it."

Something he'd said upset her. It cut at him, slicing away the moment before and replacing it with something raw and bleeding. "What, Mel?"

He lifted his hand to her cheek then, more to offer comfort than to steady her.

He was shocked when she didn't pull away.

"I guess I never thought about you and me being a united front." Her words were thick and uncertain, filled with fear and old hurts. Because he could find no other way to soothe the aching hurt in her eyes, he lowered his mouth to hers. A gentle kiss. Hesitant. A brush of lips.

Tentative and seeking. He sucked gently on her bottom lip, urging her to open for him, begging her with his mouth to not pull away.

There was fear in his kiss. Terror that she would pull away and slap at him.

But then her lips parted. Just a little, but it was enough for him to feel her breath on his tongue. She tasted sweet and sunny from the wine. He could get drunk on her taste. He deepened the kiss, slipping his tongue against hers and losing a piece of his soul.

He held himself viciously in check. Barely cupped her cheeks as he fought the turbulent need inside, as it surged up, wanting her, only her. To remind her that she was his, she'd always been his.

But this was a campaign, not a single battle.

He eased back before she could pull away. "I'm here now." His words brushed against her mouth. "For as long as you'll let me, I'm here." He stroked his thumb over her cheek. "I know I haven't been someone you can count on." He brushed his lips against hers again. "But I'd like to be."

CHAPTER EIGHT

"Go away."

Gale stood on the opposite side of a deep magenta sheet that Jamie had stapled across her doorway. Gale smiled at the petulant defiance in her voice.

She sounded like her mother. He wondered how she'd react if he told her that.

He decided against it. He was there to try and make the peace, not stir up the revolution again.

He was used to dealing with petulant kids. Hell, half his company was only a couple years older than Jamie. He could handle a cranky private.

Daughters were a whole 'nother ballgame.

He supposed it was different when said disgruntled teenager was one's own spawn, as opposed to someone else's kid. He was starting to think that dealing with a platoon full of nineteen-year-old boys was infinitely easier than dealing with his own kid.

Still, he'd never backed down from a challenge, and this one was so much more important than anything he'd done before.

He knocked on the doorframe again.

"Are you deaf? Leave me alone."

"Jamie, it's me." He wanted to say *it's your father* but the word was awkward. Like a shirt that didn't fit and cut too tight beneath his arms.

The sheet yanked open. For a moment, she looked genuinely curious about his presence, then the angry mask dropped back into place. "What do you want?"

Gale stuffed his hands in his pockets and tried to figure out how to get into that room without violating her space. She needed to invite him in, otherwise it would be defeating the purpose.

He couldn't just give her orders like one of his soldiers.

That made the entire situation trickier than anything he'd dealt with and he'd dealt with a lot.

"Can I come in?"

She scowled. "Aren't you just going to barge in like mom does?"

"Nope. Not until you invite me."

"What are you, a vampire?"

Gale covered his mouth as he laughed out loud. Holy shit, his daughter was a budding smart ass. He wondered if she knew how funny she sounded. She stepped back to throw the sheet in his face. He caught it. "I wasn't laughing at you, Jamie. Swear. I thought your vampire comment was funny, that's all."

She narrowed her eyes at him, only slightly mollified. "Fine. Come in."

He stepped into a minefield. There were clothes all over the floor and every exposed space on her dresser and bed. He fought his ingrained reaction to tell her to start picking up her shit. She wasn't one of his soldiers.

But the mess did something to his anxiety levels. His palms actually started sweating. There were clothes everywhere. Torn sheets of paper and old homework, and he didn't even want to think about what might be under the bed. Stuff was everywhere, except for a small space where it looked like she'd been curled up with a hardcover book.

His little girl was a reader. Somehow, he felt tremendous relief at that insight. "What are you reading?"

"*The Hunger Games*."

"Can I sit down?" He pointed toward the edge of her bed.

She shrugged. "Sure."

"What made you pick it?"

Her eyes lit up with excitement. "It's about this girl Katniss Everdeen. And there's a guy in it who has your name, which is weird because I've never met anyone else with your name before."

"It's not common." He shifted, not wanting to interrupt her when she was clearly in the flow of telling him about this book. It did something funny to his heart knowing she might have picked the book up because the boy's name matched his. Something that might have been guilt for not being part of her life for so long that she latched onto a character with his name.

"And Katniss and Gale have to take care of their families because they're dirt poor. And when her sister gets called to fight in the Hunger Games, she volunteers to take her place."

Gale frowned. "I'm not following. What are the Hunger Games and why would Kat—" He struggled over the name.

"Katniss," she said. "Well, the Capitol makes the twelve districts provide tributes every year as punishment for rebelling. Each year, tributes are drawn from each of the districts between the ages of twelve and eighteen. And there's only one survivor every year."

"So this is a book about kids killing each other?"

"Yeah but it's more than that. It's…it's powerful, Dad. It's so good." Gale watched her face light up in a way he hadn't seen before.

He'd never been a big reader but watching his daughter's energy, he made a decision then and there. "So can I read with you?"

She leaned back against the bed, her eyes narrowed. "Really?"

He shrugged. "Yeah, why not? I mean there are adults reading it, right?" She looked wary but not completely opposed to the idea. "I mean, why not? I can go pick up a copy, right?"

She narrowed her eyes. "Is this a trick?"

"Why would it be a trick?"

"Because I haven't talked to Mom in days. It's total bullshit that she took my door off."

"Watch your mouth."

"Why? You swear."

He shifted on the bed, drumming his fingers on one knee. "I'm a grown-ass man and in the infantry to boot. It's part of my job description. You, however, are an almost-sixteen-year-old girl. There is plenty of time for you to swear later in life when doing so isn't going to give your old man a heart attack."

Jamie giggled. Gale was honestly surprised he'd managed to get all of that out without her storming out of the room. Instead, she surprised him by laughing.

"What's so funny?"

"You. You come in here all disgruntled that I swore. I'm not seven anymore, Dad."

A lump swelled in his throat. Suddenly and unexpectedly, she'd carved a piece out of his heart with that simple declaration. "I know you're not, honey. But I would like to keep my illusions that you're not ready to hit the stripper pole just yet, if that's okay with you."

Jamie covered her mouth and laughed, doubling over until she gasped for breath.

"I had no idea I was that funny," he said dryly.

"Sorry." She swiped at her eyes, her lips still curled in a warm smile. She pulled her knees up to her chest. "Why isn't it this easy to talk to Mom?" she asked.

"Because you and your mom have forgotten how to do anything other than fight," he said. "And your mom is doing the very best she can. She's done a damn good job with you, if you ask me."

"She's a Nazi control freak," Jamie said, her eyes darkening.

"Nazis are a very specific evil," he said gently. "Calling your mother one trivializes the evil that they did."

She sobered at his correction. "Sorry," she mumbled. "I

just want my privacy."

"Honey, you scared the both of us pretty bad when you went into the hospital." He reached for her then, covering her hands with his. She was tiny, the bones in her hand small and fragile beneath his.

Something surged inside him, something that made him realize he would do violence to protect his daughter. "Your mom is still afraid for you." He waited until she met his gaze to add, "So am I."

"I'm not…I'm not doing that anymore," she said. "I'm trying to get better. Why won't either of you believe me?"

Gale opted for silence. This was so far outside of his area of expertise it wasn't even funny. The stakes, though—damn it, he couldn't screw this up. "Because we have to trust you. And sneaking boys into your bedroom when you're skipping school is not exactly a solid way to earn our trust."

She shot him a baleful look that was so much like Mel when she'd been younger that Gale paused and fought the urge to laugh. "That's so not fair."

"Trust is earned. It's actually quite fair."

Jamie folded her arms over her chest. "I'm not getting my door back any time soon, am I?"

"That's up to your mother." Gale shrugged and struggled not to grin at the sound of her disgruntlement. "You could start by talking to her. You know, act like a grown up?" He bit off the last of his thought, the part where he said *instead of a petulant child.*

Jamie made that disgusted *ugh* sound again. And Gale stood, taking the mild victory while he still could.

***

Melanie sat quickly on the edge of the couch, trying not to look like she'd been eavesdropping. She couldn't hear much from the bottom of the stairs but she'd heard her daughter laugh and figured things had to be going better than if she'd attempted to talk to her.

Another moment passed and she heard Gale's footsteps on the floor overhead.

Descending slowly. Each step brought him closer to her. Closer to where she could reach out and touch him.

That kiss had rocked her world. She hadn't expected the strength of her response to his touch. She hadn't planned on letting it get that far. In her head, she'd pulled away before his lips had touched hers.

But then the memory of his kiss wouldn't burn against her lips. It wouldn't chip at the ice around her heart and threaten to melt the wall she'd erected the day all those years ago when she'd walked away from him.

To be fair, she had been a willing participant in that kiss. No one had ever made her blood heat like Gale just had.

He descended the stairs and paused, leaning against the wall, a look of confusion and triumph on his face.

"Well?"

"I'm not sure if I won or lost," he said, walking over to the couch. "But I'm now going to the bookstore to pick up something called *The Hunger Games* because there's a character in it with my name."

"The one about kids killing each other?"

He frowned. "Yeah. You've heard about this?"

"Yeah. A couple of the agents in my office were talking about it."

"I can't believe this is a kids' book," he said. "But I offered to read it with her and she took me up on it. So there you go."

"You have made a great peace offering." Mel swirled the wine in her glass, needing something to do with her hands. "I'm jealous."

"Don't be," he said. "Remember, united front. She should be downstairs in a little while. I may have talked her into breaking the silent treatment."

"How did you pull that one off?" She hadn't been joking. The green-eyed monster settled around her shoulders and she felt petty and small and childish for not shoving it away. It wasn't fair that he could go upstairs and get Jamie to talk to him so easily.

She felt peevish that she'd been there through music recitals and school plays and lost teeth and Gale could just waltz in and talk Jamie out of a pissy mood.

She looked away, hoping to hide the amazing shot of bitterness that had just burst through her. She should be happy that he'd made progress. Happy that he was there trying.

Not bitchy that he'd gotten a prize she so badly wanted for herself.

Her daughter's affection.

"Mel?"

He hadn't approached, hadn't come any closer to where she sat on the couch. She didn't want him to see how she was feeling. She didn't want to admit it even to herself.

She pushed away from the couch and walked into the kitchen, needing a moment to pull her emotions back from the brink.

She didn't hear him follow her. She wasn't sure what she'd say or do if she turned around and he was there.

She'd invited him over to talk to Jamie. He'd talked to her. Maybe even smoothed things over.

It was what she'd wanted. So why did it hurt that Jamie was so willing to jump at her father?

She closed her eyes. She was such a bitch. Gale's hand closed over hers where she held the wine glass.

"Talk to me, Mel?"

There was crisp dark hair on his forearms, dusting the backs of his hands. His palm was rough and hard over hers but his touch was gentle.

He stroked his thumb along the edge of hers. "Tell me what I did to make you sad."

Such a loaded question. So many ways she could answer.

Maybe she shouldn't have been drinking tonight. Maybe she shouldn't have invited him over. Maybe she should have suffered her daughter's temper until it burned out.

Maybe she should never have let him back into her life.

But she had. And in doing so, she'd opened herself up to all the old hurts, all the old memories that she hadn't been good enough for him to put her first over the Army.

And now she wasn't good enough for her daughter to choose her over her father.

What a fucking disaster she was.

"I'm fine, Gale," she said, finally meeting his gaze.

"You're a terrible liar, Melanie."

He said her full name. He always called her Mel, except when he was upset with her.

She looked up sharply.

There was something dark looking back at her. Frustration, maybe. But not the warm sensuality that had looked back at her when they'd kissed.

She felt the loss like a tangible thing. The truce violated, the peace shattered.

She poured the rest of her wine and slipped her hand from beneath his and decided that for once, she would be an adult and tell him the truth. "I'm jealous." There, she'd said it and now it would be an ugly, twisted thing between them.

"Of what?"

She turned away, taking a long pull off her wine to steady herself. Or maybe give her the courage to destroy the fragile peace between them.

Either way, she knew if she opened her mouth, she was going to ruin whatever this was between them. And she hated herself for doing it.

"Jesus, Mel, you're serious?" She caught a shadow of his reflection in the microwave over the stove. He shoved his hands angrily through his hair. "I thought I could smooth things over with her and you're pissed about it?"

"I'm not angry," she said. Her words were heavy, a lead weight of failure. She lowered her forehead to the glass in her hand. It was cold and wet against her skin. "I'm sad."

"I am utterly confused right now." He paced behind her. She could hear him prowling, feel the frustration pulsing off him in palpable waves.

"About this. You can go upstairs and get her to read with you and make everything better. Nothing I do works with her and you come in and work your daddy mojo and everything's perfect." She drained the rest of the glass. "I'm sorry if that makes me a terrible person but I've done everything I know how to do with that girl and nothing I do is good enough. Nothing. And I'm sorry because this isn't your fault or your problem." *I'm just a shitty person. There's a reason I'm alone.* But she kept that to herself. Barely.

She finally turned to face him. His jaw was tight, his shoulders tense. He looked like he didn't know what to do with his hands.

"Jesus, Mel. I'm—" He stopped and she held up one hand.

"Look, thank you for coming tonight," she said softly. "I'm glad you got her to talk to you." She sighed and it did nothing to ameliorate the tension in her chest. "But you should probably go now."

Before I cry in front of you. Before I give up the last bit of my pride and ask you to stay.

But she said none of those things.

Because she'd screwed up enough in her life.

CHAPTER NINE

Gale slept like shit.

It was a bad start to any day when he didn't get at least three hours of sleep. Anything less and it was going to be a rough day for all parties concerned.

He'd been getting by on so little for so long that he'd almost forgotten how bad it felt to toss and turn all night. Most nights he simply sat up watching TV, nursing a beer until he fell asleep.

Last night, he'd been too keyed up from the argument with Melanie to do anything but pace his apartment. He'd started drinking around midnight and crashed somewhere around two.

The alarm for PT formation went off somewhere around four forty-five, just like it did every day, and he dragged his dead ass out of bed and into the bathroom.

He cut himself shaving and swore a blue streak as he tried to stop the bleeding. Blood had dripped down his cheek and onto his chest before he'd finally managed to stick a piece of toilet paper on the wound.

He managed not to slice any major arteries as he finished the rest of his face and barely remembered to wipe the blood off his chest before he left the bathroom. "What the hell?"

Beneath the blood was a bright silver hair. Actually there were several. "Wonderful. I'm turning into a silverback," he grumbled. He wondered if it mattered that first the hair on his head had started turning grey and now his chest hair was fading. Jesus, he practically had one foot in the grave.

He swiped at the blood then finished dragging on his PT

shorts and t-shirt, hoping the morning didn't get any worse. But that would be too much to hope for.

Traffic sucked because he managed to get out of his apartment five minutes later than he normally did, which meant he was still sitting in traffic as zero six hundred hours rolled by.

He'd forgotten all of his anger management techniques by the time he finally pulled into his parking spot behind the company. He didn't even bother to go into the office. He locked his keys in the truck, grabbed his PT belt, and stalked around front to formation.

His platoon sergeants had everyone already formed up but someone important was missing. "Where's the commander?" he said to Iaconelli, his headquarters platoon sergeant.

"Not sure, Top," Iaconelli said. "None of the lieutenants have heard from him either."

Gale frowned but there was no way to call his commander because he'd left his cell phone in his truck. As Mondays went, this one sucked. "All right, well here's hoping he's not dead in a ditch somewhere."

He took the company on an eight-mile run. The pace wasn't grueling; at least, not as bad as Gale could have made it. As shitty as his Monday had started off, he needed to run until his mood improved.

Which meant the formation would run with him until they quit, passed out, or died.

But no one said a word. They were too busy keeping up or trying not to puke.

Either way, the cadence behind him worked its way into his blood and helped him find his rhythm as he took his frustrations out on the Fort Hood pavement.

He couldn't figure Melanie out. She'd let him come over. She'd encouraged his talking to Jamie, and then when things had gone pretty damn good in Gale's opinion, Mel had gotten upset.

Not upset. Jealous.

And that didn't make a damned bit of sense.

He gave up the tightness in his lungs and the stiffness in his legs and became part of the formation. Part of the group. Just one piece of the whole.

There was something about running with formation that was almost peaceful. Except when he was trying to kill them.

Which he hadn't set out to do, but then Iaconelli tapped him on the shoulder and he looked back to realize he'd lost half the formation.

He looped back around and picked up the stragglers, then slowed the pace so they could finish together.

And they did, to the last man.

He released them to conduct personal hygiene and headed for the gym to shower and change. He swore a blue streak when he realized that at least some of the moisture on his face was blood instead of just sweat. And of course, his commander took that moment to walk into the locker room.

"What's the other guy look like?" Teague asked.

"Cut myself shaving."

"Shouldn't you be better at this, being part Wookie?"

Gale flipped Teague off and continued to apply pressure to the freshly bleeding wound. This was ridiculous.

"What's got you in such a shitty mood?"

"Rough weekend, that's all."

"And this rough weekend wouldn't happened to be named Melanie, would it?"

Gale looked up at Teague sharply. "Just because you've got a happily ever after with the lawyer doesn't mean I need you interrogating my love life."

"Or lack thereof?"

Gale removed the tissue. Finally the blood wasn't flowing like he'd sliced an artery.

"So when are you going to come clean with me about your concerns about Iaconelli?" Teague said after a moment.

"There's nothing to talk about, sir." He really didn't want

to have this conversation in the locker room. It wasn't crowded yet, but in a few more minutes it was going to be ass-to-elbow packed. "I'm keeping an eye on things. If I have concerns, I'll talk to you about them," he said.

When he looked over at his commander, Teague was watching him silently. "Fair enough," the other man said.

"So how's the lawyer doing with all the paperwork?"

"She said this weekend that she's never seen so much misconduct and just general don't-give-a-shitness in her entire career."

"Sounds like she's making progress."

"She's keeping busy. And with all the misconduct we keep having, she'll be busy until we deploy." Teague grabbed his towel and shower kit. "So how's the kid?"

That was the second question Gale didn't feel like answering in the locker room. "Giving her mom fits. I'm glad I finally made it here," he said.

"And I notice you dodged the earlier question about her mom."

Gale scratched his chest idly. "She's good."

"And by good I take it to mean you're still striking out with her." Teague shifted, folding his arms across his chest.

Gale sighed heavily. "I'm not exactly a stellar example of father of the year."

Teague shook his head. "This has nothing to do with you being a dad and everything to do with you holding a flame for your ex-wife."

Gale said nothing for a long time.

"Maybe. But right now we've got our hands full with our daughter."

Teague cocked one eyebrow. "You know, if you were a buck private and telling me that, I'd whip your ass for panting after a woman who doesn't fucking want you." Teague swiped his hand over his mouth. "But since you're you and you seem determined to deal with this woman in your hardheaded way,

I'll just wish you good luck. Because you, buddy boy, are going to need it if you're trying this again. Have you even been on a date in the last decade?"

"Been busy fighting a war, sir."

"So have I."

Teague headed into the showers, leaving Gale with his thoughts. He'd wanted to get to Hood to try and be a dad. He hadn't counted on things getting complicated with Melanie.

And he didn't have the slightest idea how to navigate this new terrain with his ex. Still, Teague's comment wasn't completely without merit. Sort of. The idea of taking Mel out for a date was insane. She was clearly still irritated with him about a number of things, and even when he tried to do things right, he ended up screwing them up with her. Still, he'd done far more stupid things in his life.

When he was dressed and alone in his truck, he summoned the courage to pick up his phone. He was glad he was alone so that no one could see his hands shake when he pressed the little green button.

"Hello?" Her voice was tense. He half expected her not to answer.

But she did and he felt a foolish surge of triumph.

"Hey. I wanted…" He cleared his throat. "I wanted to see if you could get away for lunch."

The empty space hung on between them for forever, maybe longer. Damn it, he should have waited to call, to let her get over being mad at him. It went on so long he looked at the phone to make sure the call was still connected.

"Sure." There was uncertainty in her voice. Things were still fragile between them. He could handle fragile. He couldn't handle silence, though. "How about Jason's Deli?"

"Sounds good. When can you get away?"

He heard her mumble something and he assumed she was with a client. "About ten-thirty?"

"Sounds good. Melanie?"

"Hmm?"

"See you soon."

He disconnected the call and wondered if he'd lost his ever-loving mind.

How exactly did one go about dating one's ex-wife?

***

See you soon.

What game was he playing? She was off-kilter now that Gale lived in town. Things that had always been in their place—old memories that had been locked away—were rising from the grave, throwing her off.

There was a gentle knock on her window and she jumped, damn near out of her skin.

Gale stood outside. His hat and sunglasses hid half his face, revealing nothing but hard jaw. He looked like every woman's fantasy soldier. Iron jaw, broad shoulders.

Too bad there was so much baggage between them.

He stepped back when she opened the door.

"Hi," he said. There was hesitation in his voice. "You look nice."

"Thanks."

Sometimes, going through the motions of conversation was easier than making real conversation.

"Thanks for meeting me," he said, falling into step with her as she locked the door and dropped her keys into her purse.

"I had time."

He held the door for her, then followed her into the restaurant. She handed him a menu, only to give up reading her own after a moment. "So listen, about the other night."

She didn't miss the way his eyes crinkled at the edges as he looked down at her. Holy Lord in heaven that was sexy.

She pulled her thoughts out of the gutter. "I'm sorry about...how I acted," she admitted softly.

The muscle in his jaw pulsed. He said nothing. "I spent most of the night trying to figure out what I did wrong."

"It wasn't you." Melanie sighed. "It was me. And I know that sounds like a cliché but it's true. I shouldn't have put that on you like I did."

"I…I don't know how to fix that," he said. He took a step closer, sliding one hand up her arm to rest on her neck. "I didn't mean to make things worse for you, Mel."

A hesitant admission. Her heart pounded in her chest a little harder. "I know you didn't. And I'm sorry I reacted so poorly."

"Okay." His thumb brushed against her jaw. A hesitant caress before he lowered his hand. They moved forward in the line and ordered. He put his hand over hers when she reached for her credit card. "Let me buy you lunch?"

He surrounded her. With one simple gesture he undid her. Chipped away at the wall around her heart a little more. "Thank you."

They got their drinks and went to find a table, settling on one behind the salad bar in relative seclusion.

"So let's play a game." He didn't look at her, though, sparking her curiosity as to what exactly he had in mind.

"A game? You never played games before."

"A lot's changed over the years."

"Apparently." She watched him snag a sugar packet from the little holder. "You don't look like the game-playing type," she said lightly.

"Maybe I'm trying something new," he said. There was that look again. That look that made her insides turn to liquid heat and made her want to do dark and forbidden things with him.

"So what's the game?" she asked as he poured a sugar packet into his unsweetened tea. She didn't remember him drinking tea.

He leaned forward, cupping his hands around hers. "Let's pretend."

He stroked his thumbs across the tops of her knuckles.

"Let's pretend what?" Her breath hitched a little in her throat.

"Let's pretend we just met."

"Gale, that's silly."

His hands tightened around hers. "Just hear me out." She stilled beneath his touch. "Look, a lot has changed. With you, with me. With Jamie. But after the other night, I realized I was the interloper. And that you were right. That I'd waltzed right into your life and expected everything to kind of fall into place because I wanted it to." He looked down at their hands. "That's not fair to you and everything you've gone through. You've done a hell of a job with Jamie, Mel." A slide of his thumb over her hand. "But I want to get to know you again. I know the girl who used to jump into the quarry with me." He cleared his throat. "I want to get to know who you are now."

Mel blinked at the sincerity in his words. The thick pressure in her lungs increased and she didn't know what to say that wouldn't screw things up any more than she'd already screwed things up with him.

But there he sat. Telling her he wanted to get to know her. Apart from their daughter.

It wasn't anything more than what it was: a simple declaration.

So why did her stupid heart start beating faster, wanting more than she'd ever allowed herself to dream of?

***

The last time he'd been this nervous, he'd been getting shot at somewhere north of Baghdad and he'd lost his lieutenant.

Okay, so maybe that was a bad analogy, but still. It took everything he had to keep his hands from shaking.

He'd just poured his heart out onto the table and Mel was

sitting there saying nothing. Looking lost and confused and a little dazed.

Maybe he'd come on too strong. Maybe he should have just left this at lunch and pushed a little more later. Once she trusted him a little more.

Once they had something more between them than awkward memories and a failed marriage and a daughter who hated them both.

But the more he'd thought about her reaction the other night, he knew he was right to lay his cards on the table. He couldn't go into this with half measures, trying to guess what she was thinking.

So he'd taken the direct approach.

And now had to sit here, waiting.

"Can you say something? Stab me in the heart with a fork, tell me to pound sand. Anything?"

Mel laughed, pulling her hand free to cover her mouth. Her eyes shimmered and he realized she'd been fighting tears. Oh shit, he'd made her cry.

"Sorry." She swiped at her eyes. "I just…I was just absorbing everything."

"Absorbing in a good way or a stab-me-in-the-heart way?"

She smiled again. "A good way. I think."

"Good doesn't usually come with qualifiers."

"It's …it's… Are you trying to say you want to date?"

That question cost her a lot to ask. She flinched from it and he saw the expectation on her face that he was going to clarify. That he was going to reject her somehow.

She'd never seemed this uncertain, this hesitant before. Even when she'd been pregnant with Jamie, she'd always seemed to know exactly what she was doing and charged full speed ahead.

It was only after Jamie was born that things had changed. Dramatically.

"I need you to come home, Gale."

"I can't. I'm in California, honey. I'm locked down at NTC."

"I don't know what to do with the baby. She won't stop crying." There had been tears in Mel's voice, and crackling over the phone line that had nothing to do with the connection.

"Can you take her to the hospital?"

She'd sounded so lost.

She'd left him less than two months after that phone call.

"Yes, Melanie. I'd like to get to know you." He swallowed the lump of nerves that blocked off his throat. "You know, if there's no one else or anything."

"I don't have a big social life," she admitted after a moment. "Jamie and work make up the bulk of it."

"Maybe we can change that?"

He leaned back as the waitress brought their food, trying to figure out if things were going well or going to hell.

He wasn't sure. She looked so hesitant. So uncertain.

There was a vulnerability to Mel that hadn't been there before. And he blamed himself for putting it there.

She folded her napkin in her lap and looked down at her salad, toying with a cherry tomato.

"Are you going back to Iraq?" There was fear, naked and raw, in her voice but if they were going to do this, she needed to know if he was going to really be around or if he was off to the great unknown once more.

"Just once more," he said.

"When?"

"A few months, I think."

She blinked rapidly and toyed with the fork beside her plate. She didn't pick it up.

Gale waited.

Waited until she looked up at him. Waited until she met his gaze. "That's terrifying," she said.

"It's not that bad. I'm used to it now," he said. "And I'm pretty good at what I do."

"You're not in danger?"

He shrugged, not wanting to travel down the wormhole of bad deployments and the number of times he'd had the shit scared out of him. "It's always dangerous."

"Jamie worries about you when you deploy."

"Do you?"

The question was out before he could stop it.

Her eyes darkened with an intensity that stunned him. "Yes, Gale. I worry about you."

"That's really nice to hear." He leaned forward, capturing her hand once more. "Really nice."

"As opposed to me wanting to stab you with a fork?" she said.

His laugh surprised him, more so than her attempt at humor. "Yeah, as opposed to stabbing me," he said after taking a sip of his drink.

It wasn't much, but it was progress. A small step toward something normal in a relationship that was anything but.

CHAPTER TEN

Gale would rather get a root canal than sit through staff meetings, but as a first sergeant, meetings were part of his duty description. A large part, sadly. How painful said meetings were, however, depended on all parties involved.

Seeing how this past weekend their battalion had apparently set records for misconduct on Fort Hood, Gale braced for at least a two-hour marathon with an option for three. And that would all be before the sergeant major got hold of them and spent another hour running a wire brush over their collective backsides.

He was going to lose his damn mind—if not from sheer boredom, then from lack of getting anything done. He was bringing evaluation reports along to read through and red line. Maybe he could get some of those done while the other command teams were getting their asses handed to them.

Gale glanced at his watch, wondering where the hell his commander was. Teague had been popping up missing lately and Gale needed to corner him and find out what was going on.

Hopefully, this wasn't a sign of trouble in Paradise. He knew Teague was seeing the lawyer but that didn't mean things couldn't already be screwed up.

He wouldn't put it past him to have done something stupid. He hoped not. He shot Teague a text, but when no response came he tucked his phone into his shoulder pocket and walked down the hall toward the battalion conference room.

And stepped into utter and complete chaos.

Gale had probably heard every variation of the expression "tension thick enough to cut" but walking into that conference room he could tell there was tension to spare.

Nichols, the Chaos Company commander, stood toe to toe with the Diablo Company commander, and neither of their first sergeants seemed inclined to pull them apart. Gale sighed. Just what he wanted to do: break up captains having a hissy fit.

He dropped his leader book on the table with a bang. "Well, ladies. What seems to be the problem here?" he said, stepping into the middle of the confrontation.

Diablo's commander, Captain Bello, took a step back. "Nothing we can't hash out later."

Nichols still looked ready to fight, but a single hand on his shoulder by First Sergeant Morgan made him, too, take a step back.

Oh good, bad blood between commanders. This was going to make everything so much more fun. He'd talk to Nichols later.

"Gentlemen, whatever is going on, I strongly suggest you squash it sooner rather than later. The battalion commander has no qualms about firing anyone," Gale said. "Give him a reason and I'm sure you'll be looking for gainful employment elsewhere."

Bello moved to the opposite side of the table with his first sergeant, leaving Nichols on the same side of the table as Gale. Teague arrived a moment later and they all took their positions around the conference room table.

"Everyone is in such a sunny mood," Teague mumbled out of the side of his mouth. "What'd I miss?"

"Chaos and Diablo were getting ready to brawl," Gale said beneath his breath. "Know why?"

"I've got some suspicions." Teague rubbed his hand over his mouth. "Tell you later."

Gale glanced around the conference room. The lawyer was nowhere to be found and the staff was slowly trickling in. The new command teams were all set now, with the exception of the support company. Apparently there had been some drama at brigade about who was going to command the unit responsible for supplying logistics to the rest of the battalion.

Kind of an important job: only beans, bullets, and bandages. No biggie. Gale shook his head, marveling at the workings in the higher echelons of leadership that kept decisions from being made.

He sat back and took in the power dynamics of the new teams, especially the first sergeants he'd be working alongside for better or for worse for the next year to eighteen months, if not longer.

Gale glanced between Nichols and Captain Bello. They must have some history together for them to be at each other's throats like that. Still, as long as Gale and his commander didn't get dragged into it, Gale couldn't see where it was any of his business.

What was fascinating, though, was the silent animosity radiating through the space. No one was talking. It was as if everyone was sizing each other up.

Gale didn't have time for who-had-the-biggest-dick games. They were short a command team and they were less than four months out from heading to the field to prep for the next deployment.

And they still had a shit-ton of personnel issues to clean up across the battalion.

He'd have to pull the new first sergeants aside and figure out what the major malfunction was. They needed to be working together, not playing childish games.

And two captains pissing on each other's legs qualified as childish games.

The operations officer, Captain Loehr, walked in and gave the warning. A moment later, the battalion commander walked in and everyone rose smartly to their feet.

"Take your seats, everyone." LTC Gilliad waited for

everyone to settle. "We should have a new support command team very soon. In the meantime, I want our continued focus on getting soldiers in the right places—if they need medical attention, make sure we're engaging at the commander level to ensure they're getting treatment. If they're having legal problems, we've been given direct access to our own lawyer. Get them out of my Army." He paused. "We just got the word that our deployment schedule has been moved up by three months. More to follow as we get more information from higher up, but I wanted you to hear it from me before the rumor mill started going ape shit. Captain Loehr?"

Gale rocked back in his seat at the news as Loehr took over the briefing. Three months earlier. That meant instead of leaving in ten months, they were leaving in seven.

He studied the paper in front of him, the words blurring as hope died in his chest.

He'd thought he'd have time to try and be the father he'd never been. He rubbed his chest as his heart twinged against his ribs. Damn it. He'd thought he had more time.

But he didn't.

He'd been lying to himself. There wasn't enough time in the world to help him fix things with Mel. To regain Jamie's trust after abandoning her and her mother.

The meeting went on without him. He heard bits and pieces of information and wrote down things he may or may not have heard correctly.

And when it was over he left, needing to put some space between him and the people that he would deploy with yet again.

He wasn't ready to go.

He'd only just gotten here.

CHAPTER ELEVEN

"So when is Dad coming over again?"

Jamie was at the kitchen sink, adding water to the blender for her morning protein smoothie before school.

Mel searched the pantry for the sugar she knew she'd bought last week but somehow now could not find. "I'm not sure. Why don't you call and ask him?"

"Um, no cell phone, remember?"

"We have a land line," Mel said, refusing to rise to the bait of her daughter's comment.

"I don't know his number. It was stored in my phone."

Mel counted to one hundred and tried to ignore the swipes. Maybe she was just being overly sensitive. Damn, but it was hard to break bad habits, like taking everything personally.

"Here." She pulled out her phone and jotted Gale's number on a piece of paper and stuck it to the fridge. "Call him."

"Are you fighting with Dad?" Jamie asked abruptly.

"No, why?"

"Because you've been in a weird mood since he left the other night." Jamie dumped strawberries into the blender and a scoop of protein powder. Mel was not a fan of milk shakes for breakfast but it was one less thing to fight with Jamie about. Her daughter was eating and that had to be good enough.

"I didn't sleep well." A convenient lie to mask the complicated truth.

She hadn't even begun to process everything that was happening in her life. She hadn't told Jamie about lunch with

Gale. Hadn't slept well that night either. Because after a lifetime of fights and blame, she wanted something more. More for him and for herself. In that brief moment at lunch, she'd seen a glimpse of what they might have become if she'd been strong enough to last through the tough times instead of breaking camp and running away the minute things got rough.

The blender roared to life, covering any further conversation. A minute later Jamie poured her drink into a tall tumbler and leaned against the counter. "Can I ask Dad over for dinner?"

"Sure." She ignored the twisting nerves in her belly at the question.

"You're acting weird."

"I'm fine. I'm just tired." She paused. "I'll drive you to school if you want."

She held her breath, waiting for Jamie to brush her off. Waiting for the bit of hurt telling her she wasn't good enough to be seen with her daughter. A daughter she'd managed to make hate her.

"Sure, Mom."

She looked up sharply but Jamie had already turned away, hunting for something in one of the drawers.

It was something so small, so trivial.

It was suddenly the most important thing in the world.

***

Gale sat at his desk, correcting evaluation reports and wondering what qualified for basic English in high school these days. If there was a properly used comma, he'd eat his Stetson. Heaven forbid any one of them would know the difference between an adjective and an adverb.

Gale wasn't a grammar fanatic by any stretch of the imagination, but he knew how to write a strong report card for one of his direct reports. "He explicticated to his soldiers that they wasn't supposed to drive fast and no one got caught" was not even remotely close to an appropriate comment on an evaluation report.

Bad writing was a good distraction from the ache in his chest.

He kept the door closed, trying to get some work done and not actually accomplishing shit. His office was a revolving door of personal trauma, gripes, bitches, and complaints—some legit, some just twisted panties. As much as he grumbled about it, he loved his job. Loved making a difference. It was a powerful force in his life. The one thing he was really good at. Right then, though, he needed time to sort through the riot in his head. He was not prepared to leave again so soon. What was Jamie going to say? What about Melanie?

Jesus, he was a mess. He turned his attention back to his evaluation reports, determined to at least get the admin processes under control, but sure enough, the minute he tried to concentrate, his phone vibrated on his desk.

"First Sarn't."

"Gale? It's Melanie."

***

She had debated about calling him. She'd gotten used to dealing with Jamie's issues on her own but something about this latest episode exceeded her capabilities on a couple of levels.

Besides, he wanted a chance to be a dad, so well, here was his chance.

"Hey, Mel." The sound of his voice warmed her. It shouldn't. She was a grown woman who'd moved beyond hormones. But hormones were exactly the reason she was calling. Just not *her* hormones. Which was a shame, actually.

"We have a small problem."

He sighed. "What did Jamie do now?"

"I…It's complicated and I'm not sure I should tell you

over the phone."

She could feel the physical shift in the silence long before he answered. "Is she…"

"No, not that."

She wished she could call her mother and ask her what to do but her mom had died a few years ago, long before Jamie had started pushing Melanie to her most recent nervous breakdown. Her dad was somewhere in Tibet doing heaven only knew what.

"Then what?" There was frustration in his voice and she couldn't blame him.

"Can you come by?" She tapped her pen against the table, nervous about his answer.

He made a rough sound. "I was going to work through lunch but yes, I can come by. Now?"

"Now works. It'll keep me from freaking out for the next two hours."

"Mel, what is it?"

"Just, just come to the house."

She hung up the phone, pacing in the kitchen. She'd been gathering the laundry from her daughter's prison cell, as Jamie had called it, before Jamie had stomped out of the house to walk to school.

Gale knocked on the door twenty minutes later.

Mel rubbed her hands on her thighs as she opened the door. "So, um, I'm trying to be rational about this but I'm not really feeling rational," she said, opening the door to him.

He walked into her living room and she led him into the kitchen where the…ahem...evidence sat like a train wreck on her island countertop.

"You're not working today?"

She shook her head, trying to ignore the warmth that built slowly in the vicinity of her belly. "I have a client in a couple of hours."

"Jesus, Mel. Did you find weed in her pocket or

something?"

"No, I think I would have been happy with weed."

"Holy shit. Meth?"

Mel shot him an odd look. "Why do you know so much about drugs?"

"Soldiers will never cease to amaze you with the shit they will smoke." He hooked his thumbs in his belt and shrugged. "As long as you didn't find any hard drugs, I think I can live with whatever has you so wound up."

Mel pointed at the small plastic wrappers on the island. "Okay, smart guy, so you're cool with condoms?"

Gale's face flushed and she could have sworn he turned a deep shade of magenta. It was hard to tell under the weathered tan of his skin. He rubbed his chest over his heart. "I think I just had a small heart attack."

"See?" She folded her arms over her chest. "So now what?"

Gale sank into one of the kitchen chairs, scrubbing his hand over his mouth. "I am not ready for this," he mumbled. "Wasn't she twelve just a minute ago? I mean we just went to Sea World last year."

"That was a lot longer ago than last year." Mel almost enjoyed watching the big man squirm. It was kind of endearing in its own way, if they hadn't been talking about their daughter having sex. "I guess we should have expected it after finding Alex in her room."

"Shit." He rubbed the back of his neck, not taking his eyes off the condoms. "Are we supposed to be glad that she has condoms and she's being safe?"

Mel flushed and turned away, opening the fridge and pulling out two hard ciders. "I'd offer you a beer but I don't have any."

"I have to go back to work but this warrants alcohol." Gale accepted. "I am not ready for our little girl to be thinking about penises."

Mel choked on the sip of cider she'd been taking. "That's so wrong. I don't even want to say the word 'penis' in the same sentence as our daughter."

"Was it too much to hope that they really had been studying biology?" Gale rubbed his thumb through the moisture beading on the side of the cider. "Have you, ah, had the talk with her?"

"We had the talk the minute she started getting pubic hair," Mel said. "But I am confident she and her friends have Googled tons of misinformation."

He frowned. "How do you know that?"

"Web history. She doesn't know how to clear it and after the hospital, I'm paranoid," Mel admitted. She wished she could trust her daughter, but the hospital stay and its aftermath had left her badly shaken and they didn't have a strong enough foundation to rebuild from. Jamie was angry, and Mel? Mel was terrified she was going to lose her.

Which was why she'd called Gale when she'd found the condoms. She'd been so focused on watching for signs of cutting, it had never even dawned on her that she'd be thinking about boys and—God forbid—sex.

Mel's brain had gone into full-blown Muppet flail upon discovering the condoms. Now that Gale was here, it was more of a slow motion flail. More like a happy Snoopy dance.

She giggled into her drink. Gale looked up sharply. "What's so funny?"

Mel paused for a moment, not sure how to describe the image of Snoopy in her head. Instead, she just smiled down at him. "I'm glad you're here."

***

Gale studied his ex-wife, noting that she looked a little more rumpled and a lot more desirable than he was used to seeing her. She was less stressed at the moment than she had been when he'd gotten there.

She'd always tugged at him. He could admit that now, after a couple of rounds of anger management therapy, and after identifying the source of the constant rage burning inside him.

He hadn't been a good enough man to hold onto her. And when he was honest with himself, everything he'd done over the last decade and a half had been to make himself a better man.

Not that he'd ever harbored illusions about her taking him back, but a man could dream.

Now, sitting in her kitchen, looking at her slightly fuzzy from the alcohol, his mind took a sharp detour away from their daughter's problem and landed squarely on another problem that he was not prepared to deal with.

His feelings for his ex-wife.

He offered a wry smile. "Sure, this is exactly what I wanted to be dealing with on my lunch break. My daughter and sex." He rubbed his heart again at the spasm. "I think this might kill me yet."

Mel laughed into her cider. Gale studied her for a moment without saying anything. She'd never been good at holding her alcohol. He smiled at the memory of the first time they'd gotten drunk together.

"What are you smiling at?" she asked.

"Remember the first time we got drunk and tried to have sex?"

"Oh God." Mel's cheeks flushed. Her eyes sparkled with the memory. "That was terrible."

"Your dad wasn't too happy with me," Gale said. "I'm lucky I didn't get shot."

"This is true. We did manage sex that night, right?"

"It was terrible sex," Gale said, taking a long pull off his cider. Jesus, he was going to have to swing by his house and take care of himself before he went back to work. He wasn't a eunuch, after all, and Mel? Mel was a sexy, beautiful woman.

His brain automatically connected the memory of the girl she'd been to the woman sitting across from him now.

"Terrible and messy, right?" She covered her mouth with her hand. "I'd forgotten about the condom breaking."

Gale looked down at the condoms, memories colliding with the stark reality of time that had passed all too quickly. "Remember how scared we were until you got your period?"

It had been a long time since they'd talked about anything other than Jamie. Time was always short, and he always had such a limited amount of it on visits. He'd focused his attention on his daughter because he'd continued to be convinced that his wife—ex-wife—didn't want anything to do with him. She'd always been cool. Distant.

This was new. In the fifteen years since she'd left him, they'd never sat around and reminisced about a time when they'd been younger and more carefree.

When they'd still been naive enough to believe that love was enough to conquer any problem the world might throw at them. Before the real world had interrupted their make-believe and forced both of them to grow up too fast.

"That was terrible. I convinced my aunt to help me go on birth control my senior year. Holy cow, was my mom mad when she found out I wasn't a virgin." Her gaze drifted back to the condoms, throbbing like a heartbeat on the kitchen counter. "So how do we handle this better than our parents did?"

"What are you talking about? My dad handed me a bunch of condoms and said good luck."

Mel lifted an eyebrow. "I'm thinking your response is going to be slightly different?"

"I'm going to break the little bastard's pecker off," Gale growled. "She's too young for sex."

"We had sex when I was seventeen."

Gale looked over at the odd tone in her voice. Her eyes were blurry, ringed with makeup she hadn't taken off last night. Her hair was in a ponytail and her sweater was slipping off one shoulder, revealing a hint of skin beneath a thin tank top strap.

His mouth went dry. He wasn't a warrior monk—not by a long shot—but looking at Melanie right then, the woman she was collided with his senses, sliding past the fantasy and reminding him of the flesh and blood woman who stood before him.

She was fucking beautiful. There were laugh lines around her mouth now but they made her smile more pronounced. The tiny creases around her eyes drew his gaze to the quick intelligence in them that had always drawn him closer when other boys had been running the other way.

He cleared his throat as his mind took a detour, wondering what else had changed in the years since she'd left him.

"Are you telling me you're okay with her having sex?" His voice grated on his ears.

"No, that's not what I'm saying," she said carefully. "I'm just saying that she's not much younger than we were when we first started misbehaving."

He glanced toward the condoms. "So what do we do?"

She took a deep drink from her cider then pointed the tip at him, a wide and mischievous smile on her lips. "I think you should talk to her. You've been a teenage boy before."

Gale laughed. "Yeah, I think I remember those days."

"Well, just tell her what all boys are thinking about. How she's probably not with the guy she's going to spend forever with and that she should respect herself enough to wait for the right person."

Gale flinched at her words. They hurt because they were a direct hit.

He'd been Mel's first but he hadn't been her forever. He hadn't gotten a chance to be her forever.

He set the half-empty drink on the counter and straightened. "Sure, I'll talk to her. Want me to pick her up from school?"

The pounding in his ears no longer had anything to do

with his daughter's condoms and everything to do with his own failings.

"I'll bring her home when we're done." He dug his keys out of his pocket and turned to go, needing to get away before some of the old anger and hurt escaped the place he'd stored it and tried to forget about.

"Gale, wait."

He didn't look back. "What?"

He didn't miss her heavy sigh. "Nothing."

CHAPTER TWELVE

Mel sat in her office, preparing for her meeting with her client. Captain Sarah Anders was recently back from Iraq, according to her e-mails. She was looking to buy in Harker Heights for the schools for her daughter. Nothing extraordinary in her requests, and she was looking well within her budget framework.

Except when she walked into the office, Mel was not expecting the younger woman to be walking with a limp. "Are you hurt?"

"Long story," Sarah said with a wave of her hand.

Mel made a mental note about the brush-off but let it ride. "Have you had a chance to look over the houses I sent you?"

"I have." Sarah pulled a few papers out of her bag. "I've pulled down a bunch of houses from the Internet that kind of give you an idea of what I'm looking for."

Melanie flipped through the papers. All the homes were modest, perfect for a woman and a single child. She saw the wedding ring on Anders's left finger. She wanted to ask where her husband was but Melanie had learned a long time ago not to dig into personal questions like that.

Things could go badly. She was there to help Sarah find a house, not be her therapist. "Well, I've got appointments scheduled at five houses today. Should we get started? Do you have your preapproval letter?"

"Yes," Sarah said. She handed Melanie another sheet of paper from a national bank. "I'm looking to stay in a reasonable price range. I want to be able to rent it after I leave Fort Hood.

And it's important that Anna be in a good school, near a good daycare." Sarah's expression faltered. Only for a moment and it was gone, but enough that Mel noticed it.

There was something more there, but Mel let it ride because honestly, it was none of her business. "I think we've got several options that will meet your requirements," Mel said, handing her a printout of the homes they were going to see. "Let's see if we can't find you a new home?"

An hour later, Mel could tell that Sarah had found the house she wanted. The captain had walked through the front door and her eyes had lit up. It was easy enough to let Sarah walk through the house by herself. Mel had her own thoughts to keep her busy.

She gave herself a mental shake as Sarah walked back into the kitchen. The floor plan was wide open, with room for a little girl's bedroom as well as a study if she needed one.

Add in that it was close to a good school and priced right, and it was a really great house for Sarah, considering her financial situation.

She knew from Sarah's financial information that the young captain wasn't broke but she wasn't flush, either. And Melanie had never once gotten someone into a house they couldn't afford. If Sarah decided this was the right house, Mel would help make sure it worked for her.

Sarah meandered through the kitchen. The countertops weren't granite or marble like in some of the nicer homes but the kitchen was a huge, welcoming space. Mel could see a little girl doing homework at the kitchen table.

Kind of like Jamie had, once upon a time. Before things had gotten complicated and twisted.

"You had a far away look just then," Sarah said, walking through the kitchen to lean on the island.

Mel smiled sadly. "I was just thinking about my daughter doing homework in here. This is a really great space."

"Why does your daughter make you sad?" Sarah asked.

"How about we leave it at difficult mother-daughter relationship?" she said.

"I live in mortal fear of puberty." Sarah smiled. "Is it as bad as I've heard?"

Mel laughed out loud. "Does the fact that I'm considering moving to Canada and letting her raise herself for the rest of it clarify the situation at all?"

"That's terrifying," Sarah said.

Mel looked down at her hands, a sudden sadness sweeping through her. "Yeah, well, I've made a lot of mistakes. And I don't know how to undo them, you know? It feels like all we do is fight." She looked up, with a shrug. "I guess we'll keep struggling through, right?"

"I think it's a parenting law that you have to." Sarah folded her arms over her chest, rubbing her upper arm absently. "I guess we just do the best we can."

"I think that's all we can do." Mel sighed. "Sometimes, I think she blames me for divorcing her dad when she was a baby." She looked up abruptly. "And hello over-sharing. Sorry. Didn't mean to dump that on you."

Sarah waved her hand. "Completely fine, believe me. If we can't bond over our children's angst what can we bond over?"

Melanie grinned. "Oh, I knew I liked you when we met. I sense a kindred sarcastic mom."

"Sarcasm is my sacred totem animal. I swear I wouldn't survive without it."

Melanie laughed out loud. "Oh, that's priceless."

Sarah walked around the island and threaded her arm through Melanie's. "So how about we go figure out whatever magic woo-woo you need to do to get me into this house and then we go share labor and delivery stories while bonding over cheesecake? Is there anywhere around here we can even get good cheesecake?"

Melanie smiled. "Oh, this sounds absolutely perfect. And yes, I know just the spot."

***

Gale was stalling. He'd already sent all the evaluation reports back to the platoon sergeants. He'd cleared out his inbox and come up with a duty roster for the next three weeks.

His desk was even cleaned off.

So why was he sitting there, staring at his computer, willing an e-mail to pop into his inbox? Something. Anything.

Anything to keep him from having to go pick up his daughter and have *the talk*.

He scrubbed his hands over his face.

"Rough day?"

Teague walked in and sat. He started to kick his feet up on Gale's desk but then decided against it when Gale glared at him.

"Fine," Teague said with a grin. He was eating from his never-ending sleeve of cookies.

"Keep eating like that. It'll catch up to you eventually," Gale said.

"Meh. I'm not worried about it. Maybe when I'm as old as you, I'll worry. Otherwise? What else am I supposed to do? I'm practicing being a responsible adult. I damn sure can't drink at work anymore." Teague sounded disgruntled but Gale knew him well enough to know he was joking. Mostly.

"Are we set to go to the range later this week?" Teague asked.

"Roger, sir. Iaconelli is running down the last of the logistic issues. And Foster is due back at work soon, too, so that'll be one less thing to worry about."

Teague chewed thoughtfully on a cookie. "I appreciate you not giving them a hard time," he said after a moment.

Gale leaned back in his chair. "They're important to you."

"It's that simple, is it?" Teague asked.

"Sometimes it is," Gale said. "Sometimes it isn't. This is one of the simple times for now."

As opposed to in about an hour when he had to figure out how to get into the right frame of mind to talk to his daughter about sex.

"So did you happen to see Tellhouse's kid on the back dock?" Teague asked after a moment.

Gale stilled. "No, why?"

"Might need to go take a look. Let me know what you think."

Gale grabbed his headgear and headed for the back of the company.

Alex stood, or rather slouched, on the back dock. His hands were stuffed into his too-baggy pants, his shoulders slumped.

But when he glanced up, Gale's shitty mood twisted in the wind and evaporated. Even the thought of this kid with a condom around his little girl did nothing to spike his anger any longer.

The kid was sporting a fat black eye. And unless he'd taken up UFC fights, Gale was willing to bet he knew the source of that black eye.

He ground his teeth, violence threatening at the tattered edges of its restraints.

Gale was going to have to have a chat with Alex's father.

Alex lifted his chin defiantly. He glared at Gale with something akin to abject hatred, then pushed off the wall and stalked back inside Tellhouse's company operations. He honestly didn't remember being such an angry kid. He glanced at his watch. He fired off a text to Mel apologizing but letting her know he wasn't going to be able to get Jamie.

He walked into the back of Assassin Company's operations. Alex sat at an abandoned desk, glaring at what looked like a calculus book.

He did not look up when Gale walked in. He continued to ignore him when Gale stopped in front of the desk.

Gale's blood pressure climbed up his neck.

He was not used to being spitefully ignored. He fought the urge to snatch the kid up out of his chair.

But that would make him no better than the kid's father or any other bully.

Alex was not a soldier. Funny how Gale needed to remind himself of that.

He stopped in front of Alex's desk. "Your dad around?"

"No."

No, first sergeant, was what Gale's brain was expecting to hear. "No" just struck him as wrong. And flagrantly disrespectful.

Alex was not a soldier. If he said it enough, his brain would stop insisting otherwise.

Gale exhaled sharply. "Well, if that had been a killing word, I'm sure I'd be lying on the floor, twitching in a pool of my own vomit."

Alex looked up. The expression of bored indifference on his face was damn near perfect. But there was a twitch at the corner of his mouth. Very faint, but Gale noticed it. He'd been dealing with pissy teenage boys for a long time.

"My dad's at battalion," Alex said. His tone was slightly less grating.

"Oh good, progress," Gale said. "Do you know when he'll be back?"

Alex shook his head. The ring in the kid's nose was rapidly driving Gale insane. And the multi-colored hair made Gale's palm twitch for a pair of clippers.

"No, but he said he wouldn't be long."

"Thanks." Gale jerked his chin in his direction. "What happened to your eye?"

"Hit myself in the head with the car door."

It sounded strangely like *I walked into a door*. An excuse Gale had heard before.

He didn't believe it any more coming from a young man than he did if it had come from a young woman.

"How do you hit yourself with a car door hard enough to get a black eye?" Gale was doing his damnedest to keep the anger out of his voice.

Alex shrugged and looked down at his homework. "I'm ADD. I get distracted a lot."

A lie if Gale had ever heard one but the kid didn't want him to push the issue.

There were other ways to skin this cat.

"Tell your dad I need to talk to him?"

Alex shrugged. "Sure."

He doubted the kid would relay the message. But he stopped near the back door to the company ops. "Alex?"

He waited until Alex looked up at him. "Tell your dad to be more careful with the door."

Alex's eyes flared wide with panic as fear registered on his damaged face. The shock in his eyes was worth relaying the message.

The fear was not.

Alex's mouth worked but no sound came out.

"I'm not going to say anything to him," Gale said softly. A lie but Alex needed a comfortable lie more than he needed to know the truth.

And the truth was that Gale was going to have a talk with Tellhouse.

And if that kid showed up with any more bruises, that talk would escalate into something else.

Gale had made his point. Alex had an ally – condoms notwithstanding.

Gale never would have thought he'd be looking out for a kid who was quite possibly trying to sleep with his little girl, but there he was.

The question now was the best way to tackle it, because while he had enough to satisfy his own beliefs that Tellhouse had hit his kid, he didn't have enough proof to go to the battalion sergeant major.

And before he made any further moves, he needed to plan them out. Very carefully.

***

Mel closed her computer, feeling quite satisfied. Sarah's paperwork was well on its way to being complete. She had never met a potential homebuyer more organized. She'd had copies of everything in a single, neat folder.

Mel wished more of her clients could be like that.

Then again, she supposed Sarah had to be organized. There was a sadness around the other woman, a sadness that was there even when she smiled.

She'd admitted to having lost her husband in the war, so it was a sadness that Mel could understand.

She hadn't lost Gale to the war—at least not permanently—but she'd lost him just the same.

The problem was, now that she had a second chance, she didn't know what to do with it. Or him.

But Sarah's stubborn determination to press on, to do the right thing by her daughter, made Mel admire her more. And made her determined that the other woman would not be alone here at Hood.

She shouldered her bag and headed out of her office, waving to Courtney, the receptionist, on her way out. The sky was darkening overhead, the threat of a Texas-sized thunderstorm rolling closer in those dark, swollen clouds.

She stopped short, though, at the man waiting by her truck.

Gale. His hands stuffed in his pockets. His pose belied the tension in his shoulders.

"I take it the talk with Jamie didn't go well?" Mel said as she approached.

The muscle in his jaw pulsed and she felt bad for his teeth. "I didn't pick her up. Sent you a text. She should be at the house."

Melanie frowned. "Then what's wrong?" He was silent, long enough to start Mel worrying. "Gale?"

Gale's chest rose as he took a deep breath. "I think Jamie's friend is getting the shit beat out of him at home."

"Alex?" Mel's breath left her lungs in a rush. "What do we do?"

Gale bit his lips together, the frustration radiating off him in waves. "I don't know. I don't have proof so I can't take it to the boss. The police likely won't look into it either."

"And calling CPS will only make it worse on him," Mel added.

Gale tipped his head, studying her with his dark brown eyes. "What aren't you telling me?" Gale said, shifting slightly.

"Jamie had a classmate in the third grade. She came home crying one day about how his parents had caused a scene at school. One of the nurses had called CPS on the father and the parents had been furious. Chris had been taken from the school kicking and screaming by his father." Mel looked away, the memory of Jamie's pain still as sharp as the first time she'd held her crying daughter. "Chris never went back to class after that. Jamie stopped asking about him eventually."

"What happened to him?"

"The school wouldn't tell me. But it hurt my heart. I remember Chris. He was such a sad little boy."

Gale shifted again and then his palm was warm on her cheek. He angled her face up until she met his eyes. "You can't stop all the bad in the world, Mel. Believe me, I've tried."

"Which doesn't answer the question of what do we do about Alex," Mel said softly. "Are you sure about him?"

Gale nodded, not lowering his hand. His palm was rough. Comforting. A source of steady heat. "Yeah. As sure as I can be on a gut suspicion." His palm slid slowly down her cheek, resting at the curve of her throat.

An uneasy tension pulsed off of Gale. He was a man of action and this uncertainty looked uncomfortable and unusual on him.

She lifted her palm to his chest. His heart was solid and strong beneath her touch. "Can you talk to his father?"

"Yeah, I'm going to talk to him. I can't sit on my hands and do nothing." He swallowed, his eyes dark and tormented. "I feel so powerless."

She did the only thing she could then. She wrapped her arms around his waist, leaning in until her cheek rested against his heart. His arms tightened around her; his cheek rested against her hair.

She stood with him in silence as the storm gathered overhead. Neither of them moved. She closed her eyes and felt the rise and fall of his chest beneath her cheek, his back beneath her palms. "You're a good man, Gale Sorren," she whispered. His arms tightened around her but he said nothing. He didn't need to.

For all his strength, the fate of one young boy had undone this man.

And it was this, this simple admission that he was willing to take a stand for a boy that was not his own, that undid the bindings around her heart just a little more.

CHAPTER THIRTEEN

Jamie looked between Mel and Gale with narrow, suspicious eyes. "Who are you and what have you done with my mother?"

Beside him, Mel tensed. Gale rested his palm on her shoulder, breaking up Mel's habitual reaction to her daughter's prodding. "If you don't want him to come over…" Gale let the words hang in the room.

Jamie looked between her parents again. There was genuine confusion in her eyes. Gale fought the urge to smile.

"You're serious? You want me to ask Alex over for dinner?"

Mel released a tense breath. "Yes. Your grades have started showing improvement and if he's one of your friends, then I'd—we'd—like to get to know him better." She tripped over the word *friend* but not enough that Jamie caught on. Her slight emphasis on *we*, though, did something funny to Gale's insides.

"So I can have my phone back?" Jamie asked cautiously.

Mel nodded, saying nothing.

Jamie still wasn't convinced but she wasn't fighting. Gale could feel the tension in Mel's shoulder. "Go call him. Before your mother and I change our minds."

Jamie bounded up the stairs with a happy squee. Mel slipped away and padded into her bedroom. Gale watched her go, a nagging sense of something being off.

So he did the only thing a sane man could do. He followed her, closing the door gently behind him.

She looked up from where she'd kicked her shoes off near the closet door. Pale soft light radiated out from the closet, softening her features. There was darkness outside as the threatening storm broiled closer, casting the bedroom in grey darkness.

"You still okay with this?" he asked softly. He hesitated to approach her. She looked wary. Skittish.

"Yeah." She tucked her hair behind one ear.

He stood near the edge of her bed, wanting badly to go to her. To do what, he didn't know…but something. Anything was better than standing there feeling useless.

He crossed the small space. He rested his hands on her shoulders, framing her neck with his fingertips. She avoided his gaze. He cupped her cheek, urging her to meet his eyes. "What?"

Her tongue flicked out, tracing her bottom lip quickly before disappearing again. The single action drew his gaze, made him want to follow that tongue with his own.

"I guess I'm just worried about Alex's father," she admitted after a moment.

"What about him?"

"What if he comes here?"

"He won't."

"You don't know that."

"You're right," he admitted finally. He sighed heavily. "I've known him a long time and this doesn't gel with what I know of him. He's not going to hurt you."

"You sound so certain." Her fingers danced over his ribs, as though she wasn't sure where to place her hands. "Why?"

"Because you're mine," he said, giving voice to the powerful feelings he could finally identify for what they were. "And if he puts his hands on you or our daughter, I'll kill him."

And then he kissed her.

It was a powerful kiss, filled with a riot of emotions that had started building in him years ago when she'd first left him. It was a kiss filled with fear. With uncertainty.

With desire.

He gave in to the maelstrom inside him, holding back only enough to be certain that he wasn't crossing the line.

Mel opened to his kiss, wanting badly to push away the sadness and the fear and the worry that had been squeezing the air from her lungs since she'd found Gale outside her office.

There was fear in her response, a tacit admission that this was something fleeting and yet, it was the only tangible thing between them.

He shifted then until their bodies pressed together, until she breathed with him and felt part of her soul take flight from the bonds of worry and sadness and daily life.

Her fingers flexed against his ribs. Gale felt the moment she gave in to the kiss, savored the moment of her surrender. Her body relaxed against his, fitting perfectly against his chest.

This was something good. Something pure. Untainted by the darkness that had caused him to seek her out today, needing her when he needed to lean. This. This was what he craved. His wife's touch. His wife's taste.

She was not his wife. That ugly piece of reality crashed into him and he stiffened.

Mel felt it instantly, her body tensing. "What?"

The words lodged in his throat. There was no way he could admit the feelings that churned inside him. That he still thought of her as his wife after all these years.

He nipped at her bottom lip, hoping to distract her. "We should do this more often."

He felt her smile beneath his lips. "You think so?" There was something light and breathless in her words.

"Very much so." He kissed the corner of her mouth. The edge of her jaw.

He traced the outside edge of her ear with the tip of his tongue. Felt the pleasure of her gasp against his cheek. His teeth scraped over her earlobe. "That's nice," she breathed.

"You like that?"

"Yeah."

He closed his eyes, pulling her tight, needing the comfort of her touch, the pleasure to drive away the darkness. He breathed in her scent, holding her close. Her pulse scattered against his cheek and for a moment, he simply held her.

"You make me crazy, Melanie," he whispered.

***

You make me crazy, Melanie.

Her full name on his lips ripped across her heart. The roughness in his voice belied the gentleness in his lips. This was a man hardened by war and violence. It was still there below the surface. Still waters and all that.

But the man who held her was infinitely gentle, concerned about a boy who was not his own.

She ran her fingers over his neck—soothing, stroking, trying to contain the leading edge of her need. They couldn't get naked right now. Not with one teenager upstairs and another on the way over.

That didn't mean she didn't want more. His touch was pure sex, dancing down her spine as he stroked his fingers over her back.

Standing there with him, the storm brewing outside, she savored the moment. This quiet, sensual pause in Gale's arms.

It wasn't as though the last fifteen years hadn't happened. No, it was something more than that. Somehow, they'd managed to break the cycle of fighting and bitterness and found a way…home.

She hesitated to think the word or to give life to the spiraling needful thing that was growing inside her. Fear licked at her, demanding that she turn away from needing, from wanting his touch. But as she stood there, wrapped in the warmth of his embrace, she let the tentative *what if* spread its wings inside of her chest and flutter against her heart.

What if meant possibilities. *What if* meant hope.

What if meant a broken heart. Again. She smothered the fear, letting the hope rise inside her.

She nuzzled his cheek, savoring the rough scrape of his beard against her skin. The sensation was something real. Something tangible against the uncertainty of what the future held.

She wasn't big on taking chances. Her entire life had been built around mitigating uncertainty, against keeping things steady and stable in her and Jamie's lives.

Gale shifted and she felt his breath hot on her neck. He made a sound deep in his throat, then she felt the warmth of his tongue tracing her pulse. It did something to her insides, turned them warm and wet and oh so aching.

She arched against him then, rubbing against him where he was thick and heavy. She wanted this man. She wanted to touch and feel and savor everything else that had changed about this man in the intervening years. Wanted to feel his body against hers. Inside her.

She wanted to close her eyes and offer herself to him. To let the years fall away until there was just him and just her.

His lips trailed over her shoulder, his fingers flicking open the buttons on her blouse. The air was cool against her skin, his lips hot.

There was something fiercely restrained in his touch. A heady mix of violence and passion trembled beneath his lips as they traced over her shoulder.

"We shouldn't be doing this right now," she murmured, her breath a gasp in her throat.

"I know." But his hand didn't fall away. His fingertips brushed her nipple, concealed in pale peach silk. It pebbled at the slightest pressure, her body craving the darkness of his caress. "I want to touch you so badly." Whispered words, heavy and thick.

***

There was something beautiful about the way she arched beneath his fingers. Gale lowered his head, flicking his tongue over her collarbone, wanting nothing more than to take that pebbled nipple between his teeth. He wanted to make her cry out, to make her body squirm as he touched her.

She was perfection in his arms. Liquid pleasure, an arch, a gasp. There was beauty in her sounds and they twisted up his insides and made him wish they were alone where he could lay her back on her bed and spread her thighs and make love to her with his mouth, his body. His soul.

There had been other women in his life but no one had ever come close to touching the special place reserved for Melanie. Her breath caught between her teeth as she smothered a gasp, his tongue tracing over her nipple. The thin fabric was dark with wetness from his tongue and he wanted. Oh how he wanted this woman.

He straightened slowly, wanting more and knowing they had to stop. But his breath froze in his lungs when he saw her. Her eyes half closed. Her fingers curled against his shoulder, her breathing unsteady. Her body exposed for his touch.

His fingers shook as he tugged her blouse closed and started redoing the tiny pearl buttons. "I don't suppose you'll let me sneak into your bedroom window tonight?" he asked against her mouth.

She smiled. "That is a very tempting offer." She curled her arms around his neck.

"Does that mean you're considering it?"

"That would be a terrible example for our daughter." She offered a mock frown. "Who you are supposed to be talking to about sex."

"I'm not actually interested in setting a good example at the moment," he murmured, his voice thick and edgy. Gale rocked against her. "But thank you. Mentioning our daughter and sex effectively killed my erection." But he was smiling when he said it. It felt so good to laugh for a change.

The doorbell rang, echoing through the house. He lowered his forehead to hers. "Time to be responsible adults?" he asked.

"Sadly, yes." But she was smiling as she adjusted her clothing and walked out, leaving him aching but with a surprising contentment teasing at the edge of his arousal.

***

Dinner was nice. Gale was honestly surprised. He'd expected Jamie to huff off at any moment but when she'd seen Alex, she'd transformed into another person entirely. Not the angry girl he'd become used to. This was someone concerned for a friend and something more. A girl trying to act cool around a boy she liked. And there they were, enabling this relationship to develop.

All because they were worried about the boy.

He watched Mel during dinner. The easy way she smiled and made the extra effort to make Alex comfortable. He caught her watching him more than once. That black eye seemed less dark, more yellow than when Gale had first noticed it, but it was no less angry or obvious.

It was Jamie's reaction that Gale watched the closest. She was trying so hard to be cool and concerned without being overly clingy. It was interesting to watch the mating rituals of the female of the species.

Yeah, that wasn't helping. She wasn't some random member of the species. She was his daughter and his daughter was swooning—was that even a word?—over this boy. Gale's heart twinged in his chest every time he thought the word "condom" and his daughter's name in the same sentence.

He glanced over and caught Mel watching him. He offered a quick wink, the absolute normalcy of the evening wrapping around him like something warm and soothing.

This was a normal he'd never experienced. He'd eaten alone for as long as he could remember, unless he was at some

Army-sponsored function. There was little point in cooking because he was inept in the kitchen to an epic level.

So this easy meal where Jamie and Alex were talking about their science teacher, where Mel told him about the houses she'd listed that week, was something beyond his realm of experience. He ate, he made the appropriate noises, but it was too new, too much unknown territory for him.

He didn't know how to truly be in the moment. He wanted to. God but he wanted this. He wanted the normal. That's why he'd gotten himself sent to Fort Hood for a chance at *this*.

So why was he feeling the crushing sense of air being squeezed from his lungs? Why the tightening around his heart, the shortness of breath?

He pushed away from the table, fighting the urge to panic. Frustration slapped at him, taunting him with the reminder that he'd never have a normal life. Not after the war and ruining everything good he'd ever attempted outside of the Army.

This house was not his home. It was not his place.

It was Melanie's place, a place she'd made without his help.

He felt useless. Unmoored and shiftless. What kind of man let his wife just leave him? And never made enough of an effort to get her back?

He scraped his food into the trash and turned toward the sink, rinsing his plate.

Mel's hand on his upper back was soft and strong. Unyielding.

She leaned against him, her forearm resting along his back. "Hey."

He stilled. Unable to move. Unable to reach for her and unable to push her away.

He was stuck. Simply frozen in space and time.

Shiftless.

Her palm slid over the U.S. Army uniform patch on his chest.

He'd given her up for the Army. He'd let her go so that he

could maybe grow into the kind of man who deserved her.

Instead, all he'd done was grow into a warrior. A leader of men.

Not a lover. Not a husband. Not a father.

A ringing sense of failure hung around his shoulders, a lead weight dragging his soul down.

"Where did you go just then?" she asked softly, her voice low so that Jamie and Alex couldn't hear.

He lifted his hand, his palm covering hers where it rested over his heart. There was so much he wanted to say, so much he wanted to feel with her.

And he was going to screw it all up again. Because that's what he did.

"I'm going to go after dinner." He squeezed her palm. "I won't leave until Alex heads home." He paused. "So you're not alone."

"What's wrong?" she asked again.

He turned, looking down into her dark, sad eyes. "You make me want things I can't have, Mel. Things I don't deserve."

She lifted both eyebrows, a storm gathering in her eyes. A storm that looked like she was going to take him apart.

Jamie and Alex slipped out of the kitchen. Gale didn't know if it was because of Mel and him or not.

At the moment, all he could see was Mel. His vision tunneled down until there was nothing else but her and the disappointment and worry he'd put on her face.

"Because I thought… I hoped." The words he needed wouldn't come. They were lodged in his throat, stuck there, blocking his air.

"You hoped what, Gale?"

He rubbed his chest where it ached. "I—"

"Come up with a really good excuse," she said, lifting her chin. "I want you here. For the first time in our adult lives, I was enjoying having you around and now you're running off? How's that even logical?"

He braced his hands on her sink. His lungs weren't cooperating. Panic ripped at him, stole the air from his lungs. His breath was ragged and scattered, failing to gulp in enough oxygen.

"Gale?"

Her voice came from somewhere very far away.

And then the black spots in front of his eyes consumed the world.

CHAPTER FOURTEEN

She caught him before his head hit the floor, staggered under his weight, crashing into the center island on their slide to the floor.

It took a lot for Mel to panic but seeing Gale sink to his knees like a puppet that'd just had his strings cut was just the thing to do it.

She was pinned beneath his weight. He was solid and heavy and he wasn't fucking moving.

Patting his cheek gently, she stomped on the panic that tore at her, terrified her into inaction. She didn't want to call Jamie, didn't want her daughter to freak out at seeing her dad laid out on the floor.

"Gale."

His skin was clammy beneath her touch. He was breathing but his breaths were slow and shallow. She slapped him a little harder. His eyes rolled around beneath his lids.

"Damn it, Gale, if you don't wake up I'm going to have to call an ambulance and Jamie is going to freak the hell out," she hissed.

He made a noise deep in his throat. Then his throat moved again as he licked his lips and tried to swallow. He blinked slowly and opened his eyes. "Shit."

Mel smiled at the disgruntled sound of his voice. "You fainted."

He frowned, his expression still a little fuzzy. "Men don't faint."

"Exhibit A says otherwise."

He rubbed his eyes with his thumb and forefinger. "What happened?"

She blinked and studied him silently. She didn't want to go back to the argument they'd had a few moments before. The feelings were raw and aching, suppressed for a time beneath the panic but still there. "We were arguing. You fainted to win the argument."

He scowled and pushed himself upright onto the heels of his palms. "I didn't faint."

"How else did you end up down here?"

She was enjoying teasing him. It was so much better than the fight they'd almost had that had sliced at her heart and attempted to rip it out of her chest.

"What were we arguing about?" he asked.

Upright, still sitting on the floor, he braced himself with his hands between her legs. He looked shaky. Uncertain.

"You don't remember?"

He scrubbed his hand over his face then looked at her. "No."

"Does this happen often? Where you faint and don't remember things?"

He looked away. "No."

She hesitated. "You're a terrible liar, Gale."

He scrubbed his hand over his face again. "I haven't passed out before. This is new."

"New and exciting medical symptoms with the added bonus of memory loss. Yay."

He shot her a baleful look.

"What?" She blinked innocently.

"You're making jokes."

"That's because I've learned to deal with abject terror with biting sarcasm." She did something impulsive then, ignoring his earlier, cutting words. She cupped his cheek, her fingers dancing over the rough stubble on his jaw, and rested her forehead against his. "You scared me."

"I'm sorry," he murmured. "I'll try not to faint on you again."

She smiled. "I'd appreciate it. I have enough grey hairs from Jamie." She paused. "And Gale?"

"Hmm?"

"Don't tell me you don't deserve happiness ever again."

She kissed him then, her lips brushing against his softly. It was meant as a gentle kiss, a hint of something teasing and light. But he captured her mouth, sucking on her lips before taking over and shifting to uncharted territory. A slide of tongues, a scrape of teeth.

His breath mixed with hers. It felt illicit, kissing him there on her kitchen floor. It felt dangerous, as if at any moment Jamie would walk into the kitchen and be scarred for life at the sight of her parents making out like horny teenagers.

But she couldn't pull away. His earlier words echoed in her memory, taunting her with a hint of losing the thing that drew her to him.

She ignored it, shut it down and pushed it away and lost herself in his taste. The roughness of his skin, the heat of his mouth.

It was Mel who broke away this time. She swiped her thumb beneath his bottom lip. "I don't think you should drive home tonight."

He narrowed his eyes, studying her. His throat pulsed when he swallowed. "Jamie—"

"Doesn't get a vote." There was fear underlying that statement—the fear of an insecure girl looking back at her from the mirror of time—the fear that he wouldn't want her enough to stay.

That she would have to leave him again to protect her own heart.

She met his gaze, hiding the fear beneath the very adult desires she let him see. This was heat. This was want.

This was her, wanting him like she'd wanted him for a very

long time.

"Stay." She traced her fingers across his cheek. "Because I am actually worried about you."

His lips curled into a slow, sensual grin.

"What?" she asked.

"I was just thinking I had a great way to take your temperature."

"You are a sick, sick man." Mel covered her mouth and laughed. "You're the one who fainted," she said. "I don't need my temperature taken."

Gale's laugh rumbled through the silence. Thick. Heavy. Filled with unasked questions and even more uncertain answers.

She knew what she risked by asking him to stay.

It wasn't just her own heart on the line. She could admit that she'd never gotten over loving this man. But Jamie? What would happen to her when Gale left again? She knew how to face the fear she'd lived with each time he'd deployed. But Jamie was old enough to understand what war was. Had been since the last deployment. And the one before that. And telling your daughter about war and being unable to promise that her father would make it home was a shitty conversation to have. But she said none of those things at the moment.

Now she studied the man sprawled casually out on her kitchen floor. His arms braced behind him, his uniform snug across his wide, heavy chest.

He was solid. Not just in his body but in something more.

The man in front of her was the man she'd wished he'd been and she'd been too scared and too immature to wait for.

***

Gale sat on the edge of her bed, staring down at his hands. He couldn't shake the knowledge that his daughter was upstairs.

In the same house.

On the same street.

And he was contemplating getting naked with her mother.

There was no contemplating. Desire, raw and powerful, rocketed through him as he sat there. He wanted Melanie. Had wanted her from the moment he'd crossed the threshold into her home.

Long before even that.

Everything he was had been building toward this. No, not the sex. That was something special, something to be cherished. No; tonight was about something more than sex.

It was potential. A potential he'd craved since the day she'd left him.

Maybe that made him a chump, pining after a woman who'd walked out on him, taking their daughter without so much as a backward glance. But he'd never given up on the girl he'd fallen in love with even when she'd given up on them. He had more faith in her than she did.

Tonight? He couldn't screw this up.

He glanced toward the bathroom where Mel had disappeared. Light poured out beneath the closed door. He heard the water running as the storm broke overhead.

Rain beat on the windows, pouring down in sheets of water, but there was no thunder. Just violent rain drowning the world outside.

He supposed the sound of the rain would drown out any other sounds.

Jesus, when had he gotten so freaked out by something as simple as taking a woman to bed? Not any woman. Melanie.

He looked away, wondering if he should get undressed or just wait or… He grinned as a deviant idea popped into his head: he should strip off his clothes and stand stark naked in the middle of the bedroom. Maybe put a bow tie around his…

The laugh choked off in his throat.

This would have been so much easier if they'd simply fallen into it. Been consumed by passion and sex and need. Someplace mindless where he'd stripped away her clothes and her inhibitions and made her moan with his hands, his lips.

Then he wouldn't have had to think. Wouldn't have had to worry about the sounds they were making and what Jamie was doing right then.

He looked down at his hands again, one leg bouncing nervously.

He didn't want to admit that the passing-out thing had freaked him out. He'd come close before. The panic was nothing new.

But he'd never passed out before. That was new.

And he wasn't opposed to taking full advantage of Mel's concern. But that concern had only gotten him as far as her bedroom. He still had to cross that threshold and… He just didn't know how to do this.

He scrubbed his hands over his face and glanced toward the bedroom door, making sure it was locked.

Then he padded toward the bathroom door and hoped it wasn't locked. The handle turned smoothly in his hand. He pushed the door open a crack and a wave of hot steam coated his skin.

He smiled. She was showering. And that gave him ideas that started with steam and ended with her hands gripping his shoulders.

He shucked out of his uniform quickly then stepped into the steaming shower.

She shrieked, covering her mouth before the sound fully escaped.

And then her gaze drifted down, over the water sluicing through the hair on his chest.

Gale was a big man. He knew it and he often took his size for granted. But he'd never felt as desired as he did right then. Her gaze lingered at his erection before trailing back up his body to meet his eyes.

He opened his mouth to say something light and teasing but nothing came out. Damn it, he was as inept as a nineteen-year-old private. Frustration was a sound in his throat as he reached for her, claiming her mouth before she could brace her palms against his chest. She tumbled against his chest, crashing into him. Her body was slick and squirming in all the right places.

The world tilted beneath his feet as he poured all of his desire, everything twisted and writhing inside him, into that kiss.

He let his hands drift from her cheeks down her slick body, pulling her closer until she was naked and writhing against him. She felt small against him. Small but perfect. She fit against him, her breasts against his chest, her hips against his erection. He closed his eyes and simply savored the feeling of Melanie in his arms and prayed that it wasn't all just a dream.

***

There was something in Gale's eyes that worried her. Uncertainty. Fear. She couldn't name it. But when he pulled her close and kissed her, she went willingly into his arms. Wanting, needing to chase away anything that took away from *this*.

This was heat. This was passion. This was long buried desire swirling around them, slicking over their skin. Her nipples dragged against his chest, pearling beneath the rough wet texture of his hair.

She loved the way this man surrounded her. Held her against him like she was a precious thing.

He leaned back, brushing her hair from her eyes. "You're beautiful," he whispered.

She smiled. "So are you."

"Men aren't beautiful."

"Men don't faint either," she said with a teasing smile.

"I'll show you fainting," he growled against her lips. He groped behind him, turning off the water.

He stepped out of the shower, dragging a towel from the rack. He was slow, but thorough, sliding the soft cloth over her shoulders. Down the swell of her breasts. Beneath their heavy weight. She'd never worried about their size but feeling Gale's steady hand palming them, they felt swollen. Tight.

She arched into his palm. Wanted to feel his thumb flick over her nipple. To make her feel and help her forget the years of loneliness that stood between them.

Something warm and wet slid over one nipple. She opened her eyes to see his head bowed in front of her. He met her gaze, his eyes dark and steady. Locked on hers, he dragged his tongue around the edge of her tight nipple. His breath cooled the wet. Her skin prickled and swelled beneath his touch, the air caught in her lungs.

"Do that again." Her voice was harsh, ragged.

A purely masculine smile curled over his lips. He shifted and dropped to his knees in front of her. He was big enough that his face was level to her ribcage. He looked up at her, and in that moment, she felt worshiped, cherished. After a moment, he wrapped his arms around her waist, pressing his face to her belly.

He'd done this once before. The night she'd told him she was pregnant with Jamie. He'd pressed his face to her belly and simply held her.

The memory collided with the reality of this big man on his knees in front of her, tearing at the fabric of what was real and what was not.

He knelt there, his hair dripping wet drops against her skin. She threaded her fingers through it then, tipped his head up, edging her knees wider as she slid down his body.

Her legs wrapped around his waist. She met his gaze, saw all the uncertainty mixed with intense desire.

"Gale." His name was a prayer on her lips.

He heard it, recognized it for what it was.

He kissed her then. And gave himself over to whatever this was for as long as it would last.

***

He was strong enough to stand with her legs still wrapped around his hips. His hands cupped her bottom, his erection teased her where she was aching and wet, their lips only parting when he rubbed against her where she was swollen and sensitive.

"Do that again." A whispered demand.

He smiled against her mouth as his knee found her bed. "I'm not sure what exactly I did," he said against her lips. "But I'm happy to repeat the experiment until I figure it out."

He framed her hips with his hands, sliding them up the gentle swell of her sides to cradle her breasts in his hands. She was heavier than when they were younger. It wasn't fair that he'd aged so well. She felt…

She looked at him then, his gaze dark and admiring as he lowered his mouth to her breast, tracing the tight peak with his tongue. She lifted her hips, hoping to find that delicious friction once more.

She knew what it was. She knew what she wanted. But Gale, damn it, had discovered some fascination with her breasts that was driving her slowly insane. She cupped his chin, dragging his attention away from her body until she could wrap her arms around his neck.

"I want you inside me." An urgent request.

He grinned and kissed her. Something light and teasing in his expression spoke of darker plans. "I'm not ready yet."

She narrowed her eyes, a mixture of denied passion and curiosity. "What does that even mean?"

He didn't answer. He snagged her wrists and tugged first one, then the other over her head. "Leave them there," he whispered against her mouth.

She arched one eyebrow at him as the position forced her spine to arch. She bent her knees to alleviate the pressure and his eyes darkened as he watched her body open for him.

He traced teasing kisses over her jaw. Down the line of the

pulse in her throat. His fingers rasped along her ribs, the harsh pads of his fingers burning her skin.

She closed her eyes as the sensations rose up like a slow fire. She thought she'd been ready.

Oh, but she'd been mistaken.

His tongue traced down her body and she felt pure male pleasure radiate from him. She could have sworn he growled as he nestled against the dark hair between her thighs.

She tensed as his breath blew across her swollen sex.

"Relax," he murmured.

Then his tongue flicked across her sex and she came up off the bed.

His laugh was pure male. And then he feasted on her. His hands held her hips captive. There was no place for her hands except in his hair, on his shoulders. Gripping, clawing as she arched and writhed beneath his sensual onslaught.

When he slipped a single thick finger inside her, she exploded in a flash of blinding passion, his name a gasp on her lips.

***

Only after he'd felt her burst against his tongue did Gale finally ease the sensual torment. There was nothing more beautiful than feeling her come on his mouth. But his body burned now, needing his own release.

It felt like coming home as he crawled onto the bed and settled his body against hers. The moment wasn't lost on him as her arms locked around his neck and her thighs cradled his ribs. He was tempted, so tempted to slide inside her and just savor that first moment.

"I suppose we need to have the responsible adult conversation," she said against his lips.

"I suppose we do." He smiled, stroking his thumb over her cheek. "Should we go raid Jamie's room for condoms?"

"That's wrong on so many levels." Mel broke out laughing, burying her face in his shoulder as the laugh rocked through her. When she could speak, she kissed him again.

He kissed her, rocking his erection against her slick, wet heat. He buried his face in her neck. "I want to be inside you right now," he said against her ear.

Still. He wanted no regrets. No mistakes. He left her momentarily and pulled a condom from his wallet and rolled it on while she waited, spread and beautiful and *his*.

Crawling between her thighs, he framed her with his arms, threading his fingers with hers. "Melanie."

She opened her eyes as he found her opening. Nudged a tiny bit. Felt her gasp and tighten, her body taut with liquid pleasure. She lifted one leg, hooking it over his hip. And with that single gesture, urged him inside her.

Urged him home.

When his orgasm ripped through him a short time later, he realized that he'd done more than start something new with his wife.

Something old had been reborn between them. As she drifted to sleep, her head on his shoulder, he wondered if she felt the same powerful emotions that kept him awake long into the night.

CHAPTER FIFTEEN

He snuck out before Jamie woke up the next morning. Dawn was still hours away as he hitched on his pants and his t-shirt and stuffed his bare feet into his boots without lacing them.

Mel watched him, half asleep, from her bed. The curve of one breast peeked out from the edge of her sheets. He was tempted to tug that sheet down and give himself five more minutes with her.

But he still had to work.

And he still wanted to avoid that awkward morning after with his daughter upstairs.

So he tugged the sheet a little higher and kissed Mel with something more fierce than sweet before he snuck out of her house like he was a teenager all over again.

Mel's father hadn't caught him.

When he'd been nineteen, that had been a mark of adolescent pride. Until she'd gotten pregnant. And then he'd learned the hard way why parents tended to frown on boys sneaking out of their daughter's bedrooms.

He started the truck and headed to his place to shower and change before PT formation.

It would have been a good start to the morning, except that Iaconelli was missing. Teague was there, though one look at his commander told Gale that now was neither the time nor the place to bring up the fact that Iaconelli might not be ready to be back in his leadership position.

He might never be. But Gale wasn't going to be the one to

tell Teague that. Not until it became absolutely necessary.

He turned the formation over to the platoon sergeants, letting them do PT in small groups, then fell into step next to Teague as they walked away from the company area and toward Battalion Avenue.

"I'm sure he's fine," Gale said after a moment.

Teague bent one leg and leaned forward into a stretch. "I talked with his other half an hour ago. He's sick. Like in he has a case of food poisoning, not like he's been drinking."

Gale nodded, saying nothing as Assassin Company ran by with Tellhouse shouting cadences alongside the formation as his commander ran up front with the guidon. He didn't hear whatever else Teague was saying. What kind of a man punched his own kid?

And what did it say about Gale that he'd never suspected Tellhouse of this kind of violence before now?

"You talk to him about his kid?" Teague said after a moment as their feet pounded the pavement in that age-old cadence.

Gale sat for a moment, trying to determine if he should lay his suspicions at his commander's feet. Finally he spoke. "He wasn't there but we had his son over for dinner last night."

"We?"

"Had dinner with Mel and my daughter. Don't get distracted."

"I'm not." Teague rubbed his hand over his face. "Do you have proof?"

Gale shook his head as they started running. They fell into step as another formation ran by, drowning out all thought until they passed. "Nothing I can act on officially. And you can't say anything to the boss yet because we don't have shit to go on. The black eye could have come from a fight at school for all we know."

"But unofficially?"

"He and I are going to have a little chat later today."

"Does a little chat involve either of those hams you call fists?" Teague asked.

Gale glanced at his commander, wondering if he knew about the violence in Gale's past. He debated asking, then decided he didn't want to know. The concrete rolled beneath their feet as they ate up the distance. "Only if he gives me a good reason. And he's not going to do that because then we end up in front of the sergeant major."

"So how do you know he won't go home and take it out on his kid?" Teague asked as they reached Clear Creek and turned around, heading back up the hill.

"Our kids are friends. Jamie will tell me." He hoped.

As plans went, it was a pretty shitty one. He was gambling that he'd be able to get his point across without having to resort to violence.

Without proof, Gale might as well be pissing in the wind. It was never about what you knew. It was always about what you could prove.

Gale would do it if he had to. But he was gambling on getting through to his old friend first.

If that failed… It wouldn't fail. If he closed his eyes, he could still see Alex's black eye and the way the kid slouched when Gale had first called him on the shiner.

He'd been relaxed at dinner last night. Not as hand shy as he'd been at the office.

"And if she doesn't?"

"Then I'll have to take it to the sergeant major."

"You could call the anonymous tip line. Child protective services can investigate."

Gale shook his head. "I have little faith in that system."

"Olivia believes in it."

"Olivia has seen it work. I've seen it fail. Badly."

"So has she," Teague said. The ground beneath their feet leveled out as they ran past the old Sports Dome. "They're trained to investigate this stuff. They can act on an anonymous complaint."

"And what if I'm wrong?"

"Are you?" Teague looked over at him as the sun peeked over the top of the III Corps headquarters.

They ran in silence for a mile, maybe more. Past the NCO Academy, past the Burger King and Popeye's that were responsible for more than one soldier busting his height and weight standards.

Was he wrong?

He could be, he admitted, if only to himself. He wasn't infallible. And no matter how certain he thought himself, he always checked his decisions, trying to see what else he could have missed.

He could be wrong about Tellhouse. He knew that. Still, his gut told him that the other first sergeant was responsible for Alex's black eye.

"I could be. But I don't think I am. Let me talk to him first. If that goes south, I'll call it in."

They circled back and slowed to a walk in front of their company operations office. "Let me know how it goes."

"You're probably going to have to deal with Captain Martini if things go badly."

Teague shrugged. "I can deal with Brint Martini. He's all hat and no swagger."

"There's a cutting assessment," Gale said dryly. "You think pretty highly of him, don't you?"

"He cheated on his pregnant wife, then divorced her in the middle of a deployment. He has no fucking moral compass whatsoever."

"Sounds like you two are BFFs," Gale said dryly.

Teague responded by flipping him off.

The day was off to a good start.

***

Gale was not prepared for the epic shit storm in his orderly room when he walked in from the gym.

Tellhouse was there. Along with his commander Captain Martini.

And the military police, apparently.

Gale zeroed in on Tellhouse, who looked just this side of blowing a gasket.

"Okay, who did something stupid?" Gale asked.

"You, apparently," Tellhouse snapped. "You plan on telling me why my kid has been taken to the MP station?"

Gale folded his arms over his chest. "Ah, your guess is as good as mine. He's your kid."

"He's hanging out with your psycho daughter. Want to tell me why he's shoplifting razor blades and cold medicine?"

"Call my daughter a psycho again and you're going to need the MPs to keep me from rearranging your vertebrae." Gale scanned the entire ops. There were entirely too many people in the office for this conversation. He wasn't ashamed of his daughter but he damn sure didn't need her struggles broadcast all over the battalion.

"I think if you're not directly involved in this conversation, you need to make yourselves scarce, time now," Gale said to the bystanders watching the brewing shit-show with rapt attention.

There was a sound of scraping chairs and feet pounding on the polished tile as the orderly room cleared out.

The MP pushed off the table, getting ready to intercede. She was tall but Gale highly doubted she'd be able to stop it if this situation devolved in the middle of his orderly room.

As Fridays went, this one had taken a pretty drastic detour. Tellhouse leaned against the dead printer, apparently not moved to violence just yet.

"My kid just got arrested at the PX for stealing fucking cold medicine for your shithead daughter. And he has razor blades in his pocket he said belong to her. So what the fuck are you going to do about this, Sorren?"

Gale took a deep breath and considered all possible courses of action that did not start and end with his fist in Tellhouse's face. "First off, why the hell wasn't he in school to begin with?"

The hypocrisy of Gale's question didn't escape him. But Jamie had been skipping school *with* Alex. Gale didn't know who'd initiated said school skipping but given that Jamie was in school right now and Alex was most definitely not, he suspected it was Alex leading the headlong charge into delinquency.

Still. Gale chose his words carefully. It was almost better that Tellhouse blame Jamie. He couldn't touch Jamie but he could damn sure take his anger out on Alex.

"Captain Martini, you might want to step outside," Gale said.

Martini puffed up, lifting his chin. "I'll stay."

"Suit yourself, sir." Gale folded his arms over his chest. "Tellhouse, I think you and I are long overdue a talk about that boy of yours."

"What about your kid?"

"This is one hundred percent not about my kid," Gale said, breathing deeply and doing everything he could to keep his temper in check.

"I'm going to whip that boy's ass when I get home if he lied to me."

"And so we've reached the heart of this conversation. You need to keep your hands off your kid."

Tellhouse froze. His jaw tightened. The MP stood up and took notice. Teague walked in from the back of the ops. He paused then moved to stand next to Gale.

He unfolded his arms from across his chest and his hands hung limply at his sides. A pit bull, ready for battle. "What the fuck did you say?"

"Alex has a black eye. He better never get another one."

"Alex hit himself in the face with a car door."

The military police officer looked between Tellhouse and Martini, then back at Gale. "First Sergeant, I'm going to need you to make a sworn statement."

Martini held up his hand. "I've got this, sergeant. I'll investigate what my first sergeant is suspected of."

The military police sergeant shook her head. "I'm sorry, sir, but this is an allegation of an actual crime. You don't have the authority to investigate this." She shifted, resting her hands on the utility belt at her waist. The effect was to broaden her stance.

Teague looked over at Martini. "You need to let this run its course, Brint."

Captain Martini was seething but his anger had nothing on the fury in Tellhouse's eyes. "That's really rich, coming from you," Martini snapped. "Your fucking first sergeant beat the hell out of his sarn't major back in Iraq and you're going to preach to me about how to run my company?"

Teague held up both hands, wiping them together. If he was surprised by Martini's statement, he said nothing. "You're on your own then."

"First Sergeant, if you can come with me?" the MP said.

Tellhouse stormed out of the company ops, followed by the MP. Captain Martini stopped about a foot away from Teague. "Watch your fucking back, Teague. I know your damn game."

Teague patted Martini's shoulder. "No games, Brint. Just don't like seeing a kid get his ass beat."

"You don't know dick about my first sergeant or what that kid is putting him through," Martini snarled.

Gale took a step forward, ready to yank his little ass away if he got the bright idea to swing on his commander.

"And I don't want to, either," Teague said. "But don't be an idiot. Let the cops investigate this one."

Martini mumbled something under his breath that sounded

suspiciously like "fuck you" and stalked out.

Teague sighed heavily. "Want to talk about Iraq?" he asked Gale when they were finally alone.

"What do you already know?"

"Cox talked to me shortly after you arrived. Said you had an incident but that you were rock solid." He met Gale's eyes steadily. "So if it's history, then it's history."

"You're not worried I might snap and lose my shit on the entire company?"

Teague shrugged. "I have way more pressing things to worry about than your mental health." He paused. "Right?"

"Not funny, sir."

Teague grinned. "Hell of a Friday morning, isn't it?"

Gale shot his commander a baleful look. "Can't wait to see what the weekend brings."

"Bite your tongue."

CHAPTER SIXTEEN

The day had gone downhill from the morning's confrontation with Tellhouse, starting at bad and ending up in complete fucking disaster.

The MPs had turned the investigation over to child protective services, a development that surprised exactly no one. Captain Martini had two other soldiers arrested for talking on their cell phones while driving, then getting lippy with the MPs, so the entire company leadership was on their way to the corps headquarters. Gale didn't envy them that at all. The corps sergeant major wasn't exactly known for shitting rainbows and unicorns.

The sergeant major had been less than thrilled to learn that one of his *new* first sergeants was under investigation and had spent the better part of an hour going up one side of all of them and down the other while they'd all stood at parade rest in his office. Gale's ass was still sore from that one.

But because of the amount of time he'd wasted getting his ass chewed, he'd gotten behind on several critical tasks, tasks that his headquarters platoon sergeant would normally have taken care of but well, Iaconelli was out sick.

He checked his patience on that one. Teague wasn't going to hear anything other than unicorns shitting rainbows when it came to Iaconelli. Which meant that Gale was going to have to come up with ways to mitigate his recovery's impact on the mission.

He gave the guy credit for trying to get sober, he really did, but as much as they needed warriors like Iaconelli, him being a little tender around the edges didn't make for an effective leader. At least not as a headquarters platoon sergeant that Gale could count on.

He was giving him the benefit of the doubt for now because Iaconelli meant something to Teague. And Gale? Gale wasn't going to pick a fight without a damn good reason. Besides, Gale didn't have any good reason not to trust Iaconelli at the moment. But something didn't rub him the right way there.

Gale was keeping his mouth shut on that one.

He toyed with his cell phone, debating whether or not he should call Mel.

He hadn't told her about the deployment moving closer. He hadn't had time to process what that meant. What it would mean to Jamie. And to whatever this thing was that was building between him and Melanie.

He wanted to hear her voice. He wanted to call but didn't want to look like an overeager teenage boy.

"Holy hell, I'm annoying myself," he mumbled, then hit her number.

"Hey."

"Hey."

"Well now, that is stunningly original conversation." He could hear the smile in her voice. "How was your day?"

"Busy," he said. He couldn't bring himself to say good because it wasn't, but she also didn't deserve him dumping his shit day on her lap. For now, it was enough that she was talking to him. "Did Jamie say anything about Alex today?"

"No, why?" Instant concern in her voice.

"He was arrested on post."

"Holy crap."

Gale swallowed, searching for the words he needed and praying Mel didn't completely lose her shit about what he was about to tell her. "He had razors. He told his dad they were for Jamie."

Silence hung on, endless and heavy. "Mel?"

"I'm here."

"You okay?"

"I don't know."

She sounded deflated. Like his words had cut the air from her lungs. He didn't want to leave her alone. Not right then. Not when their greatest fear had been resurrected in all its blood and gore. "Can I come by?" She didn't respond for far too long. "I need to talk to Jamie, Mel."

A tired sigh. "She's going to a friend's house after school."

"Not Alex's?"

"No, not Alex's," Mel said.

"I'll be there after work."

"Okay." A pause. "Gale?"

"Yeah?"

"Thank you."

***

She met him at the door, her eyes filled with worry that Gale didn't have to be a psychic to read. "She wasn't with him," he said, toeing the door shut behind him.

Mel rubbed her hands over her upper arms. Her movement was jerky and stiff. "That's good."

Gale took a step toward her. "You said you don't think she's…" The words jammed in his throat and he cleared it roughly, forcing the ugliness out. "She's not cutting again."

Mel shook her head. "No, I don't think so."

"I want to talk to her about Alex." He reached for her then as those fragile, fear-filled words brushed against her skin. "We've got to make sure she doesn't get caught up in any of his bullshit with his father."

Mel frowned, her back stiffening. "I'm well aware of the need to keep our daughter from falling in with a bunch of delinquents, Gale."

He shook his head, his hands settling on her shoulders. "I'm not worried about that. I'm worried that she'll get caught in the middle of Alex and whatever is going on with his father."

"Oh." Mel looked away, toward the kitchen. Gale followed her gaze to her cell phone on the polished granite countertop. "I can call her. She'll be mad because it's not curfew yet."

Gale shook his head. "I'm not taking her away from her night. I just want to talk to her."

Mel looked up, arching one brow. "Really? You're the cranky teen whisperer now after a few weeks?"

Gale grinned, rubbing one thumb absently over the top of her shoulder. He felt it then, a subtle movement, nothing more. A slight lean, a delicate pressure on his palm where she leaned into his touch.

She lifted her gaze to his. "I hate feeling like this," she admitted finally.

He watched her mouth move. "Like what?"

"Afraid." Her words were a rush of air across her lips. He leaned down before he could stop himself, sucking gently on her mouth.

There was a rush of breath, a slip of bodies against each other, an urgency in that first connection of body and soul.

There was fear in her touch. He felt it tremble through her and into him when he kissed her, and he wished he could take all of her fear into himself.

She'd been dealing with this situation for far too long on her own. But he didn't say that tonight. Tonight, he lifted her against him and kissed her until she forgot her name.

Until she broke away from that kiss with a gasp and rested her forehead against his.

"What?" He cupped her cheek, urging her to meet his gaze.

"I don't want to think." She closed her eyes. "Just make me feel. Something other than afraid."

He kissed her then, fierce and hard; he cupped her face until she wrapped her arms around his neck and arched against him. It was primal and primitive and raw and everything he needed. He groaned quietly as she rubbed her hips against his, until his blood pooled in his groin and he forgot to think.

He lifted her against him, slipping her thighs around his waist as he headed toward her bedroom. He captured her gasps in his mouth, savored the taste and touch of her body against his.

This was more than just sex. It was connection. It was something coming alive between them. He toed her bedroom door shut then turned, pressing her against his body and the doorframe. She inhaled sharply and he leaned back. "Did I hurt you?"

She swallowed and he was entranced by the movement of her throat. He leaned in, biting her pulse gently. "Did I hurt you?" His lips moved against her throat.

"No. Yes. It's okay." Her fingers spasmed in his hair, pulling his mouth away from her throat. "Bed." She rocked against him. "Please."

He backed up slowly, savoring the feeling of her body rubbing against his. He bumped up against the bed and she made a sudden movement and he staggered, sinking down.

"I think I like you like this," she whispered.

"Like what?" He slipped his hands beneath her top. The heat from her body scorched his fingertips. She was smooth as satin, hot beneath his touch.

"You beneath me," she breathed against his mouth.

"Jesus, don't say that," he said when he could talk.

She laughed and rocked against him. He watched, enthralled, as she bit her bottom lip. Just like that the years fell away, taking every ounce of skill he had with them. He threaded his fingers through her hair, yanking her mouth to his, giving in to the thundering need pounding in his veins.

This was a claiming. A violation of the space between them. Her fingers fumbled between them, dragging the zipper of his jacket roughly open. He didn't let her go when she yanked his shirt out of his pants or when the cool kiss of air brushed against his belly.

His stomach trembled when her fingers opened his belt. It was only then that he broke the kiss, too intrigued by the idea of her fingers on his body to give up the chance to watch her touching him.

His breath snagged in his throat. His lungs were tight, his blood suspended as she slipped the belt open then one by one, undid the buttons on his uniform pants between their bodies.

"Mel."

A slow, sensual smile spread across her lips. Her tongue flicked out, leaving moisture where she licked. "Yes?"

She pressed her palm flat against his belly, sliding lower, just a little bit.

His mouth moved but his voice apparently had gone AWOL as he watched, as he felt her fingers slip into his pants.

It took everything he had not to let his eyes roll back in his head as she found him.

"Fuck that feels good." His words were ragged, ripped from his throat.

"Yeah?"

She slipped to standing but he barely noticed. It was something so fucking gorgeous to watch her touch him. There was sensual confidence in her touch, pleasure in simply letting her do what she wanted. Take what she needed.

"What would you do…" She braced one hand on his chest while the other continued to stroke him gently. He closed his eyes as her breath traced along his cheek and brushed against his ear. "If I used my mouth on you?"

His heart stopped. Right then and there, he realized he could die a happy man.

"I'm not sure my heart could take it," he murmured when he could speak. "But we should definitely try and find out."

Her laugh was sultry and deeply sensual. "I am going to be highly disappointed if you drop dead on me while I'm going down on you," she said. There was a laugh in her voice.

"That would make two of us," he said.

And then he couldn't speak because she'd slipped him out of his pants while she'd been talking. The air was cool on his erection, her hand warm heat and skilled softness.

She loved the feel of him in her hand. There was little more empowering than making this man weak beneath her touch. She felt him tremble as she stroked him, felt his body still completely as she nuzzled his belly.

She slid her thumb over the tip of him. Felt him tense as she blew a teasing breath over him. "Mel."

"Shh."

And then there was no more talking as she took him into her mouth.

***

Gale fought to keep his hands on her shoulders as she sucked him gently. Gripped her fiercely as she swirled her tongue in some esoteric pattern that made him see stars.

And struggled to keep from ending this erotic pleasure too soon.

There was pleasure, so much pleasure in her touch. It took everything he had to lift her to claim her mouth while he groped for a condom in his pocket.

And then she was there, straddling him, her knees on either side of his hips as she slid down the length of him slowly, so slowly. He loved the feel of this woman in his arms, the fierce passion as she moved over him and took them both closer, closer to the edge.

He watched her tense, felt her tighten as she came closer to her pleasure. Reached between them to stroke her where she was soft and slick and oh so swollen for him.

And then she trembled and exploded, taking them both over the edge and into the abyss.

***

"So are you going to fill me in on what happened today?"

Mel was curled into Gale's side. The bedroom was dark, the shades drawn closed. The house was quiet, missing the sounds of sulky adolescent girl.

His heart beat slow and steady beneath her palm. For a moment she was content to lie there and let the rhythm soothe her. But only for a moment because all too soon, the ever-present weight on her chest was back, reminding her to get up, to get moving. There were things to do, daughters to worry about.

It was a hard thing for her to simply lie there in his arms and let the world go by without her.

Gale shifted, pressing his lips to her forehead. She closed her eyes, savoring the sensation. This interlude, this brief oasis of peace would end far too soon.

"Apparently Alex was arrested at the PX." She felt his throat move. "And he told his dad that the razors in his pocket were Jamie's."

His body stiffened as he spoke. A subtle tension but it was there, tightening the muscles beneath her palm. He shifted then and his hand came up to cover hers. "I don't know how to do this, Mel," he admitted softly.

"Do what?"

"Be afraid like this."

"Welcome to my life." It was Melanie's turn to stiffen. She started to pull away. "We should get dressed before Jamie comes home."

But Gale was there, surrounding her, pulling her back against his chest. His arms were strong and tight, his breath warm on her neck. It was tempting, so tempting to lie there and forget about the world. Forget about all the times she'd dealt with that fear alone. Utterly and completely alone.

It was sadly all too easy to remember that loneliness. It slipped in between them—something cold and empty where a moment before she'd been warm.

"We really should get dressed."

"While I'm all for avoiding the psychic harm of our daughter finding us naked—" he nuzzled her neck— "I want to know why you do that."

"Do what?" She was tense now, unable to enjoy the sensation of his big body surrounding hers.

He shifted suddenly and was there, pressed against her, his arms alongside her body, his hands framing her face. "Pull away."

She closed her eyes to avoid the sincerity in his eyes, searching for anything to make light of something that squeezed the air from her lungs. "Old habits?" she whispered finally. She hated this part of whatever this was. This awkwardness that crept in between them every time something good happened.

Her throat closed off and her heart ached. She wasn't ready for this with him. She wanted it, but obviously there were serious problems with her ability to live in the here and now instead of in the shitty memories of the past.

The front door chimed and Mel stiffened, looking up at Gale. "Holy shit."

They both moved like whirling dervishes, dressing in thirty seconds flat.

Mel was ready first, stepping into the kitchen and closing the bedroom door behind her as Gale tied his boots.

"Hey," she said to Jamie, feeling more awkward than she had since…since her *parents* had caught her and Gale in her bedroom. "How was school?"

The weight of her own hypocrisy was stunning.

Jamie dropped her backpack on the kitchen table with a thunk. "Fine."

And the hostility was back. Awesome. "Did you see Alex

today?"

Jamie shot her a baleful look that reminded her of Gale. "I know Dad already told you what happened."

She frowned at her daughter and leaned across the island as Jamie shuffled through her bag. "How do you know that?"

"Alex's dad threatened to whip his ass if he talked to me ever again thanks to Dad."

Gale chose that moment to step out of the bedroom.

Jamie froze, looking between her mother and her father, her mouth pressing into a flat line. "So what is this, screw with the kid day?"

Beside her, Gale stiffened but ignored Jamie's attempt at picking a fight. "Is Alex okay?"

Jamie made her disgusted sound. "I wouldn't know. I didn't get to see him tonight because of you."

"You didn't get to see him tonight because he got arrested on post today, Jamie." There was an edge to Gale's voice and Mel suddenly had a very clear idea of what his soldiers went through when they pissed him off.

"Blake didn't tell me he was arrested." There was true shock in Jamie's voice.

"Shoplifting at the PX."

"Ugh." Jamie threw her pen on the table. "He's such an idiot. I told him Blake was going to get him in trouble."

"Get him in trouble, how?" Gale asked. Mel looked up at him.

"Duh, he got arrested." Jamie looked away, suddenly preoccupied with her backpack. "He's so stupid sometimes."

She snatched her backpack off the table and stalked toward the stairs.

Mel put her hand on his arm, stopping him when he would have gone after her. "Let me," she said gently.

Gale looked down at her, saying nothing, tension etched in his jaw. She saw him breathing, slow and deep, like he was concentrating on staying calm.

Her lungs burned as she climbed the stairs toward Jamie's room. The sheet still hung on the doorframe. She was almost afraid to knock. Afraid of the fighting that she was sure waited for her on the other side of the doorway.

Still, she lifted her hand and knocked.

She lifted the sheet when Jamie didn't answer. Jamie was sitting on the bed, staring at her phone, her eyes bleak.

"Alex told me he's not allowed to talk to me anymore," Jamie said. She didn't look up. "His dad slapped him the last time Dad brought him home." She finally lifted her eyes to meet Mel's. She seemed to shrink into herself. "I don't know how to help him."

Mel inhaled a deep, steadying breath and crossed the small space, sitting next to her daughter. "I think your dad has some ideas on how to help."

"How?"

"He knows how to handle stuff like this."

"He's a soldier. He doesn't have anything to do with families."

There was a noise by the door. Gale filled it. For a moment, Mel hoped he hadn't heard Jamie's comment but one look at his expression told her that he had.

And that it had hurt.

But his expression shuttered closed. "I need proof, Jamie. I need something to take to my boss."

Jamie looked down at the phone in her hands. A quiet sniffle fractured the long silence.

"Can you really help?"

Mel's heart caught in her throat at the pain and uncertainty in her daughter's voice.

It was an eternity before Gale spoke. "I'll do everything I can," he said simply.

Mel met his gaze.

And saw that he meant every word.

But she knew in that moment with crushing certainty that

it might not be enough.

CHAPTER SEVENTEEN

"Can you really help?" It was the second time she'd asked him that.

Gale sat on the bottom step of the stairs with Jamie. His daughter sat shoulder to shoulder with him. The fact that she was sitting with him was a sure sign that either hell was freezing over or that she was really, really worried about her friend.

Gale was all for the worried-about-her-friend part because that meant the devil wasn't coming to collect his due any time soon.

And Gale had a lifetime of sins to atone for.

Starting with tonight.

He glanced over at her. In the low light that filtered in through the skylight over the front door, she looked just like her mother a lifetime ago. The same line of her mother's jaw, the same mouth.

For a moment Gale was transported back to another set of stairs, another time.

"I'm pregnant, Gale."

He swallowed, or at least he tried to, but his throat didn't work. "What do you mean, you're pregnant?"

She offered a watery smile. "Do you really want a biology lesson?" Her voice broke. "What am I going to do?"

His mind had gone blank. He'd sat next to her as those words rattled around his skull until it had finally dawned on him that she was fucking terrified and that she was waiting for him to do something other than sit there like an idiot.

He looked over at Jamie then. Watched her picking at the

side of her nail, trying to get the remains of her nail polish off one thumb.

He swallowed. And slipped his arm around his daughter's shoulder.

She didn't move, staying rigid and stiff.

Then she leaned against him, resting her head against his shoulder.

He sat, still as the stone monuments where his brothers' names had been immortalized, afraid to move. Afraid to acknowledge the terrible truth that something this simple was so powerful.

His little girl leaned on him. Her whole life he'd been gone; he hadn't been there for her but in that moment, his daughter leaned on him.

He brushed his lips against the top of her head and simply sat there, savoring the sensation of being needed by her. Wrestling with the darkness inside him that made him afraid of the powerful feelings tearing at him.

Fear. Regret.

But mostly, it was gratitude that choked him. Gratitude that was so fucking strong it threatened to break him.

He was so goddamned grateful that she was still alive.

"Alex's dad and I had a talk earlier today."

She shifted and looked up at him, her eyes filled with suspicion. "What does that mean?"

"It means that if you see anything that makes you think that Alex's dad did anything to him, I need you to tell me, okay? Even if Alex tells you not to." He squeezed her shoulders gently.

"I don't see how you're going to help, though. You can't beat up his dad because then you'll go to jail."

Gale snorted. "Well, you're assuming that physical violence is the only way to handle problems like this. There are other ways to handle these things."

"Like?"

"Like I need Alex to talk to me. Talk to someone about what's going on at home."

"He was called to the office yesterday but the lady who wanted to talk to him was weird."

"Weird how?"

"She was a soldier. Had the same patch as you."

Gale rubbed his hand across his jaw. Stubble scratched his palm. "Interesting."

Jamie looked up at him. "Interesting how?"

"I'm not sure yet."

Jamie nodded, then cupped her chin in her palm, her expression shifting. "So what's going on with you and Mom?"

Gale coughed at the unexpected question. "Ah, we're just getting along better than usual?"

Jamie shot him a baleful look. "I'm not stupid, you know."

Gale cleared his throat roughly. "And I'm not having this conversation with my teenage daughter." His voice was edgy to his own ears.

"Yeah, well, besides it being kind of gross, I kind of like having you around."

Her words trailed off, fading with embarrassment and something else he didn't recognize. He was so much better with the boys in his formation.

"Well, I kind of like being around more, too," he said quietly. "I really like it when we're not fighting."

"Ugh."

He grinned and squeezed her shoulders then pushed off the bottom step, his mind tumbling over the information his daughter had just told him.

He wasn't sure who the female at the school had been, but he had a sneaking suspicion that his commander might have had something to do with it. He made a mental note to give Teague a call if he didn't see him sooner.

It could wait. For the moment, anyway. He wasn't likely to accomplish much at this hour.

At least he hoped it could wait.

He wasn't entirely sure how this was going to work. No matter the promise he'd made to Jamie that he'd figure this out, he had no idea what to do next.

But every time he closed his eyes and saw Alex and his black eye, his shoulders hunched, his spirit bending under the pressure of being Tellhouse's kid, Gale felt that old familiar rage burn through him.

He damn sure couldn't ignore the fact that Tellhouse was putting his hands on his kid. He couldn't stand by and do *nothing* while the process took its time and Alex had to walk on eggshells in his house, hoping not to piss off his father.

Gale had lived that life once, and it had taken men like Sarn't Major Cox to help rebuild the boy Gale had been.

He hadn't been that boy in a long, long time.

But sometimes, that old confusion came back, twisting with memories and uncertainty about just what he was supposed to do. He took a deep breath and followed the light down the hallway.

He found Mel in her office. He stood in the doorway and watched her for a moment. The light from the computer screen flickered over her face, casting it in soft shadows.

He knocked gently on the doorframe.

"I'm going to head home," he said quietly. "Thank you for, ah, dinner."

She twisted in the chair, crossing her legs slowly, a warmth in her eyes. "Dinner, huh?"

His smile matched hers. "Yeah." He cleared his throat. "So Jamie figures there's something going on between us."

She arched one brow. "And what did you tell her?"

"That we were trying to get along better."

"Is that a euphemism?"

"Maybe."

She crossed the small space between them, stopping a breath away. She stood close, close enough that he could see the hair caught in her earring. He gently tugged it free. "Whatever this is, Mel…"

Her palm came up to capture his, holding it near her cheek. He gave in to the urge and cupped her cheek. "Let's just take this as it comes," she said finally.

He wasn't satisfied with that. Not by a long shot. But it was the best he was going to get right then. He was treading into dangerous territory.

He didn't know how close he could dance with her before the fire between them flared up bright and consumed them both.

So for the moment, he was content to let things ride, to not push.

Because he was a selfish bastard and he was going to break her heart when he told her about the deployment changing. Goddamn the fucking war. Why now? Why couldn't things wait a little while longer?

He'd just found his way home and he was not ready to leave it so soon.

***

"So you wouldn't happen to know anything about a female officer being at my kid's school last week, would you?"

Gale figured Monday morning—a Monday with no one in their company going to jail over the weekend for a second weekend running—was as good a time as any for him to blindside his commander with the question that had been burning in his head over the weekend.

Teague shot him a sidelong glance. "Maybe."

"Define 'maybe', sir." Gale barely restrained the dangerous edge to his voice.

"There are different ways to go about handling situations like the Tellhouse problem," Teague said quietly.

Gale said nothing as they walked out of the company ops.

It was still dark and all around them, soldiers were rushing to their respective formations. Reflective belts glittered in glow of street lamps and headlights.

Still Gale waited.

Finally, Teague spoke. "I talked to Olivia. She said she wanted to talk to the school nurse about Tellhouse's kid."

"Because of Escoberra?"

Teague nodded. "Yeah. We missed a lot in that case because people weren't talking to the right folks. So Olivia, being Olivia, decided to head to the school."

Gale swallowed hard. "And did she come up with anything?"

"She's got an appointment with an English teacher later today and the school counselor. Surprisingly, though, the military family life counselor won't talk to her."

Gale frowned. The military family life counselors were in a lot of schools, there to help the kids deal with their parents' sometimes multiple deployments.

He snorted. Man, they'd thought the deployment cycle had been bad back in the day.

"What?" Teague asked.

"Was just thinking about how much we all bitched and moaned about Bosnia and NTC rotations back in the '90s Army."

"All I heard just now was 'you young kids, get off my grass'," Teague said.

Gale flipped his commander off. "Yeah, well, we had no idea what the force could withstand. If you'd have told me back then that we'd be doing year-on year-off rotations to Iraq for the better part of a decade, I'd have had you drug tested."

"And yet, here we are."

They walked up to the formation to find Foster in the front leaning rest position, Iaconelli glaring down at him while Foster laughed hysterically.

Gale frowned. "I wasn't tracking that Foster was supposed

to be back at work yet." Foster's arms were shaking he was laughing so hard.

Teague shrugged. Gale looked at his platoon sergeant. "Do I even want to know?"

Iaconelli's smile was malicious and cold. "It's probably best if you don't ask, Top."

Gale glanced at Teague. "Do you want to know?"

Teague tipped his chin at Iaconelli and Foster, who at this point had fallen onto his stomach and had tears rolling down his face. His crutches were on the ground next to him, and his bum leg looked balanced on his good one.

"I'll admit to being mildly curious," Teague said, folding his arms over his chest.

Foster attempted to lift himself into a proper push-up form but succumbed to decidedly unmanly giggles.

"Okay, I give up," Gale finally said. "What the hell is so funny?"

Reza made a disgusted sound. "Dumb shit here swapped guard duty at the front gate with one of his buddies without telling anyone. And he thought it would be brilliant to play the Cat Game with Second Brigade's commander."

Teague made a sound that was suspiciously like a laugh.

Gale rubbed his hand over his mouth. "Please tell me you're not referring to what I think you're referring to?"

"Oh yes. The one from *Super Troopers* where they say 'meow' instead of 'now'. Yeah, Blackjack Six was, ah, not amused." Iaconelli glanced down at Foster. "Keep pushing, shithead. You owe me fifty more for corrupting the new privates."

"Those new privates?" Gale asked. Said new privates were doing push-ups near the edge of first platoon. To a man, each of them looked like they were about thirteen.

Holy shit, Gale felt old.

"Yep," Iaconelli said. "They're just lucky Blackjack Six is my former battalion commander and he called me, as opposed to our brigade commander."

"Permission to recover?" Foster said.

"Get up, smart ass," Iaconelli snapped.

Gale kept his hand over his mouth, watching the display dispassionately. There was no place for drugs in the ranks. But watching Foster and Iaconelli just then, it felt good to see Foster putting on some weight and screwing with his platoon sergeant.

It felt almost normal. As though there wasn't a war hanging over their heads or the next deployment looming a few months away.

Somehow, somewhere along the way, Gale's versions of right and wrong had gotten twisted up and he was willing to give the kid a chance. All because Foster had manned up and asked for help rather than flaring out like far too many other soldiers. Foster and Iaconelli were made for each other and, despite Foster's stupid stunt on the gate, no one had gotten hurt.

"Sorren!"

Gale turned at the sound of his name from a too familiar voice.

Tellhouse stalked across the quad toward him. Out of the corner of his eye, he saw Diablo's commander and first sarn't start to make their way in Gale and Teague's direction.

"Why do I feel like this is going to go badly?" Gale muttered.

"Well, he could just want to go bake cookies with you," Teague said lightly.

Gale shot his commander a baleful look. "Somehow I doubt it."

Before Gale knew what was happening, there was a loose semi-circle around him and Tellhouse. He felt Teague somewhere off to his left shoulder, with the Chaos Company commander Nichols close by.

"Let me tell you something, motherfucker," Tellhouse said.

His voice was deceptively mild, betraying the violence in his bunched fists. "My family is none of your damn business."

Gale swallowed the urge to step into the informal ring. Instead he shifted his weight to the balls of his feet and widened his stance. If he remembered correctly, Tellhouse was a brawler, and with him being this fired up there was no telling how things would play out.

"It is when your kid walks around the battalion area with a black eye and a bullshit story," Gale said harshly. "It takes a real man to beat up a fucking kid."

Tellhouse's face turned a deeper shade of red. "You don't know shit about my kid."

Gale finally took a single step forward and leaned in close enough that he didn't have to shout. His voice carried over the adrenaline-filled anticipation of the soldiers surrounding them. "I'm telling you now, in front of all these witnesses, that if you touch your fucking kid again, I will fucking end you. One way or another," Gale said softly.

He took a single step backward, far enough to see Tellhouse's face. "So that's how it is then?" Tellhouse's fury was still there, caged beneath the calm surface. "You forget about last deployment when I stopped your ass from killing the sarn't major? None of that matters anymore?"

"It matters," Gale said. Because it did. Tellhouse had pulled him off the sarn't major. Had shoved him away. Gale didn't remember any of it but he knew he was still here because he hadn't killed the man.

But something ugly had taken root in Tellhouse in the intervening years. Maybe it had been there all along and had just finally taken root.

Gale didn't know why, but the man who squared off in front of him just then was not the man he'd stood shoulder to shoulder with a lifetime ago. That man, Gale had trusted with his life. Before the rumors. Before Alex's black eye.

This man?

This was not the same man, and Gale was not about to let some twisted version of loyalty to a warrior who no longer existed put Tellhouse's kid in the hospital. Or worse.

"You're a real piece of fucking work." Tellhouse spat in the dirt. "Fucking hypocrite. You stand there all high and mighty and you're worse than me."

"I will be grateful to you for the rest of my life for stopping me that day," Gale said. "But that does not change a fucking thing when it comes to your kid."

"Fuck you, you self-righteous prick. I saved your goddamned career!" Tellhouse stepped into Gale's face.

"Then I'm calling in the fucking debt." Gale's voice never rose. "I'm trading my life for your son's. Don't fucking touch him or deal with me. Those are the terms." He stuck his finger in Tellhouse's chest, emphasizing his last words. "They are not negotiable."

Tellhouse reacted after the first jab into his chest. He shoved Gale violently, catching him off balance. He took a single step back, righting himself. Vaguely, Gale became aware that a crowd had grown beyond the renegade command teams that surrounded them, but he didn't have time to register more than that. He ducked backward as Tellhouse swung at him, the man's face twisted in violence and fury.

Gale took another step back, wanting to avoid the violence. Wanting to leave the temptation of bloodletting alone. Afraid of the temper lashing at its bonds, demanding he unleash the violence inside him and pound Tellhouse to within an inch of his worthless life.

He fought the beast inside him to the ground. Wrestled it into pained submission, all the while dodging Tellhouse's ham-fisted strikes.

"Come on, you fucking coward. You want to run your fucking mouth but don't want to back it up?"

"At ease!"

Gale made the mistake of glancing toward the booming

voice. Out of the corner of his eye, he saw Tellhouse's fist a moment before it connected. His lip split on impact as his head snapped back.

He kept his balance. He didn't even rock back on his heels, despite the two hundred and fifty pounds behind that connection.

He looked at Tellhouse as he lifted his index finger to his lip. Warm coppery blood trickled across his tongue.

Red flashed across his vision.

His temper lunged and thrashed. He bunched his fists at his sides, wrestling with the beast that demanded blood for blood.

He spat into the dirt as the crowd parted, revealing the sarn't major and a thin copper-skinned female first sergeant.

"What the ever loving fuck is going on here?" Sarn't Major Cox asked. His voice was just above a whisper. A warning, Gale knew, from a long history.

Gale said nothing, unable to speak, not trusting his control of his voice.

"Professional disagreement," Tellhouse said, flexing his fist.

Gale rotated his jaw and still, he said nothing.

"Then why do I have every swinging dick in the entire battalion standing around like they're watching a cockfight? Get your sorry asses back to work," he shouted at the crowd.

Soldiers disbanded like roaches in a sudden flash of light. The other commanders eased back a little bit, but not much.

Cox jammed his index finger at Tellhouse. "You. My office. Fucking yesterday." He pointed at the female first sergeant, then square at Gale. "You. Take her to battalion and get her in-processed. Then get your sorry fucking ass at parade rest outside my office. You have thirty minutes."

Sarn't Major Cox executed an about face and stalked off. Tellhouse shot a cold, hard glare in Gale's direction. "Next time, you fucking rat bastard."

In another lifetime, Gale might have hauled off and finished the fight that Tellhouse wanted so badly.

But those things never ended well. For anyone.

The crowd dispersed, leaving Gale with the new first sergeant. She had the lean body of a runner. Her hair was pulled sharply back from her face the way female first sergeants tended to and her expression was polished glass. Gale stuck his hand out. Her handshake was strong and firm. She wasn't there to play nice; she was there to kick some ass.

Gale liked her already.

"First Sarn't Sorren," he said, trusting his voice now that the object of his wrath was out of sight.

"First Sarn't Washington," she said, gripping his hand tightly before dropping it. "Might need to get that checked out," she said, pointing to his lip.

He swiped his mouth on the back of his hand. "It'll stop." He turned toward battalion. She didn't hesitate to fall into step next to him.

"Hell of an introduction to the Death Dealer battalion," she said dryly. "Is it always like this?"

Gale licked the blood from his lip and considered the range of possible answers, from the truth to the polite response. "Let's put it this way," he said mildly. "There's never a dull moment."

Washington rolled her eyes. "Guess I got here just in time."

Gale said nothing else as he led her into the battalion headquarters. The soldiers in the adjutant were professional and polite, even if he caught more than one of them whispering about the new first sergeant. You'd think they'd never seen a female first sergeant before.

Shit, all he cared about was that the support company finally had some badly needed leadership.

Maybe now they could finally get some bullets and fuel and start really training.

***

Gale had finished in processing First Sarn't Washington, showing her where her company ops was on the end of the long line of offices that was the company headquarters.

She was a bit stiff but Gale figured that was being new in the unit. She'd find her stride soon enough. He had enough faith in his fellow senior NCO to believe that she'd gotten there through the school of hard knocks. He'd given her all the first sergeants' phone numbers and added hers to his cell phone and wished her luck as she got the support company squared away.

He stood now, outside the sarn't major's office, listening to the sound of violence from inside. He was reasonably certain a coffee cup had been smashed against the wall at one point.

He *almost* felt sorry for Tellhouse, but every time he closed his eyes, he saw Alex's busted eye and heard his piss-poor excuse as he tried to cover for his sorry excuse for a father.

The cold comfort of his leashed rage kept him standing silently by, listening as Cox kicked off in Tellhouse's fourth point of contact.

It felt like forever until the door opened and Tellhouse stalked out. He didn't spare a backward glance as he made a beeline for the door.

Gale simply stood, waiting for his turn in front of the firing squad.

Cox appeared in the doorway. "Get your sorry ass in here," he snapped.

The door closed like a gunshot behind him.

Cox jammed a cigar-clenching finger in Gale's face. "You've got one shot to tell me the truth, Sorren," he said, his voice dangerous and low.

Well, he wasn't screaming. So that was always a plus.

Gale took a deep breath and searched for the words he needed. It was a long breath. "I think Tellhouse is beating up his kid."

Cox looked up sharply. The muscle in his jaw flexed violently. "Try that again?"

Gale considered his words carefully, wary of the tone in Cox's voice. "His kid and mine are friends. His kid was sporting a busted-up eye the other day. Made a really shitty excuse for what happened."

"So you go from black eye to 'one of my first sergeants is beating up his kid' how?" There it was again. That razor's edge in Cox's voice that told Gale he was on exceptionally thin ice. "That's a hell of a leap."

"Things my daughter has mentioned. The way I've seen this kid cringe away from his dad."

"And you decided you were just going to sit on this information?"

"I don't have any proof," Gale said softly, finally daring to meet Cox's cold, hard eyes. "Beyond what my daughter has told me, I've got zero proof I can turn over to investigators."

"Whatever happened between you and Tellhouse, you need to bury the fucking hatchet," Cox said after a moment.

Gale looked up sharply. That was not what he'd expected. Not at all.

"Sarn't major?"

"Tellhouse just made the same fucking accusation against you. Said your kid was cutting herself because of shit you did to her."

Gale's skin went cold, his heart shriveling in his chest beneath a band of pressure. And deep, deep inside him, the beast wanted blood.

"Sarn't major, that's bullshit and you know it," he said when he could talk.

"Is it? I know about your kid's problems, Sorren," Cox said, more softly than Gale expected. "So now I've got two first sergeants pissing on my leg, each making allegations against the other. If this wasn't fucking real life, I'd think it was a reality TV show." He pointed that cigar back at Gale. "Get whatever this shit is between you two fixed. I don't want to hear another word about it." Gale's voice was lodged in his throat. He said nothing until Cox looked up at him, his eyes cold and hard. "You're dismissed, First Sergeant."

Gale executed an about face and strode from the headquarters, his blood pounding violently in his veins.

He ignored two soldiers getting into a pissing contest about mopping the barracks.

He stalked into his company ops. Foster, who was hanging out in ops on his convalescent leave, looked about to say something smart, then wisely thought better of it.

Gale closed the door behind him as gently as if he were in church.

He stood there in the emptiness of his own space. Stood and breathed deeply, the rage pounding against his temples, demanding a release that would only feed the beast.

He threw his cap on the desk, clenching and unclenching his fists, struggling violently to get his anger under control. His skin felt hot, like it was two sizes too small. He wanted to pace, to run, to prowl, to do anything other than stand there letting the storm rage inside him.

But instead he stood. Stock still in the ocean of violence.

He stood. He breathed. In. Out.

Forced himself to slow it down. Forced himself to get a handle on the chaos inside him.

Because if he moved, if he so much as slammed a door or gave the violence the tiniest opening…he would lose everything he'd worked so hard to contain.

It was a long time before he went back to work.

CHAPTER EIGHTEEN

He didn't call Melanie that night. He felt bad about it but he didn't trust himself.

There were too many memories clawing their way to the surface, too much raw emotion for him to deal with anyone on anything even close to resembling human interaction.

He must have stopped by the Class Six on his way home. He vaguely remembered snarling at a private over something stupid.

Everything he was threatened to unravel tonight. Everything he'd tried so hard to be was coming apart at the seams.

He tried running after work. He tried losing himself in bad evaluation reports and paperwork, but they didn't distract him nearly as much as they should have and getting through them didn't last anywhere close to long enough.

He was home now. The front door was locked. His keys put away.

The gun safe locked.

He was going to crawl into the bottle tonight. It wasn't something he did often but tonight the memories were too strong.

He knew better than to fight them. Knew better than to try to stuff them down.

Tonight, bloody memories would run their stained hands across his body, reminding him of everything he wanted to forget.

Tellhouse had summoned the demons of Tal Afar and they'd come knocking, bringing a legion of other memories with them.

This didn't happen often. But when it did, Gale knew better than to be around people until he had his nightmares back under control.

He used a spoon to pop the top off a Heineken. There was probably a bottle opener somewhere in the house but he didn't bother to look. And honestly, he just wanted to fucking drink. The bitter beer burst across his tongue and burned down his throat.

He leaned on the small counter in his tiny kitchen. That morning's dishes were still in the sink. Breadcrumbs were sure to draw ants if he didn't clean them up soon.

He closed his eyes, rubbing the cold beer against his temple.

And he remembered.

Jamie standing in a pile of ants. She'd been a baby, no more than three. He'd looked down and seen the swarm tearing up her chubby little legs.

He'd never gotten a diaper off so quickly in his life. He'd swiped them off as fast as he could while she'd cried loud, wailing tears. Her little legs had turned bright red with bites.

Gale had come in for a weekend to try and spend time with Jamie. Instead, they'd spent a couple of hours in the emergency room, just to make sure Jamie was okay. God, but Melanie had been pissed at him. He'd sat in the ER holding his little girl while she slept in his lap, while the chasm between him and Melanie had grown.

He tossed back the rest of the beer. It was cold and numbed the throbbing violence inside him, pounding like the beat of a fifty cal. The rest of the memories were just getting started.

He knew this drill. Knew it well and hated that he had never moved beyond this fucking traumatic ritual.

"What do you mean she's in the hospital, Mel?"

He could still feel the ache in his knuckles where he'd

opened them up on his first sergeant's teeth. His fist tightened on the bottle in his hand, remembering how hard he'd clutched the phone in Cox's office that day.

"She's stable. They say she's okay." Her voice had broken then. *"I'm scared, Gale."* A shattered whisper. *"I've never asked you for much. I need you home."*

His throat closed off, as tight as if the memory was fresh and new and filled with vibrant pain. He was going to rip her heart out when he told her he was deploying early. He was a selfish fuck because he was only prolonging the inevitable. "I can't do this to her." There was no one to hear the pain in those words.

He left the empty bottle on the counter, popping open another. He tossed the cap in the trash and took a long pull.

Someone pounded on his front door.

There was someone at the door.

He didn't want anyone at the front door.

He'd avoided everyone on his way out of the office and he'd done it on purpose. Bad things happened when he lost his temper and damn it, he wasn't about to repeat what had happened in Iraq all those years ago.

He scraped his thumb over the green label. Maybe they'd take the hint and leave.

The pounding came again.

"Jesus," he muttered.

"Open the damn door, Top."

Gale frowned at the familiar voice. What the fuck was Teague doing here?

He padded to the front door and flipped the latch. He braced his foot on the back, keeping it from opening wider.

Teague carried a case of Heineken beneath one arm. He motioned to the bottle in Gale's hand. "Looks like you've got a head start on me."

"I'm not in the mood for company."

"Neither am I," Teague said. "Sarn't Major told me what

happened."

Gale's chest tightened and he lifted the beer to his lips, wishing he didn't notice how his own hand shook. His throat refused to cooperate and he lowered the beer. "I'm not interested in sitting around the campfire, singing 'Kumbaya'."

"And maybe I'm just offering to sit with you tonight. It's a fucked-up thing that Tellhouse did today. I always knew he was a prick but he crossed the line with this bullshit," Teague said.

Gale closed his eyes, not wanting to let his commander in. Not tonight. Not when there were already too many potent memories swirling.

But he did. He took that single step backward.

***

Gale didn't get drunk. At least not completely. He and Teague sat on the porch. A distant siren echoed off the building. The night air was sticky and thick but it was the silence between them that hung, filled with things that needed to be said. Things that lacked the ability to be put into words.

Teague shifted, leaning forward to rest his elbows on his knees. If he hadn't been sitting, Gale was worried he might have fallen over.

"You know, I thought I was going to enjoy command," Teague said. His words slurred over his tongue.

Gale took a long pull off his beer. "You mean you're not enjoying spending twenty hours a day chasing after lovesick privates who married the first girl they lost their virginity to and fending off payday loan sharks who used to be first sergeants?"

Teague shot him a glassy look. "Wait—were you in my ops today?"

Gale took another pull off his beer. "Can't say that I was."

Teague snorted and looked down at his beer. He'd been worrying the label on this one, too. It was half stuck to his thumbnail as he continued to pick at it.

Gale killed his eighth beer of the evening.

Teague handed him his ninth. "So what's the story with you and Tellhouse?"

Gale sighed and gave him the thirty-second rundown of their history. The anger he'd beaten back simmered, low and angry in his belly, as he spoke.

"I need another beer," he said mildly, draining the bottle quickly. "Because every time I think of that guy, I want to drive across town and beat him within an inch of his fucking life."

The need for violence was strong. Too strong tonight.

Gale had given in to that need once. It was not allowed to happen again.

"So I take it there will be no long hot showers together any time soon?" Teague said, taking a pull from his own beer.

Gale rubbed his thumb across the lip of his bottle. "You know what happened the last time I lost my temper," he said shortly.

Teague nodded. "I'm surprised you weren't court-martialed over that."

Gale raised the beer to his lips. "I almost was. Sarn't Major Cox got me put on assignment after he managed to get the charges dropped."

"I had no idea Cox was that powerful." Teague sniffed and leaned back in his chair, rocking on two legs.

"Cox is a good man. I hope he beats whatever demons he's fighting." Gale wished he could find the hindsight that would enable him to laugh but the memories were too raw, too ragged.

It wasn't enough that he was drinking himself stupid tonight. It wasn't enough that he'd kept himself away from everyone he cared about until he could get his emotions under control.

Teague shifted again, unsteady on those two wobbly chair legs. "Would you do it again?" he asked abruptly.

"Do what again?"

"Enlist. The war. Everything."

Gale looked over at his commander. Teague didn't do petulant introspection. The question caught him off guard, and his throat tightened as it picked the lock on memories he'd been trying to drown tonight.

"No. I don't think I would."

He thought about the time he'd missed. The years of Jamie's life. The life he might have had if he hadn't screwed things up with Mel so soon after they'd gotten married to the idea that they were both grown-ups.

The friends he'd lost along the way. The bitterness threatened to close off his lungs.

"You?" he asked his commander.

"I don't know." Teague paused. "I want the war to have been worth it. I want to know what we did mattered." He glanced over at Gale, his eyes bleak. "But I don't think it was."

Blasphemy, one so shameful Gale wasn't sure he'd heard it right. Words that felt dirty and wrong even as he silently agreed with them.

An unspoken fear rested in Teague's words. The fear that the war hadn't been worth it. That it was a waste of flesh and blood.

That their brothers and sisters had died for nothing.

Gale bit down on his lip hard, splitting the cut that had barely stopped bleeding.

When Teague handed him the next beer, he didn't turn it down.

***

"What's wrong?" Mel fought panic when she'd seen his phone number glowing in the dark. "Gale?" she said again when he didn't respond.

"I'm here." His voice was thick and slurred and slightly fuzzy.

She sat up. She couldn't remember the last time she'd seen

him drinking, let alone drunk.

"Mel?"

"I'm here," she said, cradling her forehead in her palm. "How much have you had to drink?"

"A shitload," he said. He sounded like he was swaying on his feet. She almost smiled at the idea of him struggling to stand. She didn't normally find drunks endearing but this…this was Gale.

And the soft spot she'd always had for him was exposed tonight after their afternoon together.

"Why? Are you okay?"

"It depends," he said.

"On what?"

There was no sound over the line for an impossible span of time. She glanced at the phone to make sure it wasn't disconnected. "Gale?"

"Remember that night you asked me to come home?"

Her skin went cold. Her throat tightened as her bones threatened to tear through too tight flesh. "Why are you doing this, Gale?"

Terrible disappointment burned through her lungs, ripping the bandage off old wounds. "I'm just asking a question, Melanie."

She licked her lips. "Yes, Gale. I remember."

Old hurts rose up, burning behind her eyes. It was more than just old hurts. She'd never, ever imagined fighting her own daughter like she had that night.

She'd wanted him there. Needed him.

Needed someone to stand with her so that she wouldn't have to do it alone.

But he hadn't come.

On a rational level, she knew the Army wouldn't let him.

But she hadn't been rational that night. Or for a long time after, if she was honest with herself.

She'd learned to live with the fear, with the ever-present

knowledge that her daughter could be cutting again.

"I beat my sergeant major that day," he admitted softly. "I don't remember it."

The cold wrapped around her heart and squeezed tight. "What do you mean, you don't remember it?" Broken, terrified words.

"I snapped." A harsh exhale. "When they told me I couldn't come home." Clear, brittle words. "I don't remember what happened."

"Why are you telling me this, Gale?" Broken, pain filled words.

"Because you need to know," he finally said. "You need to know that I wanted to be there for you. That I couldn't be." Another vast expanse of silence. "And you need to know what I'm capable of."

Her eyes burned. "This doesn't change anything."

Nothing could erase the emptiness she'd felt in that hospital waiting room. All those memories twisted and writhed to life from the vault where she'd locked them away. "I don't want to remember this." Her words felt like shattered glass in her throat. "I don't want to remember hating you."

"I deserve your hatred."

Mel bit the edge of her palm, biting back frustrated tears. Bitterness rose up in her, that he would do this now, after all the bad years had finally, finally turned into something good. Anger, too—that he would cut at her with the violence that she feared and hated and *lived with* every single fucking day.

"I'm hanging up, Gale." *Before I start to hate you again.* "We can talk about this tomorrow."

"There can't be any more tomorrows," Gale whispered. "We can't do this anymore."

The phone went dead. Melanie honestly wasn't sure if she'd hung up on him or if the call had dropped but she'd already slipped her feet into a pair of old sneakers and grabbed her car keys. She didn't know what the hell was going on with

Gale tonight but damn it, she was going to see for herself.

Because the man she'd just heard on the phone did not match the man she'd been falling for all over again.

And that scared the hell out of her.

CHAPTER NINETEEN

It was a damn shame that she knew how to get access to his apartment even when it was a locked and gated community, but she wasn't above using her knowledge and connections to get to him.

She knocked first. She wasn't surprised when there was no answer. She wished her hand didn't shake as she turned the key in the lock. The apartment was dark but not silent. A small flat-screen TV flickered in the corner. A pair of booted feet hung over the edge of the sofa. She approached quietly, well aware that she was trespassing. It took her a minute to recognize Captain Teague on the couch. She frowned, worried she might have broken into the wrong apartment.

The sound of a chair scraping on concrete drew her attention to the open space on the other side of a sliding glass door. She inhaled deeply, praying it was Gale and that things weren't about to get awkward.

She took a single step.

But then Gale was there, filling the door.

A brief flicker of emotion traced across his face, a flicker and nothing more before the shutters fell and she felt like she was looking at a stranger.

The sound of the TV and the other man's snoring fell away, leaving everything she was focused solely on the man in front of her. His brown t-shirt was untucked. His feet were bare beneath the hems of his uniform pants.

A beer dangled between one thumb and forefinger.

He was drunk. She could see that. Then again, she hadn't

needed to drive here to know that he'd been half in the bag when he'd called her.

His jaw tightened after a moment and he walked by her, toward the tiny kitchen. His beer clanked in the trashcan.

"Go home, Melanie," he said, not turning to face her.

She lifted her chin. "I'm worried about you."

He said nothing for the longest time. He stood there, his head bowed, his hand gripping the fridge handle. His knuckles were white, his back tense.

Finally he turned to face her. "I was wrong to try and come back into your life, Mel. I never should have tried to be a part of it. Not with you, not with Jamie. I should have let you go."

"But you're back now."

He shook his head. "But I'm not. I've been lying to you since I came back." He closed his eyes, his expression ripped with pain and sadness. "My deployment has been pushed up. I'm leaving again, sooner than I thought I was."

Mel felt the world drop from beneath her. She'd known he was going back. Had known and had avoided thinking about it.

And knew the distraction for what it was. "Nice try, Gale," she said quietly. "But this isn't about the deployment."

The muscles in his neck pulsed. It was a long time before he looked away.

"You never struck me as a coward, Gale," she said. "Whatever is going on, whatever is driving you to go full asshole, I think I've earned a right to know."

There was something here, something harsh and cutting beneath his words. Something that made her swallow her fear and take a step forward. Until she stood a few feet from him and looked up into his dark, sad eyes.

"I don't have a lot of experience with this but I always thought that the point of being with someone was not having to do it all alone."

His smile was bitter. "You never gave me a chance to do anything with you and the baby."

"You're right." That swipe hurt. It drew fresh blood from old wounds. "I didn't. And I've regretted that since the day I walked out of our life." The admission ripped from a place in her soul she'd been hiding since that terrible night all those years ago.

He snorted. "Regret is a motherfucker, isn't it?"

"Yeah." She leaned closer. "So how about we don't make new regrets." She reached for him, placing her hand over his heart. Heat radiated through the thin t-shirt to her palm. "Talk to me."

She half-expected him to push her away. To tell her to leave again.

She didn't expect the words he finally spoke.

"I can't be in your life, Mel," he said softly. "I wish there was a way but there isn't. I've…I've done…terrible things."

"You've gone to war," she said. "War demands that good men do terrible things."

She didn't lie to herself about the things he might have done. She'd followed the war closely when it first started. She knew about the terrible things that happened at war—at least as much as a civilian real estate agent could hope to know.

He reached up, squeezing her hand a moment before taking it off his chest and setting it on the cool laminate counter. "When I told you I beat my sergeant major, I didn't tell you everything." He turned away, avoiding her eyes.

She didn't step away but she let him go. Giving him the distance, the space, he needed to find the words he was searching for.

"I put him in the hospital." The words were sanitized, clean words to hide the ugly truth. "I tried to kill him." He lifted his gaze, finally meeting hers. "And I don't remember any of it."

The emotion in his words blunted the force of them as they slammed into her. "What are you telling me?"

"I black out sometimes. I don't remember things. I have

anxiety attacks." He held her gaze. "I thought I had things under control. But what happened today reminded me that I don't. And I can't be around you and Jamie because of it."

He blinked slowly, his words clear and unhindered despite the amount of beer bottles in the trashcan. "Because I'm terrified of hurting you."

"Gale." She started to take a single step toward him.

He held up his hands. "Don't, Mel."

"Then tell me what happened today. Tell me what made you decide to be a hero and rip my soul to shreds all over again." She didn't fight the emotion in her voice. The terrible grief that was threatening to overwhelm her.

"I got into a fight with Tellhouse."

Her breath caught in her throat but he continued.

"I didn't hurt him. But he told the sergeant major I was hurting Jamie."

"That's a lie."

"It might be a lie but it doesn't matter. I lost my temper, I lost control. I came home before I hurt anyone. I needed to get away. To get things reined in." His hands clenched into fists by his sides. "I wanted to make him hurt."

"But you didn't."

She took another step. Ignored the bleak emptiness in his eyes.

"You came home. You had enough control to get away from everyone and get yourself calm."

He shook his head but he didn't stop her approach. "You don't understand."

"Yes, I do." Another hesitant step. "I know all about completely losing your shit." Another step closer. "I've been in counseling for three years," she admitted. "Working on my patience, my temper." Tears filled her eyes. "She's just a child but she's pushed me so hard and so often. I was terrified I was getting close to doing something I'd regret. And then she went into the hospital." She tried to stop but the words just kept coming, tumbling out and dragging every shame-filled memory with it. "You're not the only one with a temper," she finally said.

"Mel." His hand slid around the back of her neck, tugging her close until she stepped into his arms.

Stepped one step closer to home.

He was warm and strong. Comforting her over her most secret shame.

"I don't know what you've been through," she finally said, leaning up to look at him. "But I trust you, even if you don't trust yourself. I trust you to know when you need to walk away. I trust you not to hurt me again." She cupped his cheeks, refusing to let him look away. "I trust you," she whispered.

He blinked hard. His breath huffed across her cheek. "Mel." Her name was a prayer, filled with worship.

She didn't know what to expect—whether he might pull away or leave her standing there alone, feeling stupid and abandoned yet again.

Instead, he simply gathered her to him, holding her tight.

And for the life of her, she could not figure out who was holding up who.

CHAPTER TWENTY

"You are entirely too distracted." Teague plopped down in the chair across from Gale's desk and kicked his feet up on the edge, a sleeve of cookies in one hand.

"And you are not nearly hung over enough." Gale stared at his feet until he moved them. It was an ongoing battle between them: Teague was forever kicking his feet up, Gale was forever pushing them down. Sometimes he felt like they were an old married couple.

As command relationships went, it wasn't a bad one. Gale had lived through worse, that was for damn sure. And Teague was growing on him.

He'd been planning on leaving work on time tonight. Hoping to get some time to talk to Jamie but of course, some dipshit in Second Platoon had gone and gotten himself arrested before the end of the duty day.

And the sergeant major and colonel had decided to call the entire battalion back to work to conduct extra PT. Because extra PT was sure to resolve any lingering delinquency in the battalion.

More likely it was sure to end up with guys in the aid station for dehydration. But that wasn't what had Gale drumming his hands on his desk.

He closed his eyes, his brain circling back to waking up with Mel in the bed beside him. It was strange seeing her wrapped in his sheets. Strange for them both to be fully clothed. He'd had a cup of coffee with Mel before she'd left, heading home only after extracting a promise from him not to pull any more stupid shit.

She didn't understand his fear of the thing he wrestled with.

But her faith in him was an anchor. Something stable that he'd held onto through the night as the demons and the nightmares threatened to drag him under again.

He wasn't a fool. He knew there was a hell of a lot more to getting his normal back than one night holding his ex-wife in his arms.

But maybe, just maybe, it was a start.

That start came with responsibilities. Like talking to their daughter about responsible sex.

"I'm having an existential parenting crisis," Gale mumbled.

"That's a hell of a sentence," Teague said. "Can you even spell 'existential'?"

Gale briefly considered flipping his commander off. "I finished my degree three years ago."

"Impressive. It wasn't in Underwater Basket Weaving, was it?"

Gale raised both eyebrows. "Ah, no, and fuck you for thinking us dumbass enlisted guys can only pass underwater basket weaving."

"I implied no such thing," Teague said. "I was merely inquiring into your college aspirations."

"If you must know, I got my BA in Criminal Justice."

"You want to be a cop?"

Gale shrugged. "I figure I'll have as good a shot as any at a job there when I retire."

"Or you can be a mall cop."

Gale ground his teeth. "You know how to kick a man in the soft and squishy parts, don't you, sir? What if being a mall cop was my dying wish?"

"You're not allowed to die or retire. It would leave me unsupervised and I am clearly not meant to be left alone in charge of troops." Teague held out the sleeve of cookies.

Gale held up a hand. "I'm not planning on going anywhere any time soon. I learned a long time ago that officers should not be left unattended."

"That's good to know." Teague pulled a cookie from the sleeve. "What's got your panties in a twist, anyway?"

"I have to have The Talk with my daughter." Gale scrubbed his hands over his face, dreading saying the words that were haunting him and sure to lead to an early grave. He was positive he'd already gotten more grey hair from it.

And he'd thought moving to be closer to Mel and Jamie would be a good thing.

"I'm thinking this is supposed to be a good thing? Father-daughter bonding and all that." Teague asked, "Why is this causing you to freak out like one of the lieutenants?"

Gale snorted. "You understand 'The Talk' is a euphemism for the sex talk, right?"

"There you go using those big words again. Haven't I mentioned being a product of the public education system?" Teague chewed thoughtfully on a cookie for a moment. "Isn't that usually a mom's job for daughters?"

"Apparently, her mother wants me to reinforce the fact that all boys are horny perverts and that she should wait until she meets a guy she really cares about."

Teague stared down at the cookies in his lap. "Well, boys are typically horny perverts, so I can see how that would be some sage advice," he said cautiously. He glanced up at Gale. "You look like you're going to have a heart attack."

"I might need to get my blood pressure checked," Gale said, trying and failing to be flippant. "I'm not ready for my little girl to start exploring penises."

Teague choked on his cookie and spewed crumbs across Gale's desk. "Sorry, that caught me off guard," Teague said, wiping his mouth. "I'll clean that up."

"Really, sir?" Sorren swiped the crumbs onto the floor. "Just aim for the damn floor next time."

"Next time warn a guy before you say something that funny," Teague said, still laughing.

"My daughter and penises is not funny. Some boy is going to want to do to her what I did with her mother and… I'm not ready for this," he said again.

"Did you at least talk a good game to get her mom into bed?"

Gale smiled at the long dormant memory called up far too easily. God but they'd been awkward and eager. "Yeah. I don't want Jamie to fall for the same cheesy bullshit, though."

"What's her mom say about this?"

"She doesn't want her to fall for the same cheesy bullshit she fell for, either." Gale felt some of anxiety start to fade. Not nearly enough, though.

"Is there more to this story that you're not telling me?" Teague asked after a moment.

Gale changed the subject, unwilling to have a heart-to-heart with his commander about his troubles with his ex-wife. Seeing how Teague was still figuring things out with Olivia, he was probably not the right guy to get relationship advice from.

"What has Olivia found out at the school?"

If Teague noticed the change of subject, he didn't remark on it. "Not nearly enough. The school nurse gave her everything she had, which was just short of jack shit. Tellhouse's kid isn't talking to anyone. Not the counselor. Not the teachers. No one." Teague tossed the cookies onto the chair next to him. "Nothing we can take to the boss."

Gale scrubbed his hand over his face. "We don't have anything, not even a kid willing to make a sworn statement. My kid hasn't seen anything directly. There's nothing here."

Teague folded his arms over his chest. "Fuck. Did I mention how much I hate this?"

"I'm going to pick up my daughter from school and try to figure out what to do," Gale snapped.

He didn't tell his commander what Sarn't Major Cox had

said to him the day prior about Tellhouse's allegations.

He couldn't find the words for all the ways it was fucked up.

But he needed, now more than ever, to have incontrovertible proof before he said anything else to the powers that be at battalion.

"So you want to take some of the condoms in the orderly room? You can give some to your daughter."

Gale didn't laugh. The thought was so remotely not even close to funny, his chest tightened a little more. He must have scowled. Teague held up both hands. "Okay, bad joke. Jeez."

"I'm going to take a walk."

Gale grabbed his headgear and headed out the back of the company ops. His commander had a smart mouth on him but Gale wasn't convinced the guy was as much of a fuck off as he wanted everyone to think. Teague was smarter than he let on. He also needed him to stop pissing off the sergeant major. Gale looked up in time to see said sergeant major walking out of battalion headquarters.

"Sorren," Sarn't Major Cox said by way of greeting.

"Sarn't major."

"You look like you need a cigar."

He didn't but then again, he knew this wasn't really an optional invitation. Gale glanced at his watch. Almost time for him to go pick up his daughter. But he had time to sit on sarn't major's couch.

He chopped the end off the cigar Cox handed him and waited for the lighter. He thought about bringing up Tellhouse. Thought about the different ways he could speak what he was almost certain of.

Of the different ways he could convince Cox to listen to him and ignore the lies that Tellhouse had spread.

But the words were stuck in his throat. Lodged there like a thick, heavy block that was difficult to swallow.

He needed a plan. And he needed proof.

Then he'd go to the sergeant major. Because he trusted Cox.

Or at least he had before the other day. Cox's refusal to ask him outright chafed. It burned beneath his skin like a slow poison that the man Gale had looked up to hadn't thought enough of him to ask instead of believing Tellhouse's bullshit allegations.

It burned, but still Gale couldn't bring himself to believe Cox would fail to act when Gale brought him proof. Because he would figure this out. Jamie was trusting him to look out for Alex.

They sat on the back dock of the battalion headquarters in silence. A distant boom thundered on the horizon as one of the field artillery battalions conducted gunnery.

"Sometimes I think it's easier being back in Iraq," Cox said after a while.

"Easier to deal with the enemy than all the drama back here," Gale said, looking at the end of his cigar. "This is good. What is it?"

"Coheba Red Dot. Most people hate them."

Gale tapped the ashes off onto the concrete beneath his feet. "Can't see why."

Cox did the same. "So what's eating you?"

Gale inhaled deeply on the cigar, enjoying the smooth taste and the burn in his lungs. "Where do I start?"

"Well, is it work or a woman?"

"C, all of the above. One's my daughter and one's my ex-wife."

"You have my sympathies. Ex-wife busting your balls?" Cox was on his third marriage by Gale's count.

"Nah, nothing like that." He tapped the ashes again. "It's complicated."

"It's always complicated when it's a woman. They are not simple creatures."

"Says the man who is on his third wife?"

Cox pointed his cigar at him. "Third marriage. Same woman."

Gale frowned. "How the hell did you manage that one?"

"By being an idiot the first two times?" Cox sucked on the end of his cigar. "My Leah is a pistol. She doesn't have a lot of tolerance for stupidity and well, I'm an infantryman. I've got a lot of stupidity I'm still working out of my system."

Gale chuckled. "Good point."

"What's up with your ex?"

"A lot of things."

"Start with one and we'll go from there," Cox said gruffly.

"She wants me to talk to my daughter about sex."

"And this is a problem because?"

Gale shot his mentor an odd look. "Are you serious? I haven't been a horny sixteen year old in about twenty years. And what about 'infantry first sergeant' says I know the first thing about teenage girls?"

"You're making this harder than it needs to be. It's really simple. Boys think about sex. Girls think about sex. The worst thing you can do is let her figure it out on her own. You might end up a grandfather before you're ready."

Gale's heart flipped in his chest. "Jesus, will everyone stop saying that?"

Cox snorted. "This isn't what's really bothering you."

Gale tapped his cigar again, watching the ashes drift down to the oil-stained concrete between his feet. "I never got over my ex," he admitted after a while.

"No shit, Sherlock. Tell me something I don't know."

Gale looked at him sharply. "Huh?"

"You've been pining after that woman since she broke your heart all those years ago. You don't have to read women's magazines to figure that shit out." Cox sucked on the end of his cigar. "The question becomes what do you do about it?"

Gale looked down at his cigar. He had no fucking idea.

***

It was a new level of hell waiting for his daughter to come out of the high school. He was corralled off to one side with the rest of the parents who were uncool enough to still pick their kids up from school instead of letting them find their own way home.

He spotted Jamie instantly. She walked out of school with Alex.

Gale grunted, wondering if Alex's dad knew he'd blown off the whole not-talking-to-Jamie thing.

He said nothing as they approached. Jamie looked wary, too much of her mother coming out in her eyes.

Alex, smart kid that he was, kept his hands off her and stayed a good foot and a half away from her. But as they approached, Gale studied the kid, looking for any sign that he was hiding an injury or anything else.

Too bad Gale had learned to spot shit like that from his soldiers trying to hide that they were hurt so they could stay in the fight.

But Alex gave no indication of any injuries.

Which was good.

"Alex," Gale said by way of greeting.

The owner of that name looked surprised that Gale remembered his name. "Sir."

"What happened with the MPs the other day?" Gale asked.

"I have two hundred hours of community service. If I complete it, there will be no criminal record."

"So you're going to complete it, right?" Gale said.

"Yes sir."

"You doing okay after everything the other day?" Gale asked. He felt the pressure from Jamie's gaze on him. That and the tightrope of trying to get the kid to open up to him when he may or may not have contemplated bodily harm against this same boy a short few days before.

"Yes, sir." He avoided Gale's eyes, glancing toward Jamie.

"I'm sorry if I got Jamie in any trouble." It took the kid everything he had to lift his gaze. "I panicked. She wasn't involved."

Gale said nothing, just long enough to make both Alex and Jamie squirm. "If she's accepted your apology, that's good enough for me," he said finally. He chewed on the inside of his lip. "If there's ah, anything you ever need, you can call me."

Alex didn't look away. "Sir?"

"Car breaks down, you can't reach your dad. Here." Gale pulled out his notebook and scribbled the number down on a piece of paper. "Here. For emergencies and shit."

Alex glanced down at it and Gale wished he didn't see the kid's hand tremble. But he reached into his back pocket and tucked the number away. "Thanks." Alex shot Jamie an unreadable look. "So I'll see you."

Jamie nodded. "Yeah."

Gale could see there was more she wanted to say but Alex was gone before she found the words. Gale almost shook his head. The kid was an idiot if he didn't see Jamie liked him.

And Gale was just fine with that, thank you very much. The kid could help Jamie with biology and keep all the natural experiments in his pants as far as Gale was concerned.

Who knew the thought of becoming a grandfather was a heart-attack inducing fear?

"So what's up?" Jamie said when Alex was finally out of earshot.

Gale jerked his chin toward Alex's retreating back. "He okay?"

"I guess." Jamie lifted one shoulder. "So were you just checking on him?"

Gale sighed deeply. "That was part of it. But can't a dad just pick his little girl up from school?"

Jamie raised both eyebrows and made that sound. "I know Mom found condoms," Jamie said dryly.

Gale coughed and quickly covered his mouth with his fist.

"Ah, okay." He paused. Now that everything was out in the open, what the hell was he supposed to do? "Well, do you want to go get some ice cream or something?"

"I'm not six," she mumbled.

"So you want to go get a beer or something?" Gale swore under his breath. Jamie shot him a dirty look. "Never mind. Shit."

He looked at Jamie before he started to walk around the truck toward the driver's side. She was looking down at her books, a deep unhappiness written on her features.

For one finite moment, Gale's heart broke for the daughter he hadn't raised. Guilt rose up and squeezed his heart until he thought he'd pass out.

He took a deep breath and walked over to her.

Gently he put his hand on her shoulder. Waited until she looked up at him, her eyes a mirror of Melanie's, only younger and wiser than Mel had ever been at that age.

"What do you want to do?"

***

He hadn't planned on the library. He offered up a quiet prayer that his little girl would always choose the library over the mall or dry humping in the back seats of cars.

The library, he could deal with. Wholeheartedly.

He waited for her to check the circulation desk for a new book, then chat with one of her friends.

It felt like forever before she joined him in the corner, away from all the kids. She curled one leg beneath her and sat on it. "So. Mom found the condoms and she freaked out and asked you to talk to me about sex, right?"

Gale rubbed his chest. His daughter's frank talk was…unnerving at best, but he supposed it was better than beating around the bush and hoping they came to the same meaning in their coded words.

"Yes, your mom wants me to talk to you about sex. Whose were they?"

Jamie sighed, tucking her long black hair behind one ear. "They're Kelli's."

"Who is Kelli?"

"Deacon Fred's daughter. If he finds out she's dating, he's threatened to send her on a mission to Africa."

Gale frowned. "Can he do that?"

"Her dad is some kind of really strict Christian or something. She sounds pretty sure her dad will ship her off."

"Then why risk it?"

Jamie rolled her eyes. "Because she really likes David and he really likes her."

He heard his father coming out of his mouth before he could stop it. "So that brings us to the main topic for today's conversation."

Jamie cocked her head at him. "I'm not sure I can handle you talking to me about condoms and sex, Dad."

Gale grinned at her smart-ass response. "You're supposed to listen eagerly and promise that you will remain a virgin until your old man is cold in the ground. That's how this father-daughter talk is supposed to go."

Jamie grinned and it was the first time he'd seen her smile since he'd moved here. "Yeah well, I'm not known for sticking to the script." She looked down at her hands, where she was picking at her thumbnail.

"So you're not interested in sex?"

Jamie's face flushed and for one moment, she was his little girl again and things weren't nearly so awkward. "I mean, one of the girls on the basketball team had a porno—"

Gale choked. "Jesus, what are you doing watching porn?"

Jamie's face turned bright red and she looked around wildly. "Will you say that a little louder? I don't think the fifth graders heard you."

Gale scrubbed his hand over his face. This was not going

in any way, shape, or form how he'd imagined it. But she was talking to him. He wanted that much to continue.

"Sorry," Gale mumbled. He felt at least sixteen new grey hairs start. "But seriously?"

"It was one YouTube video. And I was curious to see what everyone is always talking about," she hissed. "It looks like it hurts." She hesitated. "But I really like Alex and…I'd really like for you not to threaten to kill him or anything if he comes around a little more often."

"Well. I, ah, I had this whole speech prepared about how sixteen-year-old boys are terrible in bed and you should wait until you graduate college and your old man is dead so he doesn't have to think about some boy doing terrible things with his little girl."

It was Jamie's turn to cough. He wasn't entirely sure he hadn't heard her cover a giggle with that sound. "Really, Daddy?"

"What? It's true." Gale looked down at her hands, conscious of the fact that she was avoiding his eyes. "I know I wasn't around much when you were little but I still think of you as my little girl. And if you value my freedom at all, you'll keep horny boys away from you so that I don't go to prison for beating any of them up."

Jamie surprised him with a soft laugh. "I'll keep that in mind," she said dryly.

"Look, your mother and I made a lot of mistakes in our lives but the one thing we got right was you. We just should have waited until we were a little older." He closed his eyes, unable to believe what he was about to say next. "You're going find a guy that you really like one of these days. Maybe it's Alex, maybe it's not. But…whatever you're going to do, do it responsibly. Make sure the guy isn't an asshole. Make sure he treats you right or I'll have to kill him." He paused then looked up at her. "Make sure he's worthy of you."

In all his life, Gale had never imagined that he would have

a moment quite like this, talking about sex and boys. At least they weren't fighting and she wasn't making that God-awful sound she made when she was disgusted with him or her mother.

"Thanks, Dad," she said quietly.

She looked up at him, her eyes too young to be so wary. "So you're really going to stick around?" There was a world of caution in her words.

"Yeah. I mean, my unit is set to go to Iraq later this year and more than likely, I'm going but I'll be here for a few months before we ship out and hopefully I'll come home at the end of it." He was starting to mirror her stance, toying with his own rough fingernails, and stopped himself. He'd never been a coward before and he wasn't about to start now. "I've been gone almost your whole life. When…when you ended up in the hospital and I couldn't get home…I wasn't here for you, honey. I want to be. And I don't know everything you're dealing with and I know I haven't been here and all but…hell." He rubbed his hand over his face, the words locking behind the knot in his throat.

"Mom is glad you're home," she said softly. Jamie met his gaze. "She's been acting funny since you showed up at the house." She shot him a wry look that reminded him too much of Melanie.

Gale cleared his throat, dancing on the edge of a line of questioning he wasn't sure he was ready to delve into. "So has your mom dated much?"

Jamie shrugged. "A couple of dates here and there. Nothing serious."

He was pumping his kid for information about his ex-wife. Something about that should have struck him as unethical or sneaky, but Gale couldn't bring himself to feel guilty about it. His heart did a small flip in his chest. He should be sad for his ex that she was alone but instead, all he felt was glad.

It didn't mean he had a snowball's chance in hell at

anything more than they currently had, but it did mean he didn't have to fight another man for that chance. One less obstacle, though, was better than nothing.

"So you're not dating anyone either?" Jamie asked, curiosity in her voice.

Just your mother. But he didn't think she was ready for that revelation. He wasn't ready to have that conversation with his daughter. No, he'd spent the first few years after Mel had left him trying to be a better man. He'd gotten his education and gotten promoted and by the time he'd felt like he was ready to ask her to give their marriage another shot, a decade had passed and a war had started.

Life had worked out perfectly to keep him away from his small family.

"So are you coming over for dinner? I can probably convince Mom to have breakfast for dinner," Jamie said.

"Are you and your mom back on speaking terms this week?"

"I guess." She shrugged. "I don't want to get Alex in any more trouble with his dad so there will be no more sneaking around."

Gale frowned. That guilty feeling twisted around his heart and squeezed again. "How much trouble did he get into?"

"A lot." But Jamie didn't elaborate and Gale didn't push the issue. She looked up at him. "I've been trying to get him to talk to me about what's going on at home but he won't." She swallowed. "I'm really afraid for him."

"Yeah, honey. I get that." He leaned forward. "Tell him I was serious about the calling if he needed help or anything." He looked down at her hand, slipped it into his. "I'm not much of a dad but I'm pretty good at getting people out of shitty situations." He squeezed her hand. "So if he's too scared to call the cops or anything, he can call me."

Jamie stared at their hands for a long time. "So does this mean you're not going to try to kill him if I want to keep hanging out with him?"

Gale searched for the right thing to say. He wasn't a prude. He was realistic: if his little girl was interested in sex, he wasn't going to be able to stop her.

"Just…be responsible," he finally managed and hoped that this would pass Mel's definition of The Talk.

CHAPTER TWENTY-ONE

Mel wasn't sure how a father-daughter talk had turned into her cooking dinner for Gale and Jamie again but she wasn't complaining. She'd set up closings on three houses that afternoon, which meant that things were looking up for her financially. Last month had been tough. Signs were everywhere that the housing market was starting to struggle but Fort Hood and the surrounding areas had seemed relatively immune to the crash the rest of the country had just suffered through.

Still, Mel felt the market fluctuations in her bottom line. Some months were good. Some were not. But she'd worked hard to be able to move out of her parents' home and into her own.

She glanced at Jamie, glad her daughter didn't remember how much she'd struggled when Jamie had been little. Gale was hunched over, looking at one of Jamie's homework questions. His tan uniform t-shirt stretched across his back and she could see stark muscles beneath the thin fabric.

There was too much man beneath too little cloth. Oh, but her body noticed: stood up at the position of attention and practically begged for some alone time with the powerful man sitting with her—their—daughter.

There was a warmth inside her for her ex-husband that hadn't been there for a long, long time.

It felt good. Too good. A goodness she wanted to hold onto. She glanced over her shoulder at them. Jamie frowned at her paper and Gale tapped a pencil against a chicken scratch word.

An unexpected lump rose in her throat. It was good to have him sitting at the table with their daughter. Mel stirred the chopped up chicken and vegetables and listened with half an ear while Gale and Jamie went over the periodic table again. He was helping her memorize it and miracle of miracles, she was listening and—even better—learning it.

She refused to be bitter or jealous. She was an adult damn it, and she was going to act like it. Neither her ex nor her daughter deserved that bitterness.

That was for her alone to smother beneath cheesecake and chocolate.

She tossed the stir-fry one last time then turned off the stove. "Order up," she said. "How much does everyone want?"

She filled their plates then joined them at the table with her own. This lack of arguing with Jamie was so rare, so out of the ordinary, Mel wasn't entirely sure she wasn't dreaming the entire thing.

"So how was work, Daddy?"

Mel couldn't get used to hearing her daughter call Gale "Daddy." It was a cold reminder of the fact that their daughter was still a kid, still growing up.

Still needed her parents no matter how much she fought them.

"It was good," Gale said, washing down a bite with a drink of water. "Went to a few meetings, did a bunch of paperwork."

Jamie frowned. "That's what you do in the Army?"

Mel watched the exchange carefully. It was sad but she was waiting for her daughter to blow up and stomp from the kitchen like she did once a day at least.

"That's what I do back in garrison," Gale said.

"What's 'garrison' mean?" Jamie was glued to his every word.

Yes, this was so much better than fighting.

"Garrison is what we call it when we're not deployed." There was a patience around him now that hadn't been there when they'd been younger. It wasn't a lack of emotion or anything. No, it was an impression Mel had of still waters and what lay beneath the surface.

"And you're going to deploy again at the end of this year?" Jamie asked.

"Do you know where?" Mel asked softly.

Gale looked from his daughter to Mel, meeting her eyes. "Up north, I think," he said.

"Is that bad or good?" Jamie asked.

"I'm not sure," Gale said. He set his fork down. "It's hard saying."

"Why do you have to go back?" There was an odd note in Jamie's voice and Mel was instantly on guard. She knew that sound. It was the sound of an explosion being primed.

"Because I'm a soldier, baby; that's what I do." Infinite patience. A sense of ownership and yes, pride, in saying those words. Yes, Gale was, and always had been, a soldier. Mel remembered the day he'd told her he was joining the Army. His family had been thrilled. He'd had middling grades at best and his parents hadn't talked to him about college. He hadn't known the first thing about applying, let alone finding the money to go. They'd lain in the bed of his truck that night, wrapped in a sleeping bag he'd bought from an Army surplus store and talked about what his joining the Army meant for them.

Melanie had wanted to go to college but she'd agreed she could do that with him wherever he was stationed. She smiled at how naive they'd been. That they'd work together and share the load while they made a better life for themselves than the life they'd come from.

She still remembered her parents arguing about money. No matter that they'd both worked two jobs, there was always too much month at the end of every paycheck. And then when Mel had moved back home with the baby, things had gotten even tighter.

She missed her mom every single day. And her dad? He was out there somewhere. He'd come home eventually. She hoped. She looked up at Gale, still explaining his Army life to the daughter who'd come so unexpectedly into their lives.

Yes, the Army was part of who Gale was. He wore the Army well and if she could be honest with herself, the man looked good in uniform.

It was easy to look at him sitting across from her at her kitchen table and embrace the fantasy man in uniform that so many pined for. But the reality of loving a man in uniform was so much harder. It was long nights without phone calls; it was missed births and birthdays.

It was acceptance of being alone and sharing this man with the Army. And the Army was a demanding mistress. Mel looked at Gale then and wondered how much different things might have been if she hadn't been a coward and run away when things had gotten too overwhelming.

Then again, if things hadn't gone the way they did, maybe she wouldn't appreciate this moment, this snapshot of normalcy in the chaos of her life.

She got up and walked over to where he sat with their daughter. Leaned down and brushed her lips against his cheek, her hand resting on his strong shoulder.

"What's that for?" he asked, his hands resting gently on her sides.

"Just because."

***

"First sergeant?"

Gale looked up at his office doorway and wondered for the hundredth time why he hadn't closed the damn thing. His office was a revolving door of soldiers and lieutenants rotating in and out, each with a new crisis for him to solve.

He was used to it. There was very little he hadn't already

seen, heard or personally dealt with, so most of the issues people came to him with were easily fixed.

But the ops clerk looked at him now with an expression on his face that was a cross between confusion and hysteria. Like the soldier was literally fighting the urge not to laugh his ass off.

"Yeah?"

"There's an Alex Tellhouse here to see you."

Gale glanced at his watch. It was past three pm, so he supposed the kid could already be out of school, but it was cutting it close. Had the kid skipped school to come on post?

"Send him in."

Gale leaned back in his chair and crossed his arms over his chest, then unfolded them when he remembered he was supposed to be gaining Alex's trust, not intimidating him.

Alex shuffled to the door, his shoulders hunched, his hands stuffed in his pockets. The black eye was faded now, mostly yellow with hints of blue still there around the edges.

Alex kept his head down, his eyes avoiding Gale's. "Sir, um—"

"Stop." Gale leaned forward. "You've talked to me before. If you're going to talk to me, stand up straight and have the backbone to look me in the eye."

He kept his voice neutral but the boy flinched regardless. The edges of red blurred around Gale's vision. The kid's face flushed but slowly, he lifted his gaze to meet Gale's. He could see the struggle in the effort it took him not to look down.

But finally, he straightened and held Gale's gaze.

"Better," Gale said softly. "Now what can I do for you, son?"

"Um, sir, there's a Valentine's Day dance next week and, um, I know that Jamie got into trouble with her grades and all but I really was helping her study and… Well, I'd like your permission to take her to the dance."

The words had tumbled out of Alex all at once. Too fast and filled with uncertainty. But Gale had to give the kid some credit for coming in here and asking him.

Not that it was 1950 or anything, but it took a massive set of balls to approach a man who'd dragged you from his daughter's bedroom barely a month ago.

Gale studied the boy silently. He'd never understood these kids who put metal in their bodies, but beneath the grungy exterior, Gale had a sense that this kid wasn't as bad or as tough as he tried to appear. He supposed he could get past the metal in his ear and maybe even the fact that his hair was longer than Gale's had ever been in his life.

Except the blue and purple hair drove him batshit crazy. Maybe it was the military that had been drilled into the fiber of who he was, maybe he was just fucking old, but the multicolored hair had to go. And the black nail polish. That shit, too.

"I'll tell you what," Gale finally said. "You take some of the metal out of your head, you come back with a single color of hair, I'll think about it." He paused. "And I have to talk to her mother about whether she's still grounded or not."

Which was an excellent excuse to see Melanie again.

Alex looked at him, his eyes wide. "You didn't say no." There was genuine shock in Alex's voice.

Gale frowned to smother the urge to smile. "I didn't say yes, either. I said I'd think about it. And her grades have to come up or it's an automatic no. And no cheating, either. She earns this or it doesn't count."

Alex nodded quickly. "Roger that, sir. Sure." His lips curled into a hesitant smile. "Thank you, sir."

Gale couldn't say what prompted him to stand up and cross the small space. Alex was a tall kid but Gale dwarfed him. He didn't miss how Alex lifted his chin, as though bracing for a blow.

Gale lifted his hand to the kid's shoulder, knowing he was violating his personal space and probably half a dozen rules and doing it anyway. He gripped his shoulder. "When you're ready to talk about the shiner, I'll listen." He kept his voice gentle, his fingers easy.

The moment Alex eased back, he let him go. He wasn't there to punish the boy nor was his intent to scare him.

"It's fine, sir. Thank you for asking, though."

Gale swallowed the fierce punch of rage that flared inside him. "Just think about it."

He stood in his office door and watched as Alex walked out of his orderly room. He'd thrown the kid for a loop, first by not telling him no outright and second, by asking about the black eye.

Gale hooked his thumbs into his belt loops, then decided to take a walk. Down the docks to Tellhouse's office. It generally took a lot to get Gale's temper up, but the longer he waited for Tellhouse to get done ripping his platoon sergeants a new asshole, the higher Gale's blood pressure went.

He ignored the vibrating blackberry in his shoulder pocket and simply stood, holding his breath until his lungs burned and stars danced in front of his vision. Then he released it and started all over again, like his chaplain had taught him back in OIF 2.

He looked up as Sarn't Iaconelli walked in. Gale frowned. "You looking for a new job?" he said.

Iaconelli grinned and shook his head. "Nah. Dropping off some paperwork from the hospital."

Gale flicked his gaze down Iaconelli's body. "You weren't chatting up your significant other, were you?"

A slow smile spread across Iaconelli's face. "She may be the reason that our medical packets are moving slightly faster than frozen pond water."

"Which around here is warp speed." Gale snorted and jerked his chin toward the rest of the packets in Iaconelli's hand. "Any of those ours?"

"Three. You want them now or you want me to distro out the to-do list, and holy fuck did that sound emasculated."

Iaconelli scrubbed his hand over his face. "I need to go blow some shit up," he said more to himself than Gale.

"We're going to the range next week. You'll have ample opportunities."

A shout bounced off Tellhouse's closed door. Iaconelli glanced at Gale.

Gale met the bigger man's eyes. "I have no intentions of ever screaming at you like that."

Iaconelli grunted. "That's good because after rehab, my pride is pretty fragile. I'm not sure I could take it."

Gale fought the urge to grin. Maybe he and Iaconelli would get along after all. "I'll keep that in mind."

Iaconelli turned to go and damn near collided with the A Company commander, Brint Martini.

Martini was not a tall man but next to Iaconelli, he looked like a smurf. A mean one.

Gale made a mental note to never tell Teague about that random description. Teague would find a way to sneak a picture of Martini as a smurf into a briefing and, well they were going to be armed sooner or later. He didn't feel like having to watch his six to keep a fellow leader from fragging him when they got downrange.

"Can I help you, First Sarn't?" Martini asked.

"Waiting to talk to Tellhouse," Gale said. Iaconelli slid past him but Gale was highly aware of Ike watching the situation.

Martini narrowed his eyes and walked past Gale, toward his office. "He's probably going to be a while."

Gale drummed his fingers on the counter. "I can wait."

Tellhouse's office door opened at that exact moment and Gale thanked the Good Idea Fairy for the anger management techniques. The office was instantly flooded with rampant hostility, the kind that went far beyond an ass-chewing gone bad.

One of Tellhouse's platoon sergeants stalked out of the orderly room, his face flushed and his temper visibly boiling.

Tellhouse's expression tightened when he saw Gale in his ops office.

"You got a minute?" Gale said.

Tellhouse straightened, folding his arms over his chest and lifting his chin. His words were cold. Brittle. "What do you need?"

Gale sucked on his teeth for a second, trying to find the diplomatic way to say what was on his mind, then shoved diplomacy out of the window.

"So Alex was in my office today." Gale breathed deeply, struggling to keep his temper reined in.

"And? What'd that little fuckstick do now?"

"How about you start by calling your kid by his name? You know, work on those parenting skills we always have to talk to soldiers about."

Tellhouse stiffened, his face flushing. "You needed something?"

Gale pressed ahead, letting Tellhouse ignore the warning. He'd received it. That was enough for the moment. "He wanted to take my daughter to the school dance next week."

"You're the one who's going to end up a grandfather. Not my problem if your kid is hanging out with that fucking delinquent."

Gale's temper snapped at the end of its leash. He blinked and Tellhouse was backed against the wall, his fists twisted in Tellhouse's collar. "If I trust your kid to take my daughter out, I'm holding you personally responsible if anything happens to either of them."

"I didn't hit my kid."

"I don't believe you."

"You don't need to believe me. I can sleep at night regardless."

Gale felt his temper fraying. Tellhouse was lying to him. Standing right in front of him and looking him in the eye and lying to him. But a truce might make things easier for Alex at home. "I'm not here to fight with you. But if anything happens to my daughter or your son because you can't control your temper, you're going to have to deal with me."

"Things didn't have to be like this," Tellhouse said after a moment. "I thought we were brothers."

"We were. Until you started taking your temper out on your kid. That shit crossed the line for me."

"Even after Tal Afar?"

"Even after that."

"Guess that's the way it's going to be then." Tellhouse sat, effectively dismissing Gale. And he was fine with that. He wasn't here to pick a fight. Just to make sure there was no doubt in Tellhouse's mind about the consequences of touching his kid again.

Sarn't Major Cox would only forgive so much and Gale was reasonably certain that one of his first sergeants assaulting another one—again—was probably on the short list of things that would piss him off and get Gale fired.

The warning had been issued and received. There was little more for Gale to do.

CHAPTER TWENTY-TWO

There were no fresh bandages buried in the trash or pink-tinged towels. No strange noises from Jamie's bedroom. Jamie hadn't worn any out-of-season long-sleeved shirts either. All week, she'd been agreeable. She'd been polite. *She'd done the damn dishes.* All of which made Mel damn certain that something was up. Mel kept waiting for her to tell her she was pregnant or worse, she'd been arrested. Something terrible.

But nothing happened. So why couldn't Mel shake the feeling that her daughter was hiding something?

Mel finished folding the laundry and sorting it into piles on the couch. Her cell phone vibrated on the kitchen island.

"Hey."

She smiled at the sound of Gale's voice. "Hey."

She tried to ignore the warmth that spread across her skin from the sound of his voice over her ear. She could nearly feel his breath against her skin and she shivered. She leaned against the island, wrapping one arm around her waist while she talked to him.

She wasn't sure where things were going but it was such a departure from the way things had been. A good one. Gale the man not Gale the memory of the boy he'd been. There was power in his hands now, confidence in his touch. A smoothness in the way he stroked her body that left her breathless and shaking and wanting more. So much more.

She didn't know how to cross the chasm that had spread between them for the last fifteen years. How to build, start spanning that chasm with a bridge made of something more substantial than good sex. Oh, she knew how to touch him, how to let him into her bed, but trust? It was a hard thing to rebuild trust.

"What are you doing right now?" he asked.

She pulled the phone away from her ear and looked at it. "Laundry, why?"

"Want to meet me for a late lunch?"

She breathed slow and deep. She had to meet a client in an hour and a half. "Sure, but it has to be out towards the house. I've got a meeting soon."

"Sure. Do you still like Mexican food?"

He remembered. She wasn't sure why, but that tiny gesture made her smile and her insides melt a little more. "Yeah. We've got a great local place around the corner on FM 2410 here in Heights."

"I'll meet you there."

The phone went dead but Mel continued to stare at it long after it went dark and silent. What was so important that it required a face-to-face conversation?

Not that she was complaining. Gale had managed to get underneath her skin in a good way. A way that made her feel alive like she hadn't in a long, long time. She adjusted her top before grabbing her purse and heading out the door to lunch with her ex.

She paused at the door of the restaurant because Gale pulled into the parking lot just as she'd been getting ready to walk in. He pulled his hat on as he climbed out of the truck. She remembered being so impressed with him when he'd told her he was going to be a soldier all those years ago. He'd come home from basic training, his hair shorn off and a hard line to the edges of his body. He'd lost weight but gained strength and confidence. Even at nineteen, she'd recognized that confidence was sexy.

Now? Now she had her own confidence to match his and she was mature enough to recognize the languid feeling spreading through her body as he approached.

Arousal. Sensual, erotic and compelling. She wanted this man; despite the anger and hurt from their past, she wanted this man. The grey at his temples accented the sharp lines around his eyes and his mouth. He didn't look like he smiled often but as he approached, his body was relaxed, his expression warm.

She wondered if she could convince him to play hooky from work and come back to the house for the rest of their lunch. Whether he'd look at the invitation as something other than what it was—a need to satisfy a craving for him. She wasn't sure, though, that she would ever get her fill of him.

He smiled as he approached. "Hey."

"Hey." She ducked beneath his arm as he held the door for her and they made their way to a corner booth in the brightly colored restaurant.

"So what prompted this?" she asked after they'd ordered.

It took him a minute to answer. He fiddled with the straw wrapper on the table in front of him. "So I had an interesting visitor at work today."

She studied him while he searched for the rest of whatever he was going to say. "And?"

"So Alex? He wants to take Jamie to the school dance next Friday."

Mel twirled her straw in her ice water, poking the lemon in the bottom of the ice. "What did you tell him?"

"That I had to talk to you but also if he made his hair a single color and took all the metal out of his face, I'd think about it." He shredded the wrapper. "I had a talk with his father, too."

"This didn't involve the police, did it?" She glanced down at the remains of the wrapper on the table.

"No. We just came to an understanding." Gale's jaw flexed. "About how if he puts his hands on his son again, I'm going to put my hands on him and not in a pray to Jesus kind of way."

There was tension in his shoulders, in the way his fingers pulled at the thin paper wrapper. "I think I'm supposed to tell you that fighting violence with more violence isn't the right way to handle things as a responsible adult." She reached across the table, stilling the motion in his hands. "But men like him only respect strength. Do you think he'll listen?"

Gale's eyes didn't move from where her hand covered his. The back of his hand was covered with dark, crisp hair, rough beneath her palm. The hard callouses scraped against her skin and made her long for that roughness in other, softer places.

"I think I was pretty clear." He cleared his throat, turning his palm over until they were palm to palm. "So I, ah…I think I like this whole teamwork thing, Mel." He swallowed, willing the tension in his belly to relax. "I'd like to keep doing this."

"Doing what?"

"Seeing you. Being a team when it comes to Jamie." His fingers tensed beneath hers. "Being there for you when things get a little rough. And even when they're not." He met her gaze, his heart slow and steady in his chest. "I've missed you, Melanie."

***

He didn't know what she was going to say. He waited, every fiber in his body attuned to the touch of her hand against his. It was a simple gesture but packed with so much more than simple reassurance. There was a darker edge to her touch, or maybe it was him, reading more into the gesture than she meant.

But when he met her gaze, he realized he was not the only one feeling the heat of the touch.

"I'm not sure what you're asking." Quiet words.

He cleared his throat. "I guess I'm asking if you want to go steady. Maybe go to the dance with me?"

Her laugh was the perfect reaction, and it shattered the

tension between them. Her fingers twined with his, her thumb stroking over his knuckles. "I think I'd like that. The go-steady part. Not sure I want to go to the dance, though. I'd rather have a quiet evening at home."

"So speaking of the dance, what do we do about the walking hard-on who wants to take our daughter to one?" It was one of the reasons why he'd told Alex that he wasn't going make any decisions without talking to Mel first.

"Are you sure this boy isn't a bad influence on Jamie?"

Gale shook his head. "I think if anything, Jamie is an escape for him from some bad stuff at home. And he might be the same for her." He traced the back of her wrist with his index finger. Felt her tense beneath his touch. "I don't mean that how it came out," he said quickly. "I mean with me being gone and everything, she's got her own stuff to deal with. Maybe…maybe they're just reaching out to each other."

"I see what you did there." Her words were soft. "And yeah, I think we both did our part to mess things up with her. I'm afraid. What if things go back to what they were?"

"For her or for us?" Fear laced those words.

"Both?"

He covered her hand with his other one. "We can't save her from the world. We have to let her take a chance. And be there to catch her if she falls again. It gives Jamie a chance to earn our trust," he said quietly. "She's going to keep fighting. Maybe we need to give her a little leeway."

"We." He froze at the word but then she lifted her gaze from their hands to meet his. "I like the way that sounds, Gale."

"Yeah." His voice didn't sound right to his ears. "Me too." He cleared his throat. "Maybe, if she goes to the dance, you and I could go out. You know, dinner and a movie?"

Her fingers danced at the edge of his wrist and he had a sudden, vibrant image of her fingers curled around his wrist as he moved inside her. He was going to embarrass himself if he wasn't careful.

And then her fingers traced the sensitive skin on the inside of his wrist. His entire body stilled and he met her gaze.

"I'd like that very much," she said softly.

He didn't move, unable to look away from the strong, sensual woman sitting across from him. She wore a light silvery turquoise top that draped across her chest and accented the lines of her collarbones. There was a hint, nothing more, of cleavage.

Tasteful and professional. There was nothing tasteful and professional about the direction of his thoughts. He caught himself wondering about other lovers she'd had through the years. How had they treated her? Had she been satisfied or—

Dear lord, he was torturing himself.

"Gale?" He lifted his gaze away from her lips and back to her eyes. His fingers twitched against her skin. Deliberately, he rubbed his middle finger down the centerline of her wrist and felt an answering chill shudder through her palm and down her arm.

"What were you just thinking about?" she asked softly.

He cleared his throat roughly. "I'm not sure answering that is a good idea," he said.

Their waitress brought their food and Gale leaned back, sliding his palm from beneath hers.

She smiled, her eyes sparkling in the warm afternoon sunlight. "Now I'm really curious."

He tried to distract her by offering her some of his carne asada. She shook her head. "Nope. Not until you tell me what you were just thinking about."

She was teasing him. On purpose.

He was sitting at a late lunch with his ex-wife and, dear Lord in heaven, they were flirting. As though the last fifteen years of bitterness and frustration hadn't happened. Or maybe they still had but maybe, somehow, they'd finally found a common ground to move beyond those years into something new.

Gale took a bite and chewed slowly, considering all the ways he could answer. He took a drink then set his fork down and reached for her hand again. He caressed the soft skin on the back of her wrist.

"I was wondering if the lovers you've had over the years treated you well," he murmured.

He was captivated by the movement of her throat as she swallowed. The glistening moisture on her bottom lip that was left from her glass. There was an impossible silence between his remark and her answer.

"Why were you wondering that?"

Heat crawled slowly over his skin. His blood pounded in his veins, his heartbeat slammed against his ears. "Call it my insane curiosity," he said.

She arched one polished brow. "I don't think there is any good way for me to answer that question."

"I can think of a half a dozen ways." He watched her response to his words. The tension in her hand beneath his touch. The quick intake of her breath.

There was something primitive in the emotions rocketing through him. He knew he needed patience. Lots of it, along with a boatload of groveling if he was going to make this work.

"Yeah?"

This was flirting. A sensual heat, a seductive lure of primal eroticism between them. He swallowed. He took a deep breath. "So what are you doing tonight?"

"I've got a client in a little while. Then I was thinking I'd put the door back on Jamie's room." She looked up at him. "I could use some help with that."

CHAPTER TWENTY-THREE

Jamie looked at the electric screwdriver on the kitchen table and made that disgusted sound that Gale was starting to associate with having an anxiety attack. His, not hers.

He shot his daughter his best disapproving dad look, an expression that he was still trying out.

"Maybe instead of assuming the worst, you ask what's going on?" he said, bracing his palms against the island.

Jamie rolled her eyes but there was no fight in her expression for once. "What's going on?"

Gale looked at Mel, waiting for her to answer. Letting her claim this concession to their daughter.

"We're going to put your door back on," Mel said.

Jamie frowned and there was instant suspicion in her eyes. "Why?"

Mel didn't speak for a moment. Gale cleared his throat. "Because if we want you to trust us, we have to start trusting you."

Jamie looked between the two of them. "What's this 'we' thing?"

He looked at Mel quickly, not expecting that question. Which was really foolish because their daughter was many things, but stupid was not one of them. "We're, ah, trying out a few things."

"That doesn't make any sense." Jamie folded her arms over her chest and her look called them both on their bullshit.

"Maybe we're just seeing how things go," Mel said. He grinned down at her and she narrowed her eyes. "What?"

"I'll tell you later. I don't want to scar our daughter for life."

"Ew, gross, you guys. I'll be in my room—studying biology." Jamie paused at the bottom of the stairs. "Can Alex come over? I need some help with my homework," she called from the top of the stairs.

"Yes."

Jamie rushed up the stairs, leaving them alone. Mel looked over at Gale. "Better that they're both here where we can keep an eye on them than at Alex's house. Now, what was so funny?"

"I was thinking that telling her we were experimenting with sex might not be the wisest thing to tell our daughter."

"Experimenting? Is that what it was?"

He moved then, boxing her in against the island. She lifted her chin and refused to back down. No games with his Mel. No will she, won't she. No, Mel was a woman who went after what she wanted. She threaded her arms around his neck. "I think we need to get that door hung back up," she whispered against his mouth. But neither of them moved away.

It was good, too good to stand there with her, to feel her pressed against him. He lost himself in the sensations of her body, her touch, her scent. Everything she was surrounded him, invited him closer. Made him want impossible things with her.

It felt like only a moment had passed when the doorbell rang, interrupting the train of decidedly impure thoughts Gale was having toward his ex-wife.

"Want me to get that?" he asked her.

"We both should," she said and he didn't miss that her voice was a little breathless. It did something to his insides knowing he could affect her that way after all these years.

Alex stood on the doorstep, standing straight and tall as Gale took in the changes in his appearance.

"You didn't get a high and tight?" he said to the boy.

Alex blanched. "I cut it. And it's all one color."

Beside him, Mel elbowed him in the ribs.

"I'm kidding with you," Gale said. "What did your dad say?"

"It's probably best if I don't tell you," Alex said. But there was no fear in his words, only discomfort at being inspected.

Gale laughed at the kid's discomfort. "Okay."

"Um Jamie invited me over. Is she home?"

"She is," Mel said. "We're getting ready to put her door back on her room."

Alex narrowed his eyes.

"All that means is that we're deciding to trust her. Which means no shoplifting or any other stupid stunts to try and look cool," Gale said.

Alex had the decency to flush. "About that…"

"It's in the past. And if it doesn't happen again, it stays there." He reached out and gripped Alex's shoulder. "Whatever is going on with you, you have a safe space here. Don't give us a reason to regret it."

Alex opened his mouth but no words came out. He barely managed to hold Gale's eyes as he searched for the right words. "I won't let you down," Alex said finally.

Gale nodded and stepped aside, leaving Alex to head up the stairs to Jamie's room. Mel watched him go. "I hope this is the right thing."

"Well, everything else hasn't been working. Let's try something different." He reached down, threading his fingers with hers.

"Like hanging a door?"

Gale nodded. "Like hanging a door."

***

Melanie glanced at her watch once more and wondered not for the first time where Gale was. He'd promised he'd be there in time for Alex to pick up Jamie.

Who was she kidding? She wasn't nervous about Jamie going out on her first date. She was nervous about her own first date with Jamie's father.

She tugged at the hem of her dress and adjusted the simple pearl necklace.

"Mom?"

She stepped out of her bedroom into the kitchen. Her daughter stood there, dressed in a beautiful deep violet dress with long flowing sleeves. Her hair was curled and pinned to one side.

Mel's throat tightened. Her little girl was all grown up. After the hospital, she'd been terrified she was going to lose her daughter. "You look beautiful, honey." Her throat squeezed tight.

"So do you." Jamie fidgeted with a sleeve. "Um, I was wondering if you could do my makeup?"

Mel bit down on her lip, determined not to let her daughter see how much that simple request meant to her. They'd fought so much for so long, she was always surprised at these rare truces. "Of course, honey."

"So where are you and Daddy going tonight?" Jamie asked as she set one of the kitchen chairs in the bathroom.

"Here, put a towel around your shoulders." She draped it gently around her daughter's shoulders. "There's a really great steakhouse down in Temple."

"Do you have a reservation?" Jamie lifted her chin when Mel urged her to tip her face up.

"Yeah. It's Valentine's Day. I'm shocked he got us in."

Jamie closed her eyes as Mel dabbed tinted moisturizer across her daughter's cheeks. "I'm glad you're going out with Dad."

Mel blended the makeup into her daughter's skin. "I don't know where this is going, Jamie."

"But you're trying, right?" The hope she heard in Jamie's voice hurt Mel's heart. "I mean, I get it that you're not getting married again or anything but you're not fighting. That's a good thing, right?"

Mel dabbed pale silver eye shadow on her daughter's eyelids, then lined her eyes with dark grey liner. It was a simple look, not overdone, but it suddenly made her daughter look more grown up than she was ready to face.

It was so hard to believe she'd be leaving for college in a few more years.

She swiped a shimmery blush over Jamie's cheeks then handed her the mascara. "Don't clump it on," she said.

Jamie studied her reflection in the mirror. "Oh Mom, thank you." Her voice was breathy.

Mel shrugged. "So I'm kind of good at makeup. You look beautiful, honey."

Jamie leaned forward and expertly applied the mascara then straightened. "I didn't say thank you for letting me go tonight."

"Your dad convinced me that we need to let you spread your wings. Grades are still important and you're not off the hook there." She rested her hands on her daughter's shoulders. "I'm proud of you for not… for trying so hard to get better. I forget to tell you that sometimes."

Jamie looked away. "I get scared sometimes," she whispered.

"I know." She cupped Jamie's cheek. "But I love you. No matter how mad you make me or how much I sometimes want to strangle you. You're my daughter and I'm proud of you. All of you. You went through a dark time but you've come through it." She kissed her forehead. "And we'll be here to help you through whatever comes your way."

Jamie blinked and nodded, unable to speak for several seconds. "Thanks, Mom."

The brief interlude ended with the chime of the doorbell. Jamie rushed out of the bathroom and with a final check of her own makeup, Mel followed.

"Mom! It's for you."

Mel padded into the living room. "Why didn't you just open it?" she asked Jamie. "Just let your father in."

"You should get it."

Mel opened the door. And froze.

Gale filled the doorway. He wore a pale yellow collared shirt that accentuated his broad shoulders. A blue and gold tie drew her gaze down his broad chest to his narrow waist. He held a bouquet of roses and orchids in the cradle of one arm.

She swallowed and pulled her gaze away from his body and back up to his eyes. "You clean up well," she said, forcing a lightness she didn't feel. Her body was taut. Tense. Aching with pent-up frustration.

"Sorry I'm late," he said, leaning in to brush his lips against her cheek. "You smell nice," he whispered. His words floated over the skin of her neck.

"Thank you."

"Did Alex already show up?" He glanced over her shoulder. "Nope, guess not." He looked at the clock on the wall. "He's late?"

Jamie shot her father a wry look. "He's not a soldier, Daddy. He'll be here."

Gale offered the flowers to Mel. "These are for you. I hope you still like orchids."

"Did you keep a journal?" She smiled at his thoughtfulness. "How do you remember all this stuff?"

"It's important," he said softly.

The doorbell rang behind them. "I'll get it," he said. "I need to have a word with this young man."

Jamie looked slightly horrified. "Daddy…"

"Don't worry honey. I promise not to embarrass you."

Mel smiled as her ex stepped outside and into the cool Texas evening and wished she was a fly on the wall.

***

Gale looked Alex over without saying a word. The boy stood straight and tall under his inspection. Gale noticed his hair was solid dark brown now. He wasn't sure if the kid's hair was naturally that color or not but at least it was no longer pink and purple.

He wore a dress shirt and black jeans along with black and white Vans. Gale hid his smile.

"So where are you taking my daughter tonight?" he said, folding his arms over his chest. He was walking a fine line between playing Intimidating Dad and not scaring the shit out of the kid. He didn't see any evidence of new bruises on the boy. Which Gale was taking as a good sign.

"We're going to Olive Garden then to the dance, sir."

"And what time will you have her home?"

"I'm tracking eleven is her curfew." Alex didn't avoid his gaze and didn't slouch. Gale could see it still took him effort to break years of habit with his slouching but it said something about the boy's backbone that he was trying.

Gale figured Alex had gone through some bad stuff but he hadn't quit. That was a testament to his character, no matter how hard his father might have tried to beat it out of him.

He put his hand on the boy's shoulder. "Good. There's just one more thing you need to know, Alex." Gale chose his next words carefully. "I was a sixteen-year-old boy once upon a time. So listen carefully to my next words." He waited until Alex met his gaze. "I know exactly how your brain works. Do you get my meaning?"

Heat flashed over the boy's skin in a bright flush. "Uh, sir…"

"I'm not threatening you, son." He patted his shoulder. "But just so we're clear where you should keep certain parts of your anatomy: anything other than in your pants is probably not the right answer."

Alex nodded. Gale opened the door for him. Jamie was

waiting close by, obviously looking through the window to try and overhear what he'd said.

Gale kissed her on the cheek and waited until they were in Alex's father's car and on their way before he turned back to the living room.

Mel stood by the couch, a warm smile on her lips. "What did you say to him?"

"What your dad should have said to me," he said, crossing the small distance between them.

She lifted one brow. "Oh yeah, and what's that?"

"Just that he should think twice about putting his dick anywhere but in his pants."

"You're terrifying." Mel covered her mouth with one hand and laughed out loud. "That's rotten," she said, still smiling.

"I'm still learning how to be a father." He looked down at her, his eyes warm. "I'd rather not throw grandfather into the mix just yet."

He let his gaze drift down Mel's body and back up again. "You look incredible," he murmured.

"Thank you," she replied. Her fingers danced along the edge of the couch. "So do you." She ran her fingers over his tie before looking up at him. "What time is our reservation?"

"We've got an hour," he said, standing far too close. He could smell the faint hint of her perfume, mingling with the warm heat from her skin. Her shoulders were bare and shimmered in the low light. He brushed his thumb over her exposed skin.

"I'm sure we can find something to do with that time," she whispered. Her voice was husky. Low.

He swallowed. "There's not enough time for what I have in mind," he said. He took a risk, lowering his lips to her shoulder. There was something sweet dusted on her skin, something that tasted like honey. He traced his tongue along the edge of her dress and felt her shiver.

She tipped her neck, exposing the long slender line of her

throat. He accepted the invitation, pressing his lips to her jaw. He breathed in her scent, locking down the fierce intensity of his reaction. He traced the tip of his tongue along her jaw, nipping her earlobe and sucking on it gently.

Her palms pressed against his chest, her hands hot through the fabric of his new shirt. He'd never had much need for dressier clothing and he wondered if she'd be impressed that he'd braved the mall to go shopping specifically for this night.

He cradled her face in one palm, caressing her shoulder with his free hand.

"Gale?"

"Hmm." He bit the spot where her pulse skittered beneath his lips.

"I think I want to skip dinner." Her words were breathless.

He ran his tongue over the spot where he'd left a faint mark, then traced the outer edge of her ear, blowing on the moisture he'd left behind. "I think I want to have you for dinner," he murmured against her ear.

"It would be a hell of a way to spend tonight," she said. Her fingers clenched against his chest.

He smiled against her hair, unable to believe his good fortune that she was in his arms, trembling and aroused and so fucking sexy.

"It's up to you," he whispered, lowering his forehead to hers.

She wrapped her arms around his neck, stepping close so that the heat of their bodies melded with the brush of skin against silk. She kissed him then, surrendering to the desire burning between them.

Then she stepped away, a sly, sensual smile on her lips.

And walked slowly backward.

Toward her bedroom.

***

She felt him behind her as she lit a candle near her bed. Her body burned from his touch, her neck echoed the fierce pleasure of his lips on her skin.

She hadn't meant to lead him here. Not when he'd first arrived on her doorstep and offered her favorite flowers. But then he'd touched her and her entire body had melted in a shower of arousal and heat and pleasure.

Warmth spread across her body a moment before he touched her shoulders, his palms rough on her smooth skin. He caressed her lightly. "Melanie."

She turned in his arms. His skin glowed in the faint candlelight. The shadows in his cheeks, the darkness in his eyes. He licked his lips, his gaze not wavering from hers. "Would it be awkward if I admitted to being nervous?"

"We've done this before." She smiled faintly, lifting her palms to cup his cheeks. His skin was smooth and rough all at once—evidence of a fresh shave and too much time in the sun.

"I know. But this is different."

"Why?"

His mouth moved but no sound came out. He leaned down, capturing her lips, sucking gently on her bottom lip until they parted. His tongue slipped inside her mouth gently, seeking. Tasting. Exploring.

Driving her wild with his slow exploration of her body.

She smiled against his mouth and he leaned back. "What's so funny?" he said.

"I was just thinking you weren't this patient when we were younger."

He grinned, sliding his fingers along the edge of her throat. "A lot has changed since I was younger," he growled.

"Yeah? Like what?"

His smile was dark and filled with promise. "You'll just have to wait and see, won't you?"

She swallowed at the images that came to mind at his words, at the heat in his gaze.

"I'd very much like to get you out of this dress," he murmured. Her breath caught in her throat as he turned her. "Where's the zipper?"

She turned, lifting her hair from her neck. A tremble caught in her throat as his fingers brushed along her exposed skin. It was forever before she felt the zipper slide open, her skin cooling as air kissed it. Then his lips followed it down.

Lips and tongue made faint flicks against her skin. She closed her eyes and let her imagination run wild. This was erotic, his lips on her back. He paused at her bra, slipping a finger beneath the band before he did something and it fell open.

***

He traced a finger down the line of her spine, marveling at the sheer perfection in his arms. Her back was smooth and dusted with freckles. It aroused him endlessly as she held her hair off her neck and back, exposing herself to him. It drove him wild but he held it in check.

He'd come back into her life, trying to be a father to their daughter. But this? This was something he hadn't anticipated.

And he'd be damned if he screwed it up.

He licked down the center of her spine, drawing moisture on her exposed skin all the way from her neck to the edge of her panties and then back up, slowly pushing the dress from her shoulders.

He slipped his hands up, grasping hers where she still held her hair and wrapped her arms around his body, hugging her against him. She was soft where he was hard, warm where he felt burned. She arched her buttocks against his hips and the friction against his erection sent a bolt of desire slamming through him.

Her breasts were heavy against his forearms where he held her. He released her hands, exposing her to his touch. His hands trembled as he traced the softness of her belly, over the gentle swell of her breasts.

Her nipples puckered beneath his touch, tightening against his fingertips. They were heavier than he remembered, more beautiful.

He savored her quiet gasp when he ran his fingers over her breasts, watching in fascination as her body arched, her nipples hardened even more. His own body responded by tightening in his pants, demanding a release he wasn't prepared to seek. Not yet.

There were hours of pleasure first. He wanted to feel her coming against his mouth, his hand. A thousand different ways he wanted to explore her body and bring her pleasure.

He circled one nipple with one hand while the other drifted down her belly to the warm, moist heat between her thighs. The panties covering her were wet, slick against his fingertip. He traced the seam of her body through the thin silk. Felt her tremble even as she shifted, spreading her legs slightly. Felt her swollen and taut, open and wanting.

He wanted badly to kiss her there. To spread her wide and suck and lick until she came under his mouth. God but her pleasure was beautiful.

He laid her back on the bed, on the silvery grey comforter. Her skin glowed in the light as he slowly, so slowly pulled her panties down over her hips.

And then she was open for him. An erotic vision too beautiful for words. The hair between her thighs glistened with her own moisture. She was swollen and deep pink. He traced his thumb over the spreading seam of her. Watched her belly tremble as he touched her ever so lightly.

Saw moisture pearl on her heat as he stroked her.

***

Another stroke of his thumb over her slick heat. She'd

never felt pleasure spread from between her thighs to the rest of her body before. Never known how erotic the simple word "please" could sound on a man's lips. Not any man. This man.

It took everything she had to nod. To watch him lower his mouth to the triangle between her thighs. To see his tongue circle her where she was swollen and aching for him.

Electricity bolted through her at the first touch of his tongue to her body. Erotic heat blossomed through her as he circled her slick, swollen heat with his tongue, his mouth.

He'd never been this patient when they'd been young. There was no comparison as he made love to her with his mouth, driving her pleasure higher and higher until he had to hold her hips still while he continued his sensual onslaught.

Her body was bound and tight, walking the razor's edge, on the cusp of orgasm. She was close, so close. She'd never imagined he was this considerate, this patient.

This intensely focused on her.

He'd never been more aroused from doing this to a lover before. She was slicked with sweat, her body tight. He slid his thumb beneath his tongue. Filling her. Suckling her.

And she exploded. Her orgasm burst across his tongue, her body vibrating beneath his mouth, his fingers, his touch. A deep, primitive male desire spread inside him. He ached for his own release, but her release was another kind of reward.

It burned in his blood as she came against his mouth, her moisture spreading as she rode the final wave, shuddering and biting her lips to keep from crying out.

Never in her life had she come like that. Never had she felt pulled apart and shattered on every level, dancing on the edge of unconsciousness from the sheer intensity of the release.

Gale crawled up her body, resting between her thighs. She threaded her arms around his neck and pulled him down, tasting herself on his lips as she kissed him. "You're not naked," she whispered.

"Give me five seconds," he murmured against her lips.

She sat up, wanting to watch the man who'd brought her to such an intense and powerful release as he stripped off his clothing. Crisp dark hair spread across his chest and tapered down his belly. He was thicker everywhere, not just his chest. Hard muscles flexed and twisted as he stripped.

And then he was naked. Raw and powerful. A primitive warrior god. He stood with his feet braced shoulder width apart. His chest rose and fell with his breaths. Her gaze drifted lower to the thick erection she'd felt against her body when he'd held her against him.

She swallowed a harsh bite of arousal then opened her arms.

She shifted, arching her hips beneath him. Felt him poised at the entrance of her body. Wordlessly, she welcomed him home, her body stretching and expanding as he slid inside her.

He touched her. Deep and thick, he filled her. Completed her. Took away an emptiness she hadn't known she'd carried within her. He gripped her hands and looked down at her, their bodies joined, their souls healing the fractures from a lifetime apart.

He moved. A tiny hint of movement. She gasped, unable to look away from the intense emotion in his eyes. "Gale."

His name was a whisper. A prayer. A silent plea for more. She clenched her knees against his ribs, arching beneath him.

He withdrew slowly, his fingers locked with hers. The muscles in his neck strained as he filled her again. Slow, so slow. So much pleasure in that simple joining.

It was more than sex, more than arousal. This was connection. A coming back together after years and a lifetime apart. A new man, forged in war. A woman who'd never allowed herself to love the man he'd become. Together, they were one. Pieces of a whole. And as the pleasure rose, together they rode the wave, the pleasure, the distance between them shattered by a joining so fierce it drove them both into the darkness, entwined and falling.

Together.

***

The phone rang, dragging him out of that place between sleeping and waking that left him shaking as he groped in the dark. Melanie shifted, freeing his arm to reach for the vibrating intrusion.

"Sorren."

"Daddy?"

He sat up, his heart locked in his throat at Jamie's whispered terror. "What's wrong?"

"Daddy, you've got to come quick."

"Where are you?"

"We're at Alex's house. He forgot his wallet and his dad is freaking out. I think he's got a gun."

"Jamie, get out of the house." Gale was already moving, dragging on pants and his shoes.

Melanie was right behind him as they headed for the door.

"Daddy, I can't. He doesn't—"

The phone went dead. Gale handed it to Mel as he jammed the truck into gear and tore out of the narrow street. "Call 911."

"How far is it?" Mel finally asked.

"Three minutes." But Gale was planning on being there inside of two.

He ran over the curb. To hell with stop signs.

He didn't bother to kill the engine before racing up the front lawn. Tellhouse's truck was in the driveway. "Stay here."

"Gale."

"Mel, if he's got a gun, I can't do a damn thing if I have to worry about you along with the kids."

Mel swallowed and thank God she didn't argue.

The lights were on.

He didn't knock.

He spied into the house, his movements practiced and smooth, wishing he wasn't running into a loaded situation without any damn weapon whatsoever.

He was going to be fucking pissed if he got shot.

He was going to jail if someone else got shot.

His blood burned in his veins as the anger and the fear pounded through the constricted vessels. He took the steps two at a time and peered around the hallway toward the sound of voices.

"Dad, you don't have to do this."

Alex's voice wavered. His was the voice of a kid trying to sound like a man in a very bad situation.

Gale moved down the hall until he could see Tellhouse sitting on the floor, a bottle of Crown Royal between his legs, a 9-mil sitting on one thigh.

Pointed at his son.

Alex was crouched by his dad's feet, his eyes wide, his hand open, silently begging for the gun.

Where was Jamie?

"Dad, seriously, this isn't funny. Give me the gun."

Tellhouse didn't move except to lift the bottle to his lips again. "You think you're so fucking smart, don't you boy. Think you're too good for your old man."

"Dad, please." Alex glanced to the hall, his eyes going wide when he saw Gale.

"Tellhouse." Gale stepped into view.

"Oh look, the cavalry has arrived." Tellhouse flopped his head toward Gale. "Don't suppose I have to point out that you're breaking and entering in my house and in Texas, I have the right to shoot you."

"I think I'd prefer a much different ending to this situation," Gale said dryly. "What's up with the gun?"

"Just reminding my delinquent kid here that life's not a fucking easy ride. That sitting behind a computer is no way for a man to spend his life."

Gale ran his tongue over his teeth. "You know, the man who stopped me from killing my sarn't major would never point a gun at a fucking kid, let alone his own."

Tellhouse lifted the bottle to his lips once more. "Well, as you've pointed out, I'm not that guy anymore, now am I?"

"You want to put the gun away so we can talk about this?"

"Not really interested in talking, dickhead."

Gale inched steadily down the narrow hall. His heart pounded in his ears. Where the fuck was Jamie?

"So what, you're going to shoot your kid? Make you feel all manly to beat him up?"

Tellhouse smirked. "You know how many times the little fucker has been arrested? I've caught him with drugs, with porn. I got charged eight thousand dollars in fines because he was illegally downloading music. Eight grand. Because this little fuckstick doesn't believe in the so-called hegemonic bullshit known to the rest of us as following the goddamned rules!" His voice rose as he continued to talk. "I got a call from the fucking police tonight. Seems that Romeo over here is being investigated for threatening to blow up the school."

"That wasn't me, dad. I keep trying to explain that it was Blake and Josh."

"Right. Because they're the ones who got you arrested the other day. Because you aren't man enough to make your own fucking decisions and not hang out with fucking stoner losers."

"Tellhouse, give me the gun."

"Fuck you, Sorren," Tellhouse said. He pushed up to his feet, swaying dangerously. Gale wanted to yank Alex and shove him behind him. "You don't get to come into my fucking house and tell me how to parent my fucking kid." Tellhouse waved the gun at Alex. "I'd be better off if this little fucking pussy had never been born. He's the reason my fucking wife left me. He's not a man. He's a fucking punk ass coward."

Alex flinched with each word, as if his father were hitting him with the vicious words he hurled at his son.

"That's enough, man. He's a kid."

The gun swung toward Gale. "Or what?"

Everything slowed down. Gale's lungs squeezed tight in his chest, until his head felt like it was going to explode. He didn't think.

He reacted, slapping at the gun and lunging toward Tellhouse. Just in time to hear Jamie scream and the world fade to black as sirens wailed in the distance.

CHAPTER TWENTY-FOUR

He was cold. The kind of cold that made his entire body shiver violently. He could make his fingers work, though he was reasonably certain he couldn't feel his feet.

Fuck, he still had feet, right?

He blinked several times, his vision blurred and thick. His body still shook violently.

"Gale?"

"Cold," he whispered.

"Here." A blanket appeared suddenly, wrapped around his bare chest.

Why was his chest bare?

He frowned and blinked until his eyes cleared. Mel stood over him, her face a mask of worry. Her eyes were red, as if she'd been crying.

"Why am I in the hospital?" He frowned as everything came rushing back. "Did that fucking asshole shoot me?"

Mel made a sound that was somewhere between a laugh and a sob and then she was there, her head pressed to his shoulder, her hair soft against his exposed skin.

"Fuck. Did I die?"

"You had a heart attack," she whispered, her voice thick and filled with tears.

"A what?"

She leaned back, swiping at her face. "A heart attack."

Gale frowned again then looked down at the little sticky things pressed to his chest. "They couldn't shave my chest first?"

Mel made that sound again. “There wasn’t a hell of a lot of time,” she said, her voice watery. “You scared us all pretty bad.”

“What happened at Tellhouse’s?”

“Jamie said you went for the gun and then just collapsed. Alex managed to get the gun away from his dad before the cops showed up.”

“No one got shot?”

“No one got shot. Although from what Jamie told me Tellhouse was saying to his son, he probably could have used a bullet.”

“Where’s Tellhouse now?”

“Bell County awaiting arraignment.”

“Fuck,” Gale muttered. “How’s his kid?”

“He hasn’t left here. He’s stayed with Jamie the whole time.” Mel swallowed. “He kept asking about you.”

He couldn’t unhear Tellhouse’s hateful rant toward his kid. The kid was going to need a hell of a lot of help getting over that shit.

“How’s Jamie?”

“Scared but okay.” Mel swiped at her cheek. “You terrified all of us.”

He tried to sit up but one of his legs wasn’t working right. He looked down. “What the fuck happened to my leg?”

“You had angioplasty.”

“Speak English.”

“They stuck a tube in your leg to unblock the artery in your heart.”

“Oh.” He shivered, all the strength leaving his body as he sagged back against the bed. He was silent a long moment. “I really had a heart attack?”

“Yeah,” she whispered.

There was a knock on the door. Gale looked over as Sarn’t Major Cox walked in. “Guess who just signed himself up to be the Rear D first sergeant?”

“Oh come on, sarn’t major, that’s bullshit,” Gale said with

a hell of lot less force than he felt. Holy hell, he was as weak as a fucking kitten.

"Yeah, well, you should have thought of that before you went and had a fucking heart attack." Cox scrubbed his hand over his mouth before slapping Gale's foot. "Glad to see you're no worse for the wear, though."

Gale swallowed. "Yeah but now you're down another first sergeant."

"Yeah well, Washington is coming on board. Now that you're on your ass for the next few weeks, she'll take over as senior first sergeant."

"The boys are going to love taking shit from a female," Gale said mildly.

"We'll manage. We always do. Your commander, though, might just have given birth to kittens. He's been a little unhappy since you got your ass rushed into surgery."

"I'm sure he's capable of running the company by himself," Gale said. "Iaconelli can cover down until I get back on my feet."

Cox sniffed. "If that's what you think he's worried about, you're one dumb son of a bitch." He slapped Gale's foot. "Don't wait too long to get back to work."

"Sarn't Major?"

Cox stopped by the door.

"What happened?" He swallowed as his throat closed off but he forced the words out. "What changed with Tellhouse?"

It was a long time before Cox finally answered. "I don't know. War changes people. Sometimes it's only temporary. But sometimes…sometimes..." Cox cleared his throat roughly then looked back at him. "Sometimes we become the monsters we're supposed to be fighting."

He was gone before Gale could find anything else to say. He simply sat, unable to process the violent changes in the man he'd served with.

Mel looked at him for an explanation. "Care to explain

what just happened? Without the military jargon, please?"

"It means I'm not deploying."

"Ever?"

He rubbed his hand over his chest, his fingers colliding with the sticky thing over his heart. "Not on this rotation. I'll be in charge of the Rear Detachment."

"Is that a bad thing?" Caution in those careful words.

He looked up at her. "It's taking care of all the soldiers who don't deploy. It's a major pain in the ass that no one wants."

Silence greeted his explanation. "You sound upset about that."

He looked over at the warning underlying her words. "I'm on pain medication. I can't be held responsible for what I'm saying."

"I wasn't going to get mad." She smiled. "But I can't say I'm sad you won't be going."

Gale looked at her for a long moment, a thousand twisted things writhing inside him. Finally, he held open his arms.

She crawled into his embrace, careful not to pull or tug on any attached wires or tubes.

"I'm not happy about not going," he admitted. "I want to be there for my soldiers." He brushed his lips against her head. "But I get to be here for you and for Jamie. And that is so much more important for me."

Gale's arms were tight around her, his heartbeat strong and steady beneath her heart. "I'm so glad you're okay," she whispered.

"Me, too." He laughed against her mouth, and his thumb brushed over her cheek as he nibbled on her lips. He met her gaze.

She tried to look away but he urged her to look at him. She closed her eyes. "I'm scared of what I still feel for you," she murmured.

He brought his forehead to hers, not caring that she was in

the hospital bed beside him. Not caring if now was the right time or the wrong time. "I never got over you, Mel."

"Gale."

"No, hear me out. I meant to come after you," he said. He cupped her chin, lifting her face to his. "When you left, I meant to come after you. But after a while, when life and the Army and the war kept getting in the way, I figured it was best to let you go." He kissed her gently. "I'm sorry I didn't fight harder."

"You're here now." She threaded her fingers with his. "I'd like it very much if you'd stay."

"What will Jamie say?"

She smiled. "I'm sure we'll have good days and bad days, just like we do now."

"But you won't have to face them alone anymore," he murmured. "I want to help you carry the load, Mel." He kissed her gently. "I want the chance to grow old with you. I know I've got a lot of making up to do but I'd like that chance… Just…don't say no? And I'll ask you properly after we've done this for a few months and we're both sure that this is what we want." He caressed her cheek. "But I'd like to make you Mrs. Sorren again. In more than name."

Tears burned behind her eyes and she kissed him then, losing herself in the pleasure of this man's touch. Amazed that after a lifetime of war, he'd finally come back to her.

They got a second chance.

She wasn't going to waste a single day of it.

***

The damn sticky thing on his chest was itching. He rubbed the plastic, wondering if the nurses would freak out if he ripped them off. Seeing how the nurses were already upset with him for getting out of bed and almost ripping out his IV because he'd wanted to take a piss standing up, he figured it was better not to test their patience further.

There was a quiet knock on the door. He looked up and saw Jamie standing in the doorway. She wasn't wearing her dress. Her hair was pulled back into a ponytail, her face scrubbed clean. She looked so much younger without the eyeliner he'd gotten used to seeing on her.

"Hey kiddo."

"Hey Dad." Her voice was quiet, hesitant. "Mom went to grab some food," she said.

She looked fragile. Scared. He felt the anger rise up again, his heart pounding against his chest. "Are you okay?" His voice broke.

"I'm not the one in the hospital," she said dryly.

He grinned. "You're really nailing that sarcasm as a life skill thing," he said.

Her bottom lip quivered and she covered her mouth with her hand. He held out his arms and she crashed into him.

"Ah hell, honey, don't cry." He held her tightly, breathing her in, so goddamned grateful she wasn't hurt.

"You scared me," she whispered.

"You?" He kissed the top of her head. "You've taken fifteen years off my life."

"Sorry, I'll try not to have friends whose parents threaten to kill them in the future."

He laughed out loud and hugged her close. "How's Alex holding up?"

"He's okay for now. I think." Jamie sat up, brushing her hands over her cheeks. "Mom said you're not deploying?"

Gale shook his head. "Nope. I'll be here to be a pain in your ass for the foreseeable future."

She smiled weakly. "I think I'd like that." She fidgeted with the sleeve of her shirt.

He watched her then, wishing he knew what to say. He really needed to get better at this whole father daughter thing.

"I wanted to come home," he finally said. "When you were in the hospital. I wanted to be there for you and I wasn't."

She looked up at him, biting her lips. "I hated you." Her voice cracked over the words. "I was so pissed that you weren't there. That you were never there." She swiped at her cheeks again. "And then when you said you were moving here, I…I was happy. I…I guess it'll be nice getting to finally have a dad."

His heart lodged his throat. He scrubbed his hand over his mouth. "I want that very much." He reached for her hand. "I'm sorry, Jamie. I'm so goddamned sorry I wasn't here."

She leaned into him, resting against his chest. He wrapped her tight in his arms, holding her close. He was never going to let her go.

He'd fucked up so badly. And she still loved him.

"Maybe having a heart attack will be a good thing," he said when he was sure he could speak without embarrassing himself.

She made a sound that was halfway between a sob and a laugh as she sat up. "That's really sick, Dad."

"I'm serious. I've deployed enough." He cupped her cheek. "It's time you and your mom are my priority."

She smiled again. "So you and mom are a thing?"

He sighed heavily. "If she's willing to put up with me, yeah, I think so."

"Does that mean you're going to be spending the night at the house?"

"I'm really not ready to have that conversation," he said dryly.

"Gross." She laughed and shifted on the bed.

Gale spotted her bag near the door. "So how's the book?"

She glanced over her shoulder. "It's good."

"Read to me?"

She lifted one eyebrow. "Read to you?"

He shrugged. "Think of it as public speaking practice. You want to be a journalist, right?"

She grabbed the book and nestled down in the bed next to him and started reading. Gale closed his eyes and listened to his daughter's voice.

Heart attack or not, there was nowhere in the world Gale would rather be.

EPILOGUE

"Did your report card come in today?" Mel stirred the pasta to keep it from sticking to the bottom of the pot.

"Yep."

"Can I see it?"

"It's on the island."

Mel glanced over at her daughter. She was acting funny. Not belligerent or stubborn. Just…odd. Mel supposed she should be used to it at this point.

She opened the report card. Mostly threes and a couple of fours. "You got a four in biology," Mel said.

"Turns out when you actually do the homework, the tests are easier," Jamie said dryly.

Mel smiled at her daughter's sarcasm. Her dad was rubbing off on her. "I'm proud of you, honey. That's pretty impressive."

The front door opened and Gale strolled into the kitchen. "What's impressive?"

"Your daughter's improvement in biology. Look."

Gale studied the grades silently. Mel could feel the tension radiating off him. Worry gripped her heart. He was pushing too hard, too fast. He wanted to be back at work. Wanted to be back with his men. She knew that and it was hard not to worry that he would try to deploy. Trust was a slow thing to rebuild but they were working on it.

All of them.

"This is really great, kiddo," he said to Jamie. "How's Alex?"

"He's staying with his aunt in Lampasas and she's got him

in some counseling program with horses outside of town."

"That's good," Gale said. "Hey, can I have a few minutes with your mom?"

Jamie frowned but didn't argue. "Sure."

Mel dumped the pasta into the sink then turned to face him. "What's wrong?"

When he didn't speak for a long moment, fear twisted in her belly. "Gale?"

He swallowed and walked slowly toward her. He reached into his pocket and pulled out a small lump of tissue. "So listen. I, ah, wanted to see if you, ah, maybe wanted this?"

Her heart was a knot blocking her throat. "Gale." Her fingers trembled as she took the tissue.

"I never got rid of it. I thought about it, over the years. But every time I thought about actually doing it, something stopped me." He reached for it, unwrapping the tiny diamond ring he'd given her once upon a time. "I mean, I want to get another stone. Something nicer and all… And it's fine if you don't like it anymore and all…"

"Gale."

He lifted the ring from her palm and slipped it over her finger.

"I would very much like it if you'd be my wife." Quiet, questioning words. "Again."

She adjusted the ring, seating it where it still fit even after all these years. Then she looked up at him, threading her arms around his neck. "I'd like that very much, too." She brushed her lips against his. "I love you, Gale Sorren. I think I always have."

He lowered his forehead to hers. "I love you." His voice broke a little on the words.

He kissed her then because he was never a man of many words and right then, he lacked the words he needed. Instead he showed her—with his mouth, with his body, with his every action—how much he loved her. How much he'd never stopped loving her.

And he would spend the rest of his life showing her just that.

THANK YOU!

Thank you so much for reading! Word of mouth is incredibly important to helping authors like me reach new readers so please tell a friend if you've enjoyed this book. Reviews help other readers decide whether or not to pick up a book. If you'd consider leaving a review, I appreciate any and all of them (whether positive or negative or somewhere in between).

I generally don't post about a new book until I'm sure about the release date. If you'd like to make sure you never miss a new release, sign up for my newsletter at http://www.jessicascott.net/mailing-list.html

You can read more about soldiers coming home from war in the rest of the Homefront series.

Homefront: First Sergeant Gale Sorren & Melanie
After the War: Captain Sean Nichols & Captain Sarah Anders
Face the Fire: Captain Sal Bello & First Sergeant Holly Washington

Want to know what life is like for a soldier home from war adjusting to life on campus? Check out my Falling Series:

Before I Fall: Noah & Beth
Break My Fall: Abby & Josh
If I Fall: Parker and Eli

If you'd like to read about my own experiences in Iraq and the transition home, please check out **To Iraq & Back: On War & Writing** and **The Long Way Home: One Mom's**

Journey Home From War.

Want more stories about soldiers coming home from war and the families who love them? Check out my Coming Home series:

Because of You: Sergeant First Class Shane Garrison & Jen St. James

I'll Be Home for Christmas: A Coming Home Novella: Sergeant Vic Carponti & his wife Nicole

Anything for You: A Coming Home Short Story: Sergeant First Class Shane Garrison & Jen St. James

Back to You: Captain Trent Davila & his wife Laura

Until There Was You: Captain Evan Loehr & Captain Claire Montoya

All for You: Sergeant First Class Reza Iaconelli & Captain Emily Lindberg

It's Always Been You: Captain Ben Teague & Major Olivia Hale

All I Want For Christmas is You: A Coming Home Novella: Major Patrick McLean & Captain Samantha Egan

If you'd like a special preview of **BEFORE I FALL**, turn the page.

Before I Fall

Chapter One

Beth

My dad has good days and bad. The good days are awesome. When he's awake and he's pretending to cook and I'm pretending to eat it. It's a joke between us that he burns water. But that's okay.

On the good days, I humor him. Because for those brief interludes, I have my dad back.

The not so good days, like today, are more common. Days when he can't get out of bed without my help.

I bring him his medication. I know exactly how much he takes and how often.

And I know exactly when he runs out.

I've gotten better at keeping up with his appointments so he doesn't, but the faceless bastards at the VA cancel more than they keep. But what can we do? He can't get private insurance with his health, and because someone decided that his back injury wasn't entirely service-related, he doesn't have a high enough disability rating to qualify for automatic care. So we wait for them to fit him in and when we can't, we go to the emergency room and the bills pile up. Because despite him not being able to move on the bad days, his back pain treatments are elective.

So I juggle phone calls to the docs and try to keep us above water.

Bastards.

I leave his phone by his bed and make sure it's plugged in to charge before I head to school. He's got water and the pills he'll need when he finally comes out of the fog. Our tiny house is only a mile from campus. Not in the best part of town but not the worst either. I've got an hour before class, which means I need to hustle. Thankfully, it's not terribly hot today so I won't arrive on campus a sweating, soggy mess. That always makes a good impression, especially at a wealthy southern school like this one.

I make it to campus with twenty minutes to spare and check my e-mail on the campus WiFi. I can't check it at the house - Internet is a luxury we can't afford. If I'm lucky, my neighbor's signal sometimes bleeds over into our house. Most of the time, though, I'm not that lucky. Which is fine. Except for days like this where there's a note from my professor asking me to come by her office before class.

Professor Blake is terrifying to those who don't know her. She's so damn smart it's scary, and she doesn't let any of us get away with not speaking up in class. Sit up straight. Speak loudly. She's harder on the girls, too. Some of the underclassmen complain that she's being unfair. I don't complain, though. I know she's doing it for a reason.

"You got my note just in time," she says. Her tortoise-shell glasses reflect the fluorescent light, and I can't see her eyes.

"Yes, ma'am." She's told me not to call her ma'am, but it slips out anyway. I can't help it. Thankfully, she doesn't push the issue.

"I have a job for you."

"Sure." A job means extra money on the side. Money that I can use to get my dad his medications. Or, you know, buy food. Little things. It's hard as hell to do stats when your stomach is rumbling. "What does it entail?"

"Tutoring. Business statistics."

"I hear a but in there."

"He's a former soldier."

Once, when my mom first left us, I couldn't wake my dad

up. My blood pounded so loud in my ears that I could hardly hear. That's how I feel now. My mouth is open, but no sound crosses my lips. Professor Blake knows how I feel about the war, about soldiers. I can't deal with all the hoah chest-beating bullshit. Not with my dad and everything the war has done to him.

"Before you say no, hear me out. Noah has some very well-placed friends that want him very much to succeed here. He's got a ticket into the business school graduate program, but only if he gets through Stats."

I'm having a hard time breathing. I can't do this. Just thinking about what the war has done to my dad makes it difficult to breathe. But the idea of extra money, just a little, is a strong motivator when you don't have it. Principles are for people who can afford them.

I take a deep, cleansing breath. "So why me?"

"Because you've got the best head for stats I've seen in a long time, and I've seen you explain things to the underclassmen in ways that make sense to them. You can translate."

"There's no one else?" I hate that I need this job.

Professor Blake removes her glasses with a quiet sigh. "Our school is very pro-military, Beth. And I would consider it a personal favor if you'd help him."

She's right. That's the only reason I was able to get in. This is one of the Southern Ivies. A top school in the southeast that I have no business being at except for my dad, who knew the dean of the law school from his time in the Army. I hate the war and everything it's done to my family. But I wouldn't be where I am today if my dad hadn't gone to war and sacrificed everything to make sure I had a future outside of our crappy little place outside of Fort Benning. There are things worse than death and my dad lives with them every day because he had done what he had to do to provide for me.

I will not let him down.

"Okay. When do I start?"

She hands me a slip of paper. It's yellow and has her

letterhead at the top in neat, formal block letters. "Here's his information. Make contact and see what his schedule is." She places her glasses back on and just like that, I'm dismissed.

Professor Blake is not a warm woman, but I wouldn't have made it through my first semester at this school without her mentorship. If not for her and my friend Abby, I would have left from the sheer overwhelming force of being surrounded by money and wealth and all the intangibles that came along with it. I did not belong here, but because of Professor Blake, I hadn't quit.

So if I need to tutor some blockhead soldier to repay her kindness, then so be it. Graduating from this program is my one chance to take care of my dad and I will not fail.

Noah

I hate being on campus. I feel old. Which isn't entirely logical because I'm only a few years older than most of the kids plugged in and tuned out around me. Part of me envies them. The casual nonchalance as they stroll from class to class, listening to music without a care in the world.

It feels surreal. Like a dream that I'm going to wake up from any minute now and find that I'm still in Iraq with LT and the guys. A few months ago, I was patrolling a shithole town in the middle of Iraq where we had no official boots on the ground and now I'm here. I feel like I've been ripped out of my normal.

Hell, I don't even know what to wear to class. This is not a problem I've had for the last few years.

I erred on the side of caution - khakis and a button-down polo. I hope I don't look like a fucking douchebag. LT would be proud of me. I think. But he's not here to tell me what to do, and I'm so far out of my fucking league it's not even funny.

I almost grin at the thought. LT is still looking after me. His parents are both academics, and it is because of him that I am even here. I told him there was no fucking way I was going to make it into the business school because math was basically a foreign language to me. He said tough shit and had helped me apply.

My phone vibrates in my pocket, distracting me from the fact that my happy ass is lost on campus. Kind of hard to navigate when the terrain is buildings and mopeds as opposed to burned-out city streets and destroyed mosques.

Stats tutor contact info: Beth Lamont. E-mail her, don't text.

Apparently, LT was serious about making sure I didn't fail. Class hasn't even started yet, and here I am with my very own tutor. I'm paying for it out of pocket. There were limits to how much pride I could swallow.

Half the students around me looked like they'd turn sixteen shades of purple if I said the wrong thing. Like, look out, here's the crazy-ass veteran, one bad day away from shooting the place up. The other half probably expects the former soldier to speak in broken English and be barely literate because we're too poor and dumb to go to college. Douchebags. It's bad enough that I wanted to put on my ruck and get the hell out of this place.

I stop myself. I need to get working on that whole cussing thing, too. Can't be swearing like I'm back with the guys or calling my classmates names. Not if I wanted to fit in and not be the angry veteran stereotype.

I'm not sure about this. Not any of it. I never figured I was the college type - at least not this kind of college.

I tap out an e-mail to the tutor and ask when she's available to meet. The response comes back quickly. A surprise, really. I can't tell you how many e-mails I sent trying to get my schedule fixed and nothing. Silence. Hell, the idea of actually responding to someone seems foreign. I had to physically go to the registrar's office to get a simple question answered about a form. No one would answer a damn e-mail, and you could forget about a phone call. Sometimes, I think they'd be more comfortable with carrier pigeons. Or not having to interact at all. I can't imagine what my old platoon would do to this place.

Noon at The Grind.

Which is about as useful information as giving me

directions in Arabic because I have no idea a) what The Grind is or b) where it might be.

I respond to her e-mail and tell her that, saving her contact information in my phone. If she's going to be my tutor, who knows when I'll need to get a hold of her in a complete panic.

Library coffee shop. Central campus.

Okay then. This ought to be interesting.

I head to my first class. Business Statistics. Great. Guess I'll get my head wrapped around it before I meet the tutor. That should be fun.

I'm pretty sure that fun and statistics don't belong in the same sentence but whatever. It's a required course, so I guess that's where I'm going to be.

My hands start sweating the minute I step into the classroom. Hello, school anxiety. Fuck. I forgot how much I hate school. I snag a seat at the back of the room, the wall behind me so I can see the doors and windows. I hate the idea of someone coming in behind me. Call it PTSD or whatever, but I hate not being able to see who's coming or going.

I reach into my backpack and pull out a small pill bottle. My anxiety is tripping at a double-time, and I'm going to have a goddamned heart attack at this rate.

I hate the pills more than I hate being in a classroom again, but there's not much I can do about it. Not if I want to do this right.

And LT would pretty much haunt me if I fuck this up.

I choke down the bitter pill and pull out my notebook as the rest of the class filters in.

I flip to the back of the notebook and start taking notes. Observations. Old habit from Iraq. Keeps me sane, I guess.

The females have some kind of religious objection to pants. Yoga pants might as well be full-on burqas. I've seen actual tights being worn as outer garments and no one bats an eye. It feels strange seeing so much flesh after being in Iraq where the only flesh you saw was burned and bloody...

Well, wasn't *that* a happy fucking thought.

Jesus. I scrub my hands over my face. Need to put that shit

aside, a.s.a.p.

Professor Blake comes in, and I immediately turn my attention to the front of the classroom. She looks stern today, but that's a front. She's got to look mean in front of these young kids. She's nothing like she was when we talked about enrollment before I started. She was one of the few people who did respond to e-mails at this place.

"Good morning. I'm Professor Blake, and this is my TA Beth Lamont. If you have problems or issues, go to her. She speaks for me and has my full faith and confidence. If you want to pass this class, pay attention because she knows this information inside and out."

Beth Lamont. *Hello, tutor.*

I lose the rest of whatever Professor Blake has to say. Because Beth Lamont is like some kind of stats goddess. Add in that she's drop-dead smoking hot, but it's her eyes that grab hold of me. Piercing green, so bright that you can see them from across the room. She looks at me, and I can feel my entire body standing at the position of attention. It's been a long time since a woman made me stand up and take notice. And I'm supposed to focus on stats around her? I'll be lucky to remember how to write my name in crayons around her.

I am completely fucked.

Chapter Two

Beth

It doesn't take me long to figure out who Noah Warren is. He's a little bit older than the rest of the fresh-faced underclassmen I've gotten used to. I'm not even twenty-one, but I feel ancient these days. I was up late last night, worrying about my dad.

I can feel him watching me as I hand out the syllabus and the first lecture notes. My hackles are up - he's staring and being rude. I don't tolerate this from the jocks but right then, I'm stuck because Professor Blake has asked me to tutor him. I can't exactly cuss him out in front of the class.

Which is really frustrating because the rest of the class is focused on Professor Blake, but not our soldier. Oh no, he's such a stereotype it's not even funny. Staring. Not even trying to be slick about it like the football player in the front of the classroom who's trying to catch a glimpse of my tits when I lean down to pass out the papers.

Instead, our soldier just leans back, nonchalant like he owns the place. Like the whole world should bend over and kiss his ass because he's defending our freedom. Well, I know all about that, and the price is too goddamned high.

And wow, how is that for bitterness and angst on a

Monday morning? I need to get my shit together. I haven't even spoken to him and I'm already tarring and feathering him. Not going to be very productive for our tutoring relationship if I hate him before we even get started.

I take a deep breath and hand him the syllabus and the first lecture worksheet.

I imagine he's figured out that I'm his tutor.

I turn back and head to my desk in the front as Professor Blake drops her bombshell on the class.

"There will be no computer use in this class. You may use laptops during lab when Beth is instructing because there will be practical applications. But during lecture, you will not use computers. If your phones go off, you can expect to be docked participation points, and those are a significant portion of your grade."

There is the requisite crying and wailing and gnashing of the teeth. I remember the first time I heard of Professor Blake's no computer rule. I thought it was draconian and complete bullshit. But then I realized she was right - I learned better by writing things down. Especially the stats stuff.

I look up at Noah. He's watching the class now. He's scowling. He looks like he might frown a lot. He looks...harder than the rest of the class. There are angles to his cheeks and shadows beneath his eyes. His dark hair is shorter than most and he damn sure doesn't have that crazy-ass swoop thing that so many of the guys are doing these days.

Everything about him radiates soldier. I wonder if he knows how intimidating he looks. And why the hell do I care what he thinks?

I'm going to be his tutor, not his shrink.

He shifts and his gaze collides with mine. Something tightens in the vicinity of my belly. It's not fear. Soldiers don't scare me, not even ones who look like they were forged in fire like Noah.

No, it's something else. Something tight and tense and distinctly distracting. I'm not in the mood for my hormones to overwhelm my common sense.

I stomp on the feeling viciously.

I'm staring at him now. I'm deliberately trying to look confident and confrontational. Men like Noah don't respect weakness. Show a moment's hesitation and the next thing you know they've got your ass pinned in a corner while they're trying to grab your tits.

He lifts one brow in response. I have no idea how to read that reaction.

Noah

I had to swallow my pride and ask some perky blond directions to The Grind. I hadn't expected Valley Girl airheadedness but then again, I didn't really know what I expected. I managed to interpret the directions between a few giggles and several "likes" and "ahs" and "ums". I imagined her briefing my CO and almost smiled at the train wreck it would be. We had a lieutenant like her once. She was in the intelligence shop and she might have been the smartest lieutenant in the brigade, but the way she talked made everyone think she was a complete space cadet.

She'd said "like" one too many times during a briefing to the division commander and yeah, well, last I heard, she'd been put in charge of keeping the latrines cleaned down in Kuwait. Which wasn't fair but then again, what in life was? Guess the meat eaters in the brigade hadn't wanted to listen to the Valley Girl give them intelligence reports on what the Kurdish Pesh and ISIS were up to at any given point in time.

My cup of coffee from The Grind isn't terrible. It certainly isn't Green Bean coffee, but it's a passable second place. Green Bean has enough caffeine in it to keep you up for two days straight. This stuff...it's softer, I guess. Smoother? I'm not really sure. It isn't bad. Just not what I'm used to. Nothing here is.

I wonder if there is any way to run down to Bragg and get some of the hard stuff. Hell, I am considering chewing on coffee beans at this point. Anything to clear the fog in my brain.

But I need the fog to keep the anxiety at bay, so I guess I'm fucked there, too. Guess I should start getting used to things around here. No better place to start than with the coffee, I guess.

The Grind is busy. Small, low tables are crowded with laptops and books and students all looking intently at their work. It's like a morgue in here. Everyone is hyper-focused. Don't these people know how to have a good time? Relax a little bit? There are no seats anywhere. The Grind is apparently a popular if silent, place.

The tutor walks in at exactly twelve fifty-eight. Two minutes to spare.

"You're not late." I'm mildly shocked.

She does that eyebrow thing again, and I have to admit on her, it is pretty fucking sexy. "I tend to be punctual. It's a life skill."

"Kitty has claws," I say.

She stiffens. Apparently, the joke's fallen flat. Guess I'm going to have to work on that.

"Let's get something straight, shall we? My name is Beth, and I'm going to tutor you in business stats. We are not going to be friends or fuck buddies or anything else you might think of. I'm not 'Kitty' or any other pet name. I'm here to get a degree, not a husband."

My not-strong-enough coffee burns my tongue as her words sink in. She's damn sure prickly all right. I can't decide if I admire her spine or I think it's unnecessary. Hell, it isn't like I tried to grab her ass or asked her to suck my dick.

The coffee slides down my throat. "Glad we cleared that up," I say instead. "I wasn't sure if blowjobs came with the tutoring."

She grinds her teeth. There isn't much by way of sense of humor in the tutor. She has a no-nonsense look about her. Her dark blond hair is drawn tight to her neck, and I can't figure out if she is naturally flawless or if she is just damn good with makeup.

There is a freshness to her, though, that isn't something I

am used to either. Enlisted women, the few I've been around, either try way too hard with too much black eyeliner downrange or aren't interested in men beyond the buddy level.

But this academic woman is a new species entirely for me, and as our standoff continues, I realize I have no idea what the rules of engagement are with someone like her. At least not beyond her name is not Kitty and she's not here for a husband. Oh and can't forget the no blowjobs thing. She made the rules pretty clear.

She is fucking stunning and I suddenly can't talk.

She clears her throat. "So are we going to stand here and continue to stare at each other, or are we going to get to work? I have somewhere to be in two hours."

I motion toward the library. "Lead the way."

Beth

He's watching my ass as I walk in front of him. He's just the type who would do something like that. The blowjob comment caught me completely off guard. I hate that. I hate that I couldn't come up with any brilliant, sarcastic response, either. I always think of smartass comebacks fifteen minutes too late.

So now I am even more irritated than I was when he'd been staring at me class. What the hell had Professor Blake been thinking?

I lead us to a small table out of the way, where there won't be a lot of disruption. Stats is one of those things that takes a lot of concentration. At least it did for me until I learned the language.

I pull out the worksheet from class. Homework and lessons. "So let's get the business stuff out of the way," I say. I hate the tone in my voice. I'm not normally a ball-busting bitch, but he's set me off and if being cold and curt is the only way to keep him in line then so be it. "I'd like to be paid each meeting. Cash."

"What's your rate?"

I sit back. How the hell did that question catch me off guard? I don't know. I work part-time at the country club next to campus, but the tips are hit or miss. The thing about the wealthy? Some of them can be downright stingy. Most of the time, I make okay tips. When it isn't, I tried not to be bitter about how they don't need the money like I do.

I just smile and take their orders.

I'm stuck. Noah is not my first tutoring job, but my other jobs were paid for by the university. I have no idea how much to charge for freelance work.

"Fifty dollars an hour, three times a week," he offers abruptly.

I cover my shock with my hand. "Huh?"

"Fifty dollars an hour. I saw a sign in the common area charging that much for Spanish. Figure Stats should be at least that much, right?"

My voice is stuck somewhere in the bottom of my chest. Fifty bucks an hour is a lot of groceries and medication. It feels wrong taking that kind of money, even from Mr. Does-the-Tutoring-Come-with-Blowjobs.

"Will that be a problem?"

I shake my head. "No. That's fine." There's a stack of bills that need to be paid. The electricity is a week overdue. I'm counting on tips tonight to make a payment tomorrow to keep them from shutting it off. Again. Between that and the money from tutoring - I could keep the lights on. I can feel my face burning hot. I turn away, digging into my backpack to keep him from seeing my humiliation, not wanting him to see my relief.

"Same time, same place? Monday, Wednesday and Friday?" My computer flickers to life.

"Works for me. How much pain should I be prepared for?" He sounds worried. He should. Professor Blake is one of the top in her field, and that's no small feat considering she came up at a time when women were still blazing trails in the business world.

"Depends on if you do the work or not," I say. I can't

quite bring myself to offer him comfort. I'm still irritated by the blowjob comment. "So let's get started." I lean over the worksheet. "What questions do you have from class today?"

I look up to find him watching me. There's something in his eyes that tugs at me. I don't want to be tugged at.

He looks away. He's strangling that poor pen in his hands. Clearly, I've struck a nerve with my question.

I wish I didn't remember how that felt. The lost sensation of not having a clue what I was doing. I didn't even know what questions to ask.

I don't want to feel anything charitable toward him, but there's something about the way he shifts. Something that makes him vulnerable.

I run my tongue over my teeth. This isn't going well. "Okay look. We'll start with the basics, okay?"

I open my laptop to the lecture notes.

He finally notices my computer. "I haven't seen one of the black MacBooks in years," he says.

He's not being a prick, but I bristle anyway. "It might be old but she's never failed me."

"It can run stats software? Isn't that pretty intense processor-wise?"

I don't feel like telling him that to run said stats program, I have to shut down every other program and clear the cache. I don't want to admit that there's just no money to buy a new computer. I can't even finance one because I don't have the credit for it.

Business school is about looking the part as much as it is about knowing the game, so none of those words are going to leave my lips.

"It gets the job done," I say. "Now, the first lecture."

"I get everything about what stats is supposed to do. I got lost somewhere around regression."

"Don't worry about regression right now. We're going to focus on understanding what we're looking at first up. Basic concepts."

I look over at him. He's scowling at the paper. I can see

tiny flecks of gold in his dark brown eyes. He drags one hand through his short dark hair and leans forward. He's practically radiating tension, and I can feel it infecting me.

Damn it, I don't give a shit about his anxiety. I don't care. I can't.

"So the normal distribution is?"

I take a deep breath. This stuff I know. I draw the standard bell-shaped curve on his paper. "The normal distribution says that any results are normally..."

Noah

She knows her stuff. She relaxes when she starts talking about confidence intervals and normal distributions. Hell, I can't even *spell* normal distribution.

But she has a way of making things make sense.

And her confidence isn't scary so much as it is really fucking attractive.

I'm watching her lips move and I swear to God I'm trying to pay attention, but my brain decides to take a detour into not stats-ville. She's got a great mouth. It's a little too wide, and she has a tendency to chew on the inside of her lip when she's focusing.

I look down because I don't want her to catch me not paying attention. I need to understand this stuff, not stare at her like a lovesick private.

I'm focusing on confidence intervals when something dings on her computer. She frowns and opens her e-mail. It's angled away so I can't look over her shoulder, but something is clearly wrong. A flush creeps up her neck. She grinds her teeth when she's irritated. I tend to notice that in other people. I do the same thing when the anxiety starts taking hold. At least when it starts. It graduates quickly beyond teeth grinding into something more paralyzing.

I glance at my watch. It's almost time for her to go. I have no idea how I'm going to get my homework done, but I'll figure it out later. I'm meeting a couple of former military guys some place called Baywater Inn in a few hours. Plenty of time for me to get my homework done. Or at least attempt it. Because, of course, LT put me in touch with these guys, too.

But watching her, something is clearly wrong. I want to ask, but given how our history isn't exactly on the confide-your-darkest-secrets level, I don't.

She snaps her laptop closed and sighs. "I've got to run and make a phone call. Are you set for your assignment for lab?"

"I'll figure it out."

Her lips press into a flat line. "You can always look it up online."

"Sure thing."

She's distracted now. Not paying attention. I watch her move. There's an edge to her seriousness now, a tension in the long lines of her neck. A strand of hair falls free from the knot and brushes her temple. I want to tuck it back into place, but I'm pretty sure if I tried it, I'd be rewarded with a knee in the balls. And I like them where they are, thanks. I've come too close to losing them to risk them now.

I pull out my wallet and hand her two twenties and a ten. She hesitates then offers the ten back. "We didn't do the full hour." I refuse the money. "Keep it. Obviously you've got something to take care of. Don't worry about it."

She sucks in a deep breath like she's going to argue but then clamps her mouth shut. "Thank you."

She didn't choke on it, but it's a close thing. I am suddenly deeply curious about what has gotten her all wound up in such a short amount of time.

Maybe I'll get a chance to ask her some day.

I definitely have the impression that Beth Lamont isn't into warm cuddles and hugs. She strikes me as independent and tough.

And I admire the hell out of that attitude, even as she scares the shit out of me with how smart she is.

ABOUT THE AUTHOR

Jessica Scott is a career Army officer, mother of two daughters, three cats, and three dogs, wife to a career NCO, and wrangler of all things stuffed and fluffy. She is a terrible cook and even worse housekeeper, but she's a pretty good shot with her assigned weapon. Somehow, her children are pretty well-adjusted and her husband still loves her, despite burned water and a messy house.

Photo: Courtesy of Buzz Covington Photography

Find her online at http://www.jessicascott.net